The Electric Boner

Nathaniel Lewis

Copyright © 2018 Nathaniel Lewis

All rights reserved.

ISBN: 9781720184287

CONTENTS

BOOK I: THE RISING

Part I	2
Part II	32
Part III	86

BOOK II: THE COMING

Part I	137
Part II	173
Part III	205

BOOK I: THE RISING

PART I

Chapter one

Nick Sherman awoke. His mother was yelling from downstairs. "Time to get up!" As far as he could tell, he was already up. He reached down and gave it a gentle squeeze. It was nice there in bed. It was soft and warm and there was nothing unpleasant going on there, though he could smell scrambled eggs being cooked. He didn't like breakfast and he especially didn't like having to get out of bed.

"You're going to be late!" Ug. That was another thing he didn't like: going to school. Somehow, it was all like scrambled eggs: sickly yellow, gross, unimaginative. But you had to keep stuffing yourself with it, because there was nothing else to do.

Someday, probably, he would be able to do what he wanted, whatever that turned out to be. After all, his mother had money. Something like eight million dollars, growing somehow, somewhere, in some kind of fund that Nick didn't understand, at a rate much faster than she was spending it. The money came from a distant uncle who had invented something to do with those swiveling, adjustable height computer chairs. Nick didn't really know. All he knew was that one day he was going to be rich, because if you had money and kept it, they gave you more money, and if you didn't have money, they made you pay even more for stuff: cars that always needed to be repaired, overdraft fees, payday loans, medical bills from eating shitty food and no insurance. Although Nick and his mother still lived frugally, at least they didn't have to deal with that kind of stuff anymore. And they didn't have to deal with The Asshole anymore. He'd left a while back. Before the money, of course. That fact always made Nick smile.

He made it out of bed, into the bathroom, and downstairs, where he sat at the kitchen table, his plate already laid out for him. He looked at his eggs, shuffled them around with his fork. Might as well get it over with. He dug in and shoved them in his mouth.

"Anything exciting going on today?" asked his mom, Fran.

"Nah," said Nick, shoving in another mouthful. He thought of his bed up there, empty and waiting for him.

"Are you coming home after school?"

"Dunno."

"Well, call if you don't."

"Yeah." One more bite and it would be done. He wouldn't have to eat breakfast again for a whole day. He got it down without chewing. He felt it slide into his stomach and sit there, a burden.

"Do you need a ride?" asked Fran. She could have bought him a car, no problem, but she didn't. It was annoying, but then, what had he ever done to deserve a car?

"Nah," said Nick. "Hugh's picking me up." On cue, they heard a clattering outside, as though someone had strung together a hundred and fifty empty tin cans and was dragging them along down the street. That was Hugh, in his 1998 red Volkswagen Jetta. "Here he is now. Don't want to keep him waiting."

"Bye, honey. Have a great day! I love you."

"See ya," said Nick. He grabbed his backpack and headed out the door.

He had to get in through the back of the Jetta, because the passenger side door didn't work. He crawled to the front seat and Hugh put it in first. With much noise and exhaust, it lurched forward. The noise increased as the RPM needle shot up. You had to go straight from first to third; there was something terribly wrong with second.

"Well good morning, Nick," said Hugh, once they had made it to fourth. "Look at this," he said, pulling a joint from the compartment between the seats. "Do you know what this is?"

"It looks a lot like a joint."

"It's more than that. It's a fucking super joint. Silas's brother brought this shit back from California."

"Shit," said Nick, "I can't."

"Hold on, I don't think you heard me. Or I didn't hear you, one or the other. I've been saving this all night for you, all morning too. I can't wait until you get a permission slip from your mom, or whatever your problem is."

"I've got Ricksclyde first period."

"So? Dick's bride? The old fuck can't see past his nose."

"He doesn't have to... he can smell me out. He *always* calls on me when I'm high. I keep changing seats, but it doesn't matter. He's a hunter. He just knows. And we're on goddamn *Huckleberry Finn* and I tried to read it, but I couldn't do it. So it's a guarantee he's going to call on me. And if I'm straight, I can fake it somewhat, but if I go in there high, I'm done for. I need the grade."

"Jesus Christ, Nick. I keep telling myself there's going to be some kind of reward for all this, for putting up with your bullshit all the time. Fuck it. I'm going to have a few hits. I do *better* in class when I'm high, because I know how to keep my head out of my ass."

Nick laughed. "Sure. Headed straight for Harvard."

"Harvard shit," said Hugh. He lit the joint, took a deep drag and let it out. "Harvard is for pussies." He took one more hit, then snuffed out the joint in the ashtray. "Which makes it a perfect fit for you."

They arrived at the school and the Jetta jerked to a

halt in the parking lot at the bottom of the hill. They walked up the hill. It was a January day in Clairmont, Maine, but it felt like more like early fall than the middle of winter. "What is this shit?" said Hugh. "Global warming?"

Nick shrugged. Whatever it was, if he could make it through first period English, he thought that maybe he could enjoy it.

Chapter two

Today was the day. And tonight, he would sleep. Jonathan Huskfield tilted his head back and tossed the pills into his mouth. They were his own special blend, designed to keep him awake while retaining maximum focus. Nevertheless, three months of daily use had taken its toll. He had begun to malfunction in small, ordinary ways, like putting his shirt on backwards and not noticing until midday, when the chaffing of the tag had become irritating enough to draw in his attention. He found that he had lost the ability to walk and chew gum at the same time, so to speak. He could focus deeply on one thing at a time, but only one thing. That was just as well, as there was only one thing that he truly needed to focus on.

He swirled the test tube around and held it up to the light. The dash of pepper. Brilliant. Tonight, he would be ready to taste the soup. More evidence of his brilliance: he had been working on it in a large batch, enough to feed thousands. More importantly, enough to make him billions of dollars. Besides, the process was so delicate that it simply made sense to produce it in a large batch. Of its success, he had no doubt. A lesser man might have been unsure and made a small test sample. But then he would have wasted a full year. That's how long it took to make it, whether you were making enough to fill an eyedropper, or enough to fill a swimming pool.

And now he held the final ingredient in his hand. He poured it into a container, screwed on the lid, put it in the pocket of his coat and walked out of his lab room. In the main lobby, he bumped into something, a human body. It was Johnston. "Watch where you're going, woman," he said. He was amused by the cloud of rage that passed over her face. She gave the most forced smile he had ever seen. That made him smile in earnest.

"Good morning, Doctor," she said. "Off already? You'll never get anything done at this rate."

"I'll be back around lunchtime," he said. "I'm thinking chicken salad. See that it's on my desk." Her face turned red. He loved to pretend to mistake her for his intern. It put her in her place, the haughty bitch.

He exited the research facility and got in his Corolla. It would be nice to finally get his *own* research facility, and not have to write those obnoxious articles any more. With the money he was going to make, he could buy the entire state of Maine. He did like it there. There were less people around to bother him.

He drove down the road toward town to the small shed that he had purchased. He got out and undid the padlock with his key. He opened the door and there it was: his masterpiece. He opened the container and poured its contents into the tub. He watched green spread out into the milky white mixture, like a drop of ink in water, until finally the entire substance was green. He smiled. It was just as he predicted. Other than the mishap with XB15, it was always just as he predicted.

He put on his gloves and dipped the empty container into the tub. The green fluid rushed into it. He pulled out the container and there it was: his monumental achievement, sitting there in his hand. He screwed on the lid, wiped off the container, and put it in his pocket. Then he took off his gloves, threw them on the ground, and left the shed.

It wasn't until he was sitting at his desk again, writing

in his notebook, that he realized he had left the door to the shed wide open.

Chapter three

The lunch bell rang and there was Lucy. Lucy Littleton. Nick couldn't imagine anything more perfect. He had tried, with his box of tissues beside him on the nightstand, but it always came back to Lucy. She was put together in the fashion of God's good plan. Not just her body, with its full breasts and fulsome behind, but her happy laugh, too, and the way she leaned forward in class, as if Ricksclyde were chanting some magic spell that only she could hear, while the rest of them heard dull and dusty words from a petty old man. There was nothing cruel about her – nothing except for the fact that Nick could never have her. He had watched her grow from a little girl with a cute brown pony tail into the very embodiment of his sexual desire. He knew that he was not alone in his admiration, and would sometimes torture himself with jealousy when he saw her talking to this or that guy.

She was walking toward him. In his fantasies, he was good with the talk. Now, he stood as an atomic mess of nerves and headless desire. Then she said his name. "Nick!" He felt the pulse in his wrists pounding, his stomach pulling inside itself, a stone weight in his head.

"Yaw?"

"Are you going to Jake's party on Saturday?" she asked, smiling. Her smile was beautiful. Her lips and her cheeks were full and alive.

"Yaw."

"Awesome! I'll see you there."

She walked off and Nick didn't dare watch her, but he wanted to. He wanted to stop time and catch up to her and tell her that she was beautiful and that she was like a strand of Mozart or something laughing and dripping with sex in a world that was like a dank hole in the ground. He wanted to spin her around and kiss her lips and talk to her and listen to her laugh. But he didn't. He didn't know how.

He walked outside and found Hugh sitting in his Jetta. "Jesus Christ," said Hugh. "This stuff... we can't go back there. Let's get the fuck out of here."

"Alright. Listen. You hear about a party at Jake Canter's on Saturday?"

"What about it? You want to go hang with the pussycats, maybe drink some Juicy Juice and play Yahtzee all night?" Hugh backed out of the parking lot.

"Jake's alright."

"He's going to be a professional bank teller when he grows up is what he is." Hugh laughed. "Don't worry about me. I would never get in the way of true love. We'll go, if you want to go so bad. At least there'll be a keg there."

"Alright. So what's the plan?"

"The plan," said Hugh, "is that we fire up the rest of this monster joint, and see what happens."

They passed the joint back and forth and drove in silence. Then Nick said, "I am seeing these little red cartoon coins with pure green leaves in the center of them."

"I shouldn't be driving," said Hugh.

"Let's go for a walk."

There was a park a few blocks away. Hugh drove to it, employing the entirety of his concentration. They made it there, after what seemed like three and a half hours. Hugh parked and they crawled out of the Jetta.

"It looks like somebody got really high and tried to park a really shitty car here," said Nick, laughing.

"Fuck it," said Hugh. "I'm not getting back in that thing. If they want to take it away, that's alright with me."

They walked along the edge of the park. Nick looked out at the bay, cold and full of gentle motion. "That's nice," he said.

"That's bullshit," said Hugh. "Nothing's happening. Things want to happen, not stand around with dick in hand."

"There's enough happening, and there's more happening than what we can see. Why can't we just be content with that?"

"And I thought Ricksclyde was dull. Let's go."

They walked along in silence. Soon they were out of the park, and heading further out of town. Then they were out of town, on the industrial fringe, populated by fish factories and other buildings, some of them abandoned and run down, businesses from a time past that had eventually failed or found a better place to be.

They passed by a small shed with its door open. Nick stopped. "What?" said Hugh. "What the fuck?"

"I don't know," said Nick. "What the fuck *is* that?"

Chapter four

Sarah Johnston slammed the door to her office and flung her purse to the floor in a rage. Fucking Jack Huskfield! One day, he would see. All of them would see, all of the puffed-up, cocksure men strutting around as if the world was rightfully theirs, and all of the frail women who groveled at their feet and served them, too. The fault lay with them all. But not with Sarah. She was strong, and driven, and the patriarchy was just another problem to be solved. She could solve a problem – not by waving a cock around, but by studying it, applying her mind, and finally conquering it. When she thought of it like that, she was able to take a deep breath, sit down, and look at her notes.

She sighed. The cancer cells were coming back. With each new formulation, they took a little longer to come back, but they came back nevertheless. No matter. It might take another twenty years, but *she* was going to be the one who cured cancer. Let's see who gets the Noble Prize then. Let's see who is remembered and celebrated throughout history then.

Suddenly, she felt the weight of her tiredness. She hadn't slept all night. She had been at the lab, working, always working. Jack had been there too, but she couldn't say what the bastard was working on. He never *did* anything. Every few months, he would publish an article, obscurely hinting that he was getting closer to understanding and curing Alzheimer's. But Sarah knew that it was a sham. The few glimpses she had caught of him actually working had been of him playing around with chemicals, God knows why. She had seen him once, asleep in his lab with a half-dissected brain inches away from his own head. Other than that, he seemed to do nothing but sexually harass all of the female employees in the building, and make crude jokes with the males. It was disgusting.

Sarah put her head down on her desk and closed her eyes. She couldn't believe that she had once admired Jack. That was before she met him, of course, before she came to work in this godforsaken town. She remembered reading his first book, 18 years ago, when she had been working on her Bachelor's degree at MIT. It was a brilliant study of the brain, revolutionary. It had thrilled her, inspired her.

Maybe just an hour nap. She could allow herself that. Then she could take a fresh look. She began to drift off, and the past began to seep into her brain, to take it over, like the cancer cells did to the healthy ones.

Then she was eight years old. She was living in Boston, walking home from school, and passed the bar where her father liked to get drunk after hanging drywall all day. At first, for the first month after the divorce, Sarah would look through the window and see him there. Sometimes he saw her too, but he always pretended that he didn't. So eventually she had stopped looking.

THE ELECTRIC BONER

On this day, after she had passed the bar, she heard her father's voice behind her. He had come out of the bar and was standing in front of the door, weaving a bit. "Kid," he said, "c'mere aminnit." Sarah regarded him indifferently for a moment, then shrugged and walked over to him.

"Lissen kid," he said, "you got stuck with an ass for an old man. It ain't fair, but that's the way life is, kid: it ain't fair. I jus wanna make sure you know it ain't your fault. You don't let all that get you down. You don't ever let some crummy asshole get you down. You got smarts. Your old man's stupid, but he's got eyes. You got smarts, and you gotta use them. Just... aw shit, kid, just take care, okay?" Then he walked back into the bar and she never saw him again.

She walked home and her mother's boyfriend was having a beer at the kitchen table. She looked at him and wondered why her mother was wasting her time with him, why her mother had wasted her time with her father. She could have been doing so many other things. Sarah went to her room and opened her math book. Everything there made sense, and it was perfect. She sat down and read through it, all of it, doing all of the problems, and getting all of the answers correct. She felt the thrill of excelling, of understanding. She loved it. It was the only thing that she loved, the only thing she wanted.

Then she was at MIT, her second year there. Kenneth Lawton was talking to her after class. He made some kind of joke about quarks, and Sarah laughed. Later, they were making love in his apartment. It was her first time. Then they lay together naked, and talked. Sarah told him all about herself, about how her mother had gotten her one of those science kits when she was 10, and she had gotten bored with it in five minutes and made the volcano experiment more interesting by building a rudimentary motor that powered a pinwheel that blew over an origami swan, which set off a long series of events that she could no longer remember, but which involved all of the chemicals in the kit and the kitchen, and resulted in the paper cup of vinegar spilling and trickling down into the stupid volcano.

The naked intimacy, which she had never known before - as she had hardly bothered to have friends or talk much to anyone -, became another thrill for her, the only other one besides study. The next year, when Kenneth had graduated and gone off to London, she attempted to duplicate that thrill with other men, but it didn't work. They had no problem fucking her, but the warmth and intimacy were absent. They didn't make her laugh, they didn't make her want to tell them things, and she sensed that they didn't want to hear what she had to say anyhow. They were all self-absorbed, and it was as if she might as well not even be there. So she stopped bothering with them, and threw herself deeper into her studies than ever before.

She felt a greatness within herself and she nurtured it, and fed it with success after success. It wasn't enough to have the second highest grade in the class, she had to be first. In this fashion, she got her BA, then her doctorate. She had no trouble landing a job at a major pharmaceutical company, as head of research. It was there that she met Roland Matthews.

Roland was able to give her everything that Kenneth had, and more. His jokes were funnier, his penis larger, and his mind was almost as sharp as Sarah's own. Not wanting to repeat her past mistake, she married him, so that she could hold on to the thrill and keep it always. But slowly, without really noticing it, the thrill began to fade. Instead of talking about herself, and her history and aspirations and feelings, she began talking more and more about work. Then the sex had stopped being interesting, and more of a nuisance than anything. Then even talking about anything with him, or going out to dinner, became a nuisance.

THE ELECTRIC BONER

Then Roland himself became a nuisance. His salary was half again as much as hers, and she was twice as accomplished, twice as capable, twice as good. It didn't make any sense. It was because he was a man, and she was a woman, she realized. To put an end to things, one night she went back to her office, because she had forgotten her purse. There she found Roland, fucking the receptionist on her desk.

Sarah flew into a rage, and began throwing things around. She grabbed the stapler from the desk and began hitting Roland over the head with it. The receptionist was screaming, covering her naked breasts. Stupid bitch. After Roland slumped over unconscious, Sarah began beating her. Then she left them there, covered in blood. The next day she was fired, but Roland and the slut had decided not to press charges. He was promoted to her position, and was now making twice as much as she had. Of course, they got divorced.

Sarah was beginning to discover the third and final thrill of her life. Rather than destroying her, what had happened with Roland only spurred her on to excellence. She moved to New York City, took another job, and began to become more interested in conducting her own research, after hours. In this way, she was able to publish a series of papers on cancer, which put her in contention for a Nobel Prize. She lost out narrowly to Michael Dreeves, which enraged her. But she had made a name for herself, and was offered a job working with the esteemed Doctor Jonathan Huskfield in a government research facility in some backwoods town in Maine.

She jumped at the chance to work with the only man she had ever looked up to. When he turned out to be a chauvinistic slob, the idea that had been fermenting in her mind - through her experiences in life, through the history of the world, through what her handful of friends scattered throughout the world had confirmed – came to fruition. Men Ruled the World and They Were Shitty At It. It infuriated her to think that such incompetence could rule *her* life, and it became her final thrill and everlasting fuel to think that one day she would change all that and put men in their place.

She fell asleep.

Chapter five

"Some kind of green toxic shit," said Hugh.

"What do you think it's doing here?" asked Nick.

"Who gives a shit?"

Nick laughed. "Weren't you the one who wanted some action?" He stepped into the shed.

"You call this bubbling tub of shit *action*? Let's *go*," said Hugh. He was trying to act bored, but there was a definite edge to his voice. Nick felt it too, a strange unease at the sight and the putrid smell of the green toxic shit. At the same time, he felt an overwhelming curiosity. He felt that combination of dread and fascination a lot, high or not.

As he peered over the edge of the tub, the vapors stung his eyes. There was a swirling of colors in his head, and then blackness. Out of that blackness, he saw an image of the Earth, getting larger and larger as it zoomed in, and kept zooming in like a satellite image, and then it was like he was in a plane, flying past the tops of trees, and then it was like he was at the top of the old church in Clairmont, Maine, looking down at the intersection with the only traffic light in town. Nick saw the streets littered with corpses, grey, blue, green, bloated, stiff, rotting. Then the corpses began to rise, and then they began walking around like they were alive, like everything was normal. One of them made a deposit at the ATM. One of them went into the bakery and came out with a green, moldy loaf of bread under his arm. His face was falling off. Then, all at once, they converged, beneath the traffic light. They began grabbing at each other, and fucking each other. Then some began to crawl on the ones who were fucking each other, and those ones started fucking, and then some crawled on top of them, and the pile kept getting higher and higher. Then the last one was standing face to face with Nick on top of the church and it raised its bone hand and pointed at him and growled, "You're next."

"Like Hell," said Nick.

"What's that?" said Hugh, who was still just outside the door.

The image was gone. Nick stared into the green toxic shit for a moment, and then said, "This is it."

"Oh God. What? This is what?"

"This is the essence. This is what happens when we're not content to just sit and watch the waves."

"I've heard some pretty fruity shit come out of that mouth of yours, Nick, but that has got to take the cake."

"This is all of our nasty bits, put together, stewing away for thousands of years."

"Listen, there isn't some medication you've been taking, haven't told me about, and for some reason decided to kick it this morning - is there?"

"Hold on. I'm going to capture it." Nick pulled out his phone, centered the tub, and shot it.

"Great," said Hugh. "I'm sure I'll see it on the cover of National Geographic next month. Can we get the fuck out of here now?"

Nick took a last look. The bubbling liquid seemed to hold him in a trance. He was staring at it, and it seemed somehow to be getting closer to him, though he wasn't moving his head.

"HEY!" someone shouted. The voice was like an explosion of glass in Nick's being, and he dropped his phone into the tub.

"Shit! My phone!"

"What are you punks *doing*? Get the hell *away* from

there!"

"Fuck your phone! Time to go!"

The phone was bobbing along on top of the green toxic shit. Nick plucked it out, dripping with the stuff. He wiped it off on his pants and shoved it in his pocket. Then there was a hand on his shoulder, pulling him out of the shed.

"Let's *go* you asshole!" said Hugh, spinning him around. Nick saw a man running toward them. He had a grey beard and large glasses and was wearing a white coat, like a doctor. They ran as fast as they possibly could.

Chapter six

Jack reached in his pocket for the padlock, put it through the loop, and clicked it shut. He watched them scamper off. He might run them down in his Corolla and teach them a lesson, but it would be the wrong lesson. It would be the lesson that he had been taught, again and again, ruthlessly and relentlessly, as a child. It would be the lesson that had landed him in the emergency room when he was 12, with three broken ribs; that had left him embarrassed and in tears in front of all of the girls he had found lovely; that had left him standing in the mirror at age 22 with a kitchen knife in his right hand, envisioning with such clarity Langer's lines, until his hand shook so bad that he knew he couldn't do it.

Jack had another lesson to teach the world. It was that true power lay in the mind, and that with that power, you could conquer the physical and have anything you desired. Too bad for them that they had rat shit for brains – that wasn't his problem.

He drove back to the lab, walked to his lab room, and put the container - which contained his future - in a drawer. That was prudent. With the important thing always occupying his mind, he might forget that the container was in his pocket and bump into something and break it. That could be disastrous.

But wasn't there something he was forgetting? He searched his mind. Ah, yes, of course. The wine. And the candles. After all, it was a special night, and he wanted it to be lavish, exquisite. Soon, he would be able to send out a whole team to address such trivialities, but for now, he had to attend to them himself.

He left the lab and drove to the supermarket. He hated it there, amongst all those people. Even the ones who fancied themselves exceptional – the doctors, the lawyers, the ones making six figures – were nothing but puffed-up cockroaches. Check that. They *all* fancied themselves exceptional, even the bag boys. But what had they ever done? What had they ever done except what they were trained to do? They should bend down on their knees and thank God that innovators like him existed, people who could make their worthless lives a little more comfortable, a little longer, a little healthier.

He saw a young man with a muscular upper body, manually rolling himself along in a wheelchair, deftly grabbing things from the shelves and putting them in the basket that had been fashioned at the chair's side. Such grace, in the face of such adversity. *That* was exceptional.

Jack felt a shock of guilt. He knew that he could help this man walk again. He had the research in his notebook, on his desk. It was a byproduct of his work on the serum, which had been a byproduct of his work on Alzheimer's. He watched the man roll down the aisle and out of sight. Soon, friend. Let me get what's mine, let me enjoy it, and then I can resume my work in helping you. It will be better this way – I can focus on it without distractions, without having to write those silly articles, without having to play their game.

He got the wine, the most expensive Pinot Noir they had, the candles, and some chicken salad for lunch. He got in line and looked at the checkout clerk. She was young and beautiful. He could never dream of having a woman like her, with his awkward body, his awkward ways. But maybe he would keep a bit of the serum for himself, and have her anyway. Why not? It would be part of the reward for his life's work, and down payment on the truly great things he had yet to do. No doubt, the money would bring the women in droves, but this way seemed more honest to him. He hated whores.

"How are you today, sir?" she asked, smiling at him.

Yes, she was a keeper all right. Sweet and righteous. He would treat her well, in his fashion. "Fine, fine, my dear," he said, smiling back.

He got his things and left. For the rest of the day, he checked his notes for the thousandth time. He studied them for hours, making sure they were correct. Everything was in order. It was going to work. He cleaned up the room, putting all of the chemicals away in the closet. By the time he was done, it was 9:23 PM. The lab would be empty. It was time.

He set up the candles and lit them. He had gotten the lavender ones, his favorite scent. Then he opened the good red and poured it into his glass. He swished it around and took a sip. Then, laughing, he poured some into the other glass.

"Sarah," he said softly. "Where are you?" He took another sip, and then bellowed: "SARAH! COME!"

Chapter seven

Sarah Johnston awoke. She thought somebody was calling her name and lifted her head. It was dark. How long had she been asleep? The clock said 9:32. Some hour-long nap that had been. She turned on her lamp, squinted her eyes, and slowly began to come back to herself.

THE ELECTRIC BONER

"SARAH!"

It sounded like Jack. What was the old bastard up to? Maybe he was having a heart attack? She stood up and stretched out. Oh, if only she hadn't just woken up. Then maybe she could move a little faster. She smiled and slowly made her way to the door.

The hallway was pitch black. Some brilliant architect had decided to put two light switches on each floor. But that was just as well. She couldn't check on Jack in a dark hallway. She'd have to walk all the way back to the main entrance, turn on the light, and then go check on him. Maybe by then, he'd be dead.

Then she heard a door open and close. She walked softly in the direction of Jack's lab room, opposite the light switch. She listened. After a few minutes, she heard a soft moaning. The moaning was getting louder. Then she reached room 110, and saw a faint flicker of light coming from below the door. She put her ear to the door and heard Jack talking in a low voice. "Oh yes," he was saying, "suck it you little bitch."

She had to cover her mouth to keep from laughing. Sarah, that was also Jack's intern's name. One of his favorite jokes. She was beginning to see the humor in it. A blowjob was just as good as a heart attack, maybe even better. Only, she wouldn't make the same mistake she'd made with Roland, who had denied the fact that he had been fucking the receptionist in the office, on her desk. Oh, the wonders of modern science! Her cell phone would clear it all up. Just one little snapshot, and Jack would be revealed for the pig he was.

She reached in her pocket, but it wasn't there. She almost let out a curse, but stifled it and stalked back down the dark hallway. She went into her office, and there it was, on the floor amidst the scattered contents of her purse. She emitted a quiet curse, and bent down to pick it up. Then she heard Jack scream.

"YOU BITCH!!" The sound echoed down the

hallway as she stuck her head out into it. Dear God, please, please don't ruin this. She moved quietly and quickly down the dark hallway. When she was almost to the corner, she heard a terrible scream, as of a large animal being slaughtered and protesting with its entire being. She froze. She heard the door open again, and then all was quiet. Still, dark, quiet. She stood without moving, frightened. Finally, her scientific curiosity got the better of her and she slowly turned the corner.

She saw the door to room 110 standing open, illuminated faintly by a flickering light coming from inside. As she got closer, she saw a streak of blood across the face of the door, and she saw that the door knob was covered in blood. She reached into her pocket for her knife. She always carried it with her, in case some asshole tried to attack or rape her. And she had 10 years of mixed martial arts weekend classes under her proverbial belt, so that the asshole would have another thing coming.

She was nearly at the door when she saw the bare and bloody footprints disappearing into blackness further down the hall. She gripped her knife tight and looked in the room. There were dozens of candles lined up on the tables, and a glass of wine spilled next to Jack's hand. Jack was slumped over in a chair, with his back to her. She saw the pool of red on the floor next to him, and couldn't make out if it were blood or wine.

"Jack?" she said softly. He didn't answer. She turned on the lights and walked over to face him. He was quite dead. His entrails were spilling out of him, his colon touching the floor. She screamed, then put her hand over her mouth and turned around in terror. She picked up a candle and carried it to the hallway. She could see a little further, down to where the footsteps turned another corner. There was a streak of blood along the wall.

She backed into the room and locked the door. Then she opened her phone. But she saw two things which delayed the call. First, she saw Jack's notebook, laying open on one of the tables. She walked over to it. She had better take that with her, to carry on the legacy of Jack's work. It wouldn't be of any help to the police, surely.

Then she saw something below the table in a pool of blood. It looked as though somebody had bitten it in half and spit it out. She walked back over to Jack. Yes, there was the other half. She began laughing, quietly at first, and then louder, and finally the sound filled the whole room. It was all there was.

Chapter eight

Nick lay in bed and did what he always did at the end of a bad day. It was what he did at the end of a good day, too. He wasn't quite sure whether this had been a good or a bad day – more strange than anything. He was trying not to think about his vision of the undead orgy. That was nothing more than some kind of pot trip – it had been the most potent joint he'd ever smoked.

Jerking off was great because you didn't need to be good with the girls to do it. You didn't need to be good with the talk, you didn't need to have the good looks. Nick knew that he looked alright, but it never helped him. He always sort of left his body altogether whenever a pretty girl approached him. But here, now, all he needed was a functional dick.

When he wanted to speed things along – and he almost always had to, because Fran was forever walking around, making her footsteps heard at just the worst moments – he got things started by looking at porn. He pulled out his phone and found his favorite site. It worked. It worked every time.

He spit on his hand and started stroking it. When he was getting close, he always liked to finish in his head. He closed his eyes and there was Lucy. They were sitting together on a grassy hill in the sunshine. He said something clever and she threw her head back and laughed. Her hair was out of its ponytail and fell down below her shoulders. It was golden brown in the sun. Then she looked at him with her deep blue eyes and, still laughing, pushed him back onto the grass. She lifted his shirt and began kissing his stomach, working her way down.

She pulled it out of his pants and slowly licked the shaft, circling the head with her tongue, all the while looking him in the eyes. Then she grabbed it, pulled her head away abruptly, and then gave the tip a quick peck. She looked at it for a second, smiled at him, and then lunged at it. Then it was all the way in, it had disappeared in her mouth, touching the back of her throat. Then she pulled back, looked at it again, looked at him again, leaned in, and began bobbing away, gently twisting on it with her hand, slurping loudly, swirling her tongue around it.

He came so hard that he felt some of it splash on his neck. At once, the bliss left him, and there was only darkness. He hated this part. He opened his eyes and looked down to see how much of a mess there was. Then a shudder ran through him, and he felt queasy. *What the fuck?!*

His dick was green. He was still holding his phone in one hand, and watched as the green toxic shit trickled out of the charging port, straight onto his dick. He did a quick clean up, pulled his shorts back on, and leaped out of the bed. He didn't know if he was going to make it.

He ran past his mother, who was just coming up the stairs. "Nick? Are you okay?"

He made it just in time. The vomit came in bucket loads. It was green. The toilet bowl filled up and he had to flush, but it kept coming.

"Nick! What's wrong?!" yelled his mother.

The last load came, he flushed, leaned his head on the bowl for a moment, then stood up. "It's alright mom," he said through the door.

"I'm taking you to the hospital!" she said.

"I'm fine!" he said, looking down at his green dick. "Probably just your goddamn scrambled eggs."

He rubbed some soap and warm water on it and, mercifully, the green washed away. He looked at himself in the mirror. *All* of the color had washed out of him. He looked and felt like a ghost.

He left the bathroom, gave Fran a wan smile in passing, and flopped back on his bed. He couldn't think. An impossible tiredness overtook him and he closed his eyes.

Chapter nine

Her story was in line with what he saw, but he got the sense that she was keeping something from him. But there was no reason to hold her any longer. Whatever the case may be, Lt. Mikhail Duvlosky didn't believe that she had anything to do with the murder.

"Thank you for your help, Ms. Johnston," he said. "You go home and get some rest. But do me a favor, and don't leave town until we have this cleared up. You know… in case we have any more questions."

She nodded and walked down the hallway, out of sight. Mikhail walked back to room 110. The medical examiners were still fussing with the body. It didn't take a PhD to know that Huskfield was dead, but he didn't blame them. It was all so strange and gruesome. Marie had told him that murders didn't happen but once a decade in Clairmont, and that's exactly why she had wanted to move back. Mikhail had seen his share of murders in Philly, but never anything like this.

He stood in the back of the room and mentally reviewed what Johnston had told him. 9:32 PM she had been awakened at her desk, and heard Huskfield call her name. She then walked down the hallway to his lab room, but stopped when she heard a door open. She then heard what sounded to her like some kind of sexual activity. Not wanting to intrude, she had turned back to her office. When she heard screams, she had run to room 110, to find the door open and bloodied, with the bloody footprints leading out of it. Concerned, she had rushed in to find Huskfield like this. Eviscerated and dismembered. She had then immediately dialed 911 and returned to her office to wait for them.

It was there that she had recalled that Huskfield's intern was also named Sarah, and that it was probably her he had been calling. But Johnston didn't think she had done *this*. How could she have? She was just a 21 year old girl, and as far as Johnston knew, she held no particular ill will against Huskfield.

But, Mikhail knew, sex can do strange things to people. Two people got together and they lived a life behind closed doors that nobody else in the world knew about, or could guess. Passions rose, all sorts of passions. Passions that gave life and passions that took it.

Still... Mikhail looked at the photograph that Rogers had found on the 8th floor - that's where the interns had their work area, and it was actually the seventh floor *below* grade. This Wilkins girl *looked* so sweet, so harmless, bright-eyed and beautiful. Could she really have done *this*?

He heard footsteps behind him. "Sir?" It was Miller. Poor Miller. He had never seen anything even close to this before. None of them had.

"What have you got?"

"The footprints lead out of the parking lot and into the woods. It's a pretty clear trail."

"Take Rogers and Phillips. This is our main and only suspect," said Mikhail, handing Miller the photograph. Miller raised his eyebrows and gave Mikhail a questioning look.

"It doesn't make sense to me, either. But the footprints fit, and it's all we've got. Just go in there expecting anything. Whoever it is, is obviously capable of some pretty heavy shit. Just stay in contact. I need to stay here and keep things organized, keep the crime scene intact. The damn paramedic kid already vomited all over the floor."

Miller nodded, then handed back the photo. "Don't worry, Lt," he said. "Whatever's out there, we'll get it."

Chapter ten

Sarah walked into her apartment, set her purse on the kitchen table, pulled out a chair, and sat down. She smiled. She had been horrified at first, that was true, but that was only an animal reaction. She wasn't an animal. She could process the raw data, and give it meaning. Once she had done that, she grew elated. She pulled the notebook out of her purse and set it down on the table. It was thick. Old Jack had been a busy boy after all.

She opened it up and began flipping through the pages. There was a Nobel Prize, and there was a Nobel Prize, and there was one. Oh, that one might be used to help the paralyzed regain use of their limbs. And that one really *did* show a clear path to the remedy for Alzheimer's. Each page was more amazing than the last. After a while, she had to put it down and get up to make some tea. It was like having 30 orgasms in a row, each one more intense than any that had ever been delivered to her by a penis.

How was this possible? Why hadn't he published any of this? The questions haunted her as the kettle began to whistle. The old bastard had been up to something, there was no doubt about that. But what? She poured her tea and sat back down at the table.

As she turned the pages, the ground-breaking research began to be interceded with chemical formulas. But the formulas didn't fit with what had preceded them, or what followed. They were intricate, bold formulas, combining things that she had never heard of being combined before. Just looking at the physical shape of the periodic symbols and the lines connecting them mesmerized her. It was like a work of art, each one of them, just the shape of the lines on the page. And when she considered what those lines represented…

For the first time in her life, she didn't know, scientifically, what she was looking at. She realized now that somewhere in the back of her mind, she had understood that each of her attempts to cure cancer would fail, before she had even run the tests. She had known exactly what her formulations would amount to, but she had tried them anyhow, unable to face the fact that she couldn't solve the problem. This all came to her now, at the kitchen table, looking over Jack's notebook. She knew science, but she didn't know this.

But as she looked at it, for the third time, the fourth time, the seventh time, slowly a picture began forming in her head. Everything was related after all. The very last page was related to the very first page, and all the ones in between it. She set down her teacup, which had been emptied for the twelfth time, and looked at the clock. It was 4:56 in the morning. She remembered waking up and looking at the glowing red clock in her office and it had said 9:32 PM. Then an image of Jack's chewed-up penis came to the center of her mind, and all at once she had it.

After that, it didn't take much consideration. Help the crippled regain the use of their dicks, help senile old men find theirs again? Why? So they could go waving it in everyone's face again? No, those things were petty in the grand scheme. She *was* going to be the one who cured cancer, after all. And that cancer, of course, was men.

Chapter eleven

Nick awoke with a throbbing dick. It was still dark. He looked over at the clock, saw that there was some weird number there, some number that meant he should still be asleep, flipped over and closed his eyes again. He reached down, as a sort of comfort-reflex, into his boxers and wrapped his hand around it.

Last year, Nick had put an overhead light in the living room, at Fran's request. She could have afforded to hire 25 crews to build 25 different houses for her, but she had asked Nick to do it. The year before, one of their light switches had blown, and Nick had read on the internet how to replace it, and convinced her to let him try it. He'd had a Hell of a time convincing her, but in the end she relented. And he'd fixed it, and it felt good. It was a good balance to all of the time he spent in his head – to use his hands and make something work. After that, he started volunteering for more projects. The clogged-up kitchen drain was so easy that he almost didn't get any satisfaction from it. Almost. So when Fran had asked Nick to wire the new light, he knew that it was for his sake. He knew that she knew it made him feel good to do things like that.

The problem was, the project was more than he had anticipated. He had to dig around in the insulation in the attic, where it was probably two or three hundred degrees Fahrenheit. He had to cut through drywall with a utility knife. He had to fuck around with making the connections to the light, bending the wires just so while he was dripping with sweat. When it came time to cut the feed wire and make the junction box in the attic, he had to crawl back down, head down to the basement, and shut off the breaker, thinking all the while that that should have been the first thing he had done. When he got back into the attic, itching hopelessly with the bits of fiberglass that seemed to multiply and get deeper every time he scratched, he cut the supply line, so he could make the splice.

The problem was, he had turned off the wrong breaker. As he cut the line with the uninsulated pliers he had on hand, he felt the jolt of electricity run though his body. He recoiled from the wire, jumping back and landing between joists, so that his legs crashed through the drywall, and dangled down into the second floor bathroom.

That jolt, and that feeling of helplessly dangling, were like a gentle handjob compared to what he now felt. His eyes shot open and his back lifted off the bed, causing him to arch his body in amazement. This was the definition of shock. A little drool trickled onto his pillow. He let go of his dick and all at once his body relaxed.

His mind was static for several minutes, until slowly thought trickled back into it. What the fuck was that? A nightmare? Epilepsy? To comfort himself, without thinking, he reached back down to his cock, which was still hard and throbbing, hungry. The shock ran through his body once again. He felt something wet coming from his nose, and released his grip.

The third time was deliberate, to test a theory. That time, he swore he saw a little glow of light come from down there. But he couldn't say for sure. His brains felt like the scrambled eggs he'd had for breakfast. He released once again.

He flipped on his lamp, feeling weak and beyond tired. He pulled down his shorts and looked at it. It looked normal. It looked normal, but it was an electric boner.

Chapter twelve

"That Johnston's face weren't much to look at, I'll give ya that. But did you see that ass? Flip 'er around and she coulda had seven eyes and a horn growing out 'er goddamn head for all I care," said Gerald Phillips, laughing. Rogers gave a half-hearted chuckle, and then it was back to nothing but branches snapping. Christ, these guys were acting like somebody had just rammed something up *their* asses. Were they really scared of a little girl?

"Look," said Miller. He shone his flashlight at a big oak tree, smeared in blood.

"Bout as subtle as a elephant," said Jerry. Wilkins had left them a nice little trail, alright. Even in the dark, he could have found it half-drunk. In a way, it felt like just another hunting trip with Miller and Rogers. But in another way, it didn't feel that way at all.

They picked through the woods for another fifteen minutes in silence. Jerry couldn't take it anymore. "Hey, I ever tell you guys about the old whore who walked into a bar, sat on a bar stool, and sunk to the ground?"

"Shut up," said Miller. "Just shut up."

Jerry didn't like that at all, but he decided to give Miller a break. The poor fucker *was* scared. So was Rogers. "You got it boss," said Jerry. "I'll shut up, but we find the bitch, she gives us any trouble, can't say the same about my Glock here." He held it up in the darkness.

That got another nervous laugh from Rogers. Hell, it was better than nothing. Tough crowd tonight.

Miller led them on. The trail was erratic, like the one a deer makes when you wound it, but miss its vitals and it runs off scared. Instead of ducking under the branches, she had simply snapped them off. Some of them were pretty big branches, and that might have worried Jerry, if he didn't know he was looking for a little girl, and if he didn't have two armed men alongside him. She was probably just on crank or something. These kids get hopped up on crank and they start doing all sorts of crazy shit. But nothing he couldn't handle.

After an hour, they reached a small clearing and there was Wilkins. She was naked and covered in blood. She was looking around, dazed. Doped up on *something*. Then she slowly turned to face them.

"Christ," muttered Rogers, "look at her *eyes*."

"Forget 'er eyes," said Jerry, "look at them *tits*." But when he caught the reflection of his flashlight in her eyes, he shuddered. They were wrong.

"Ma'am," said Miller. "Stay where you are, and put your hands up, slowly."

"Yeah," said Jerry, trying not to look at those eyes. "Put 'em up real high like, make them tits kiss the sky."

Jerry saw her smile, and she began walking toward them.

"Shit," said Rogers. "She's insane."

"Ain't they all?" said Jerry. But he found himself taking a step back.

"I'm not going to ask you again," said Miller. "If you don't stop right there, we're going to have to use force."

She took one more step forward, then slid her hand down to her crotch. She began rubbing it, and with her other hand, she pointed at Miller, and then flipped her finger over and beckoned him to come.

"Think she likes you," said Jerry. His previous misgivings were gone. He had a hard-on.

Miller had his taser in hand. "What the fuck?" he said.

Jerry thought it over. "Look," he said. "Ain't no one ever gonna know. What's the harm? She *wants* it. So we give 'er what she wants, then take 'er in and everybody wins."

"Shut up, Phillips," said Miller.

"She ripped that guy's *dick* off," said Rogers.

"Only cause it weren't big enough for 'er," said Jerry. "Wait'll she gets a look at the Jerrinator." He started walking toward her.

"Phillips," said Miller, "you stop right there or so help me, I'll taze you *both*."

Jerry ignored him. He walked up to Wilkins, who was still rubbing herself, and grabbed one of her tits. Her smile broadened.

"Maybe he's right," said Rogers. "Maybe we ought to give her what she wants."

She stuck her lips out and Jerry leaned in to kiss them. They were nice and full and warm. Now the only thing he was afraid of was that he might cum in his pants. Then he felt an incredible pain and he wanted to scream out "YOU WHORE" but the only thing that came out his mouth was a gush of blood. He fell back, on his ass, and when he hit the ground, it hit him: the bitch had bitten his tongue off. He sprawled onto the ground.

She spat out Jerry's tongue and it landed next to his head. He could see her feet. They started moving, toward Miller and Rogers. He looked over and saw Miller's feet. Then he saw the taser fall down next to them. He heard a shot, and blood splattered against his face.

"Fuck!" he heard Rogers scream. He lifted his head and he saw that Wilkins had Miller by the neck. Her right thigh was bleeding where Miller had shot her. Then she unzipped his pants and pulled out his dick. She started stroking it.

Rogers ducked out behind her and swung the butt of his Glock at the back of her head. She didn't even flinch. Miller was trying to say something, but he couldn't. But Rogers got the message. He flipped the gun around and put it to the side of her head. Then he fired.

Jerry saw the side of her head open up as the bullet tore through it. Chunks of brain and skull flew through the air, catching glints of the moonlight. Then the wind picked up, out of nowhere, and it started to snow. More than started to snow. It was a sudden blizzard.

He squinted and caught one more glimpse, before the snow blotted everything out. He saw Miller, and he saw Wilkins. She was still choking him, and stroking him.

PART II

Chapter thirteen

Nick awoke and reached down like he always did, but stopped himself just in time. Maybe it *had* just been a nightmare? He didn't want to find out, not just then. And he had a feeling that it was as real as the snow piled on the skylight, blocking both the sky and the light. He heard the wind howling outside. That meant there was probably no school. Somehow, the prospect left him feeling flat. For the first time he could remember, he was eager to get out of his bed, eager to go downstairs and see his mother.

He waddled down the hallway and into the bathroom. He pissed, and his boner retreated. He had to do it, had to find out. He grabbed his soft dick between his thumb and forefinger and gave it a shake. Nothing happened. Well, that was good, anyway. It was something. Maybe everything was back to normal?

Fran was in the kitchen, making pancakes. She turned and smiled when he came in. "School's cancelled," she said.

"I figured," he said.

"How are we feeling this morning?"

"Alright," he lied. It was comforting, though, seeing her there, the same as always.

"Are you sure? You were pretty sick last night. You weren't drinking, were you?"

"No, mom," he said.

"Pancakes?"

"Alright."

She slid three huge ones onto a plate and set it down

on the island. There was no way he could eat all that.

He took them into the living room and turned on the TV. It was on a local station, the morning news. He was about to change it when he saw an image on the screen of the guy who had chased them away from the green toxic shit yesterday. He turned it up.

"...was found in his lab last night, gruesomely murdered. Police suspect this woman, 21 year-old Sarah Wilkins, of being involved."

The guy's picture was replaced by a picture of a beautiful young woman, healthy and smiling. Nick felt something stir in his pants and shoved half of a pancake into his mouth.

"Wilkins was an intern for Huskfield, and it is reported by a witness that he had called her name just seconds before he was brutally slaughtered. The search for Wilkins was cut short early this morning, as the unexpected blizzard swept in and made it impossible to continue. Police are cautioning people to stay at home until the storm passes, but are asking for any information that might lead them to Sarah Wilkins. If you have any such information, please call the number listed on the screen. That's..."

They kept showing that damn picture of the girl. His cock was straining against his jeans. He thought it was going to break the zipper. He'd never been more anxious for breakfast in his life. He kept shoving it in. He felt it filling his stomach, making him sluggish. But his dick was at full alert. They finally went to the weatherman, but it was too late. The girl's image was seared into his brain, floating around in the center of it, making its way down through him, past the mass of pancakes, and into what felt at the moment like the very center of his being.

Finally he couldn't take it anymore. He walked back into the kitchen and slid the empty plate across the island. "Thanks mom, that was great. You know what, I think I'm going to get a head start on this report I have due next week."

His mother raised an eyebrow. "Are you sure everything's okay, honey?"

"Sure. Jesus, a guy can't even do his homework anymore without getting the third degree?"

Fran laughed. "I was beginning to think they didn't even *give* you homework anymore."

Nick hurried up to his room and flopped on the bed. He unzipped his pants and kicked them off, then threw down his shorts. That gave him some relief. He lay there looking at it. The thing had always been a mixed blessing at best. It had always seemed somehow like it wasn't a part of him, but at the same time it was very much a part of him. Sometimes it seemed like a ridiculous piece of meat hanging there as a joke. Sometimes it seemed like it was all there was in the world. Now it seemed that way, and it was awful. He was afraid to touch it, but it was a worse boner than any one he'd ever had. It *begged* to be touched.

He reached slowly down with just his index finger and brushed it lightly against the head. Then everything was white, pure white, and for half a second he couldn't feel anything, and then he felt it. He felt the pain stab through his body in a sudden burst, and then he started tingling all over. He had to bite down on his pillow to keep from screaming.

When he opened his eyes again, it was soft. The image of the girl had been sort of whitewashed out of his brain. From the blankness emerged an image of the guy whom they had seen yesterday... this Huskfield. "Gruesomely murdered." What the fuck was going on?

Chapter fourteen

Most likely, there was still time. The blizzard had

provided her that assumption. Sarah didn't believe in God and she didn't believe in luck. But she knew an opportunity when she saw one, and this one was so big that it almost *was* as if there were Something up there, finally making things happen for her.

The storm had caught everyone sleeping. The roads weren't yet plowed and she had to drive carefully in her Prius. She drifted dangerously a couple of times, but there was no oncoming traffic to worry about, and she thought she could manage. She couldn't see ten feet in front of her, but she didn't have to. She knew where she was going. It was the most probable location.

As it was, it was still a theory. The reciprocating saw in the passenger side seat would help prove that theory true or false. She had cut through flesh and bone plenty with a similar version. This one was cordless, but it was all she could manage without taking a trip to the lab. She'd bought it when she had demolished the walk-in closet in her bedroom. She'd had no need for such foolish vanity, and she'd had no need to hire someone else to do the work for her… some crew of foul-mouthed, cigarette-smoking, sweating and stinking men.

She crested the hill going down into town. As far as she could she – which wasn't very far, she knew – it was deserted. A little adversity sent them all crawling under their beds. A little adversity made Sarah as sharp as a hawk.

She pulled her Prius alongside the curb in front of Finnegan's Pub. She had been inside once, when she had first moved to town. It was like any another bar in America. It didn't matter if it was a working class bar, or an exclusive club where people with money and power went. It was just men waving their cocks around, and women with no self-worth grabbing at them. She'd had a glass of Pinot Grigio by herself and then left, disgusted.

It was where they all went, all of her coworkers, on a Wednesday night or a Friday night. Surely it was etched into the intern's brain. It was a simple, primal equation: the closest place where she was likely to find the most number of dicks. If Sarah was right about this, then she was most certainly right about the rest. Though the one last test would confirm it all.

She picked up the saw and got out of the car. With the snow blowing directly in her eyes, she couldn't even see the ten feet. It was the noise she heard, through the blast of the wind, that alerted her. A persistent thudding sound. Sarah stepped slowly toward it. It wasn't until she had almost bumped into the body that she saw it.

She saw the hands first, covered in a veil of red, where the snow had thinned out the blood. The hands were beating and clawing against the plate glass window of the bar, where Sarah saw a sign hung: CLOSED DUE TO INCLIMENT WEATHER.

Then the hands stopped and with her eyes Sarah followed the bloody hands to the naked arms, to the naked breasts, whiter than the snow but for the splatter of gore, and up the bruised and blood-streaked neck to the head. The head was only partially there. A good portion of it was missing, the raw brain exposed. Sarah almost dropped her saw.

She closed her eyes and thought of all the times that Jack had spoken to her as if *she* were the intern. As if she was nothing. And she thought of this Wilkins following him around like a puppy dog, even flirting whorishly with him. That was all she needed. When she opened her eyes, the hands were reaching for her neck. They were moving slow. Sarah spun around them to the intern's back.

She put her finger on the trigger and laid the saw to Wilkins' neck. The blade skipped around at first, chewing the flesh. Then it found its track when it found the bone. Wilkins was jerking her head around wildly, but that only helped the cut, and saved Sarah the trouble of wiggling the saw around.

All Sarah could see was red and white, as the snow stung her eyes and the blood flew into her face. Then she felt a cold hand close around her neck. She couldn't breathe, but she kept working the saw as best she could. Then she felt the hand relax its grip and fall away.

Exhausted, Sarah wiped the blood from her face with the back of her hand. She saw the body lying on the ground, with the severed head next to it. She picked the head up by hair that had once been smooth and blond, but was now a gargled mess of dirt and gore. She looked at it. It was snapping its teeth at her. She gave it a good slap.

Chapter fifteen

Trying to find a needle in a haystack was child's play. Mikhail thought that whoever had come up with that saying should try stomping around in the woods through a foot of snow during a blizzard, looking for… something. Was he looking for the bodies of his men? He hoped not, but they had stopped responding to their radios hours ago. They weren't answering their cell phones, either.

He didn't know what he was looking for, and he didn't know where to look for it. His men had gone off into the woods and reported that the perpetrator had left a clear trail. But whatever trail there may have been was now buried. And it didn't help that he couldn't see his fingertips if he stretched out his hand.

All at once, the snow and the wind stopped. Everything was suddenly very clear and still. Mikhail turned around and there was somebody, less than a yard behind him. He tensed up and prepared to strike, but relaxed when he saw it was Henderson. Of course it was. Who else would it have been?

"There's a clearing up ahead," said Mikhail. "Let's go check it out." They tramped through the snow, ducking branches until they made it. Mikhail's heart sank when he saw the research lab in the distance. "Goddammit," he said. "We're back where we started."

"Least that shit storm stopped, Lt. Never seen anything like it. No warning, nothing. There's a lot been happening I've never seen anything like it before."

Mikhail pulled out a cigarette and offered it to Henderson. Then he lit one up himself. He radioed Richaud. "This is Duvlosky. Status?"

"Well, we're out here in the middle of the woods," came the cracked voice from the other side. "No GPS here. We're lost."

"Well, just keep going. You're bound to get somewhere eventually. And let me know the second you find anything."

"10-4."

"What now?" asked Henderson.

For an instant, Mikhail pictured himself in bed with Marie, warm and happy. "We go back," he said. "We keep looking. We've got three men who went in there." He looked at Henderson's face. "Look," he lied, "I'm sure they're fine. Their equipment probably just malfunctioned."

"Yeah," said Henderson in an unsure voice. "You're probably right."

"Tell you what. Let's take a break and finish these smokes, then we'll go back in." Henderson needed a break, Mikhail could tell. Mikhail needed one too, probably, but now he didn't feel like it. The sudden silence to the storm had energized him. He had men to find, and a murder suspect.

They threw their butts into the snow and headed back into the woods. They hadn't made it very far when the call came from dispatch. "Female body found outside of Finnegan's Pub. Headless body."

"What did you just say, Denise?" asked Mikhail over the radio.

"Headless female body found outside of Finnegan's

Pub," repeated Denise.

Mikhail turned back. He could still see the clearing. Most of his remaining men were searching the woods. Sweeny was at the lab, keeping an eye on the crime scene. Only Jacobs was free, sick with the flu.

"Henderson and Duvlosky are on it," said Mikhail. "And Jacobs. Go to his house and drag him out of bed if you have to."

"Got it," said Denise.

They turned around once again and made it to their car. They drove into town, to Finnegan's. When they were almost there, Mikhail got the call. It was Richaud. At first it was hard to make it out. There was a lot of noise in the background.

"We... we found them. It... there was just a hand sticking out of the snow. Phillips' hand. We had to dig them out. They're... oh Jesus Christ have mercy... they're dead, all of them. Phillips, Rogers, and Miller. They're... they're in pieces. They're torn apart. Something tore them apart."

They could see Finnegan's at the bottom of the hill.

"We have to go back," said Henderson. "Oh God, we have to go back."

"No," said Mikhail. "There's nothing we can do for them. Don't you understand? They're dead." Then he picked up the radio and opened up the channel. "This is your Lieutenant. What happened tonight, this morning – it's the stuff nightmares are made of. But this isn't a nightmare, this is happening. I want all of you, except Sweeny and Cooper, to converge at the crime scene. Richaud, you arrange this. Then write down exactly what you see. Take pictures, I want everyone to max out his cell phone's memory in pictures. Then get the coroner to come and remove the bodies. Help him if he needs it, I'm sure he does. Then I want you all to go home and do whatever you do best when you get home. Do you understand?"

"Yes," said Richaud.

"Yes," said Cooper.
"Yes," said Jackson.
"Yes," said Sweeny.
"Yes," said Jacobs.
"Yes," said Clayton.
"Yes," said Henderson, who was sitting right next to him.

That was the entire police force of Clairmont, Maine. Mikhail had known them for three years. The rest of them had known each other for most of their lives, if not their entire lives. And they had known Phillips, Rogers, and Miller just as long.

Mikhail pulled into a spot in front of Finnegan's. He saw Mickey MacDaniels standing just outside the door, with a snow shovel in his hand.

"Officer Duvlosky," MacDaniels said, as Mikhail got out of the car. "I was clearing out the snow and I hit something. There she is."

Mikhail studied the headless, naked body. Jacobs pulled up and walked over, sniffling.

"Hell," said Henderson. "I mean... goddamn, what do you make of it? She tears the guts out of some guy, rips his dick off... Jerry, Steve, and Kevin... are killed in the woods... and now this? She ends up here, with her head cut off?"

Jacobs coughed. "She had someone with her, or people," he said. "And they worked together, and then something happened and the others left her here like this."

"But there was just the one set of footprints going into the woods," protested Henderson.

"Just one set of bloody footprints," corrected Jacobs. "Maybe the others were more careful than she was. Maybe they heard her name mentioned in the news and considered her a liability."

Henderson thought about that. "Hell," he said, "we don't even know for sure that this *is* Wilkins. Maybe it's another one of her victims."

"What I want to know," said Jacobs, "is where is her *head?*"

Mikhail lit a cigarette. "It's Wilkins," he said. "See there? That birthmark on the left side of her neck? Now look at the way the skin is torn, but the bone cut cleanly. What would do that? Think about it. Think about cutting a hole in the wall and putting in a new door. Think about the way a Sawzall skitters around unless you have the material firmly against the base plate. But once it catches something solid, it finds its way. Without an outlet… using common sense… there's no other explanation."

They were both staring at him. "What else, Lt?" asked Henderson.

"I don't know what else. I know that there's something very strange and very horrible going on in our town." He tossed the butt into the snow. "And I know I want to have another talk with that woman from the lab," he said. "There was something she wasn't telling us. Sarah Johnston."

Chapter sixteen

"You know that you can tell me anything," said Fran, turning down High Street.

Nick was tempted. He knew how she would react. She would call in the police, the FBI, the fucking United Nations. A part of him wanted that. He felt like he couldn't handle it on his own. He felt like crawling back into the womb, where it was safe. Another part of him wanted to pretend that nothing out of the ordinary was happening. He had come to a compromise.

"I know, mom," he said. "And I don't know what to tell you. I'll probably hang out with Hugh all day. He can give me a ride home." It was Friday, and no school, so she didn't really have a reason to object.

"What are you two going to do?"

"I don't know, mom. We just hang out and talk, that's all."

"They're saying now that three police officers have been murdered, along with the scientist."

"They're also saying that they got the killer."

"Just be safe, honey. Be smart."

"I always am."

"Yeah. Sometimes a little *too* smart."

"My genetics aren't my fault," said Nick. They pulled into Hugh's driveway. "Yes, I'll check in with you. Have fun."

"Bye," she said as he got out of the car. "Love you."

"Me too," he said.

Hugh's dad answered the door as Fran drove off. "He's upstairs playing his video games," said Frank. "Tell me, Nick. What good are video games? You know what we did for fun when I was your age? We built *cars*. We took a goddamn engine and looked at the thing and figured out how it worked. All you kids want to do is turn the key and zoom off. But you don't know where you're going. It's a wonder you can find your own dicks."

Hugh's old man was a ball buster. He said so himself, whenever he had the chance.

"Yes, Mr. Macmillan. The Greatest Generation."

"You tryna be funny?"

Nick realized he may be off by a few years. "No sir. I didn't mean it like that. I only meant that you're right. Compared with us, you guys really *are* the greatest generation."

Frank seemed to like that. Nick knew what to say to make the adults like him. It was only his own generation that he had troubles with. "Go on now," said Frank. "Go zap your brain out with those goddamn video games."

Nick headed over to Hugh's room. Hugh was killing something on the screen. Nick closed the door. "Listen," he said. "We need to talk."

Hugh kept shooting. "Which one is it, mom, the sex talk, or the drug talk? I haven't done either, I swear it."

"Goddammit. Can't you ever be serious?"

"No Nick," said Hugh gravely, "I always *did* want to be Sirius, until I learned that it was like a million light years away. I couldn't do that to you – I couldn't leave you here to fend for yourself."

"Fuck it. Nevermind. I don't know what I was thinking."

Hugh put down the remote and turned to look at Nick. His broad smile dropped. "Alright," he said, "What is it?"

Nick sighed. "I've got a… a…"

"Dick in your mouth?" suggested Hugh.

"That's it. See you later." Nick turned and put his hand on the door knob.

Hugh laughed. "Sorry, I couldn't help myself. Alright, let's start over. I'm all ears."

"I've got an electric boner."

"What's that? What did you just say to me?"

"I was whacking off, and some of that green toxic shit got on my dick. It was in my phone, from when I dropped it in that bubbling tub."

"Uh huh," said Hugh. "Go on."

"That's it. Whatever that shit is, it turned my dick into a live wire."

"So what's the problem?" asked Hugh. "And why are you telling me? You should be out there using that line on the girls. I'll admit, it's a good one, I wish I'd thought of it. Now maybe you'll finally get your first peck on the cheek."

"You don't believe me," said Nick.

"I'll tell you what I believe. I believe that maybe they were right: maybe marijuana really *can* put a man out of his mind."

"Touch it," said Nick. "Touch it and see."

"Look, I know you have trouble with the ladies, but I don't think this is the answer."

"It's got to be hard, though."

" 'It's got to be hard,' he says. I know how it works."

"Touch it," said Nick. His voice had an edge to it, and he could almost see his words cutting through the air of Hugh's sarcasm.

"You're seriously asking me to touch your dick?" asked Hugh in a voice that was just above a whisper.

"You're not going to believe me until you do, so let's just get it over with."

"Shit. Look, no, okay, I believe you. I do. An electric boner, you say? Ah, I think I had one of those once. Just rub some baby oil on it and it'll clear right up."

Nick walked over to Hugh's laptop. Hugh already had a porn site up. Nick felt it stir. On the list of things he didn't want to do, this had to be near the very top. But he couldn't face this alone, whatever it was, and despite his sarcasm, there was nobody in the world he would rather face it with than with Hugh.

"This is going to happen, isn't it?" asked Hugh with great concern.

"Just close your eyes and reach out your hand."

"Look, if this is some kind of shitty joke… well, I guess you got me." Hugh closed his eyes and stuck out his hand.

Nick dropped his pants and underwear, and there it was, sticking out in the air, like an alien creature. Nick knew he had to act fast. There was no way he could keep it up for long in this situation. He leaned forward and brushed it against Hugh's hand. Hugh's eyes shot open, as did his mouth. His head snapped back and he was staring at the ceiling. Nick went soft right away and pulled up his pants. After a full minute, Hugh seemed to recover somewhat, though he was pale and trembling a little.

"Motherfucker," he said. "The electric boner."

THE ELECTRIC BONER

Chapter seventeen

The bag with the head in it was on the kitchen table. Sarah had gone home to clean the blood off her before heading to the lab. As soon as she had stepped into the apartment, she had realized how exhausted she was. She took a hot shower and got in some fresh clothes. Then she made a cup of tea and sat at the table drinking it. She had a long day ahead of her, and decided that it was prudent to re-gather her strength.

So far, her theory was working. She only had to cut open the brain, have a look in there, and then she could start the real work, the work of duplicating the substance. She couldn't allow herself to despair over how long *that* would take. It was one logical step after the next. That's how problems got solved.

She finished her tea and stood up. She felt refreshed. She was ready for the next step. Then she heard a knock at her door. She looked down at the bag and stood very still.

"Ms. Johnston?" said a voice from the other side of the door. "This is the police. We saw your car outside and we'd like to talk to you for five more minutes about what happened last night."

Sarah walked over and opened the door, but not all the way. There was a fat middle-aged one with a drooping face, and a younger one, fit and handsome. "Hello, officers," she said, "I'm afraid that now's not a good time. Perhaps we could arrange something for later?"

The young one smiled. "Oh, we'll just be five minutes and then we'll be out of your hair. I promise. It's very important. May we come in?"

"I'm sorry, but I can't let you in right now. You see, I'm just finishing up with a small batch of bacteria. It's a very delicate process, and if I don't get back to it posthaste, it will all be ruined. I'll have to start all over again, have another shipment sent."

The young one raised his eyebrow. The older one just

stood there, not seeming to understand anything. "You're conducting experiments in your apartment?"

"I couldn't go back to the lab just yet, after what happened there. And as I said, this work is very time-sensitive. So now if you'll excuse me…"

She started to close the door, but the man put his hand against it to stop it. Sarah felt the rush of fury. Such an arrogant prick! Waving his cock around! He smiled again, a stupid, cocky smile. "We wouldn't want to get in the way of scientific progress," he said. "We'll just stand in the corner and ask a few simple questions while you work."

She clenched her teeth and forced a smile. "I'm afraid that's out of the question. A sterile environment is of the utmost importance. Your germs are seeping in through the door, as we speak."

"Another time, then," he said, and took his hand off the door.

"Thank you for understanding, Officer…" she looked at his name tag "…Duvlosky." She shut the door, then went back into the kitchen. She circled the table, with her fists clenched. Then she stopped, took a deep breath, and composed her thoughts.

A man like that, he had to be married. They sought control wherever they could find it, and marriage was just another outlet, a place where they could be… *men*. She pulled the phonebook out of a drawer and opened it on the kitchen table, next to the head. There it was… 327 High Street… Duvlosky… Mikhail and Marie. She must be a pretty little bitch. Men like that always got the prettiest little bitches they could find.

"What's that, Marie?" she said to the phonebook. "You want to be my first volunteer? How kind. But a little patience, my dear. Just be a little patient, and I'll be along for you before you know it."

THE ELECTRIC BONER

Chapter eighteen

"I'll never be the same," said Hugh, running his hand through his hair.

"Right, I feel so sorry for you," said Nick.

"So you think it was the green toxic shit?"

"It had to be. And I'll tell you what else. Have you seen the news today?"

"Why the fuck would I watch the news?"

"Well, that guy we saw yesterday, the one who chased us off..."

"Yeah?"

"I guess he was a scientist or something. And they found him all savaged up, in his lab, murdered."

"No shit?"

"No shit. It's got to be related, somehow. The green toxic shit, my dick, his murder."

"What are you going to do?"

"I was hoping you'd tell me that."

"Hmm... that's a tough one. All I can say for sure is that you absolutely made the right decision coming to your old pal Hugh for advice. I'll need to think on it. But let *me* do the thinking. You just forget about it for now."

"Sure, no problem. Lots of guys lead normal lives with a couple hundred volts' charge running through their dick."

"We'll start by getting a few drinks in you," said Hugh. "No pot. You get too *thinky* with pot. Thinking isn't going to help you, not your kind of thinking anyway. *My* kind of thinking, as what leads to a solid plan of action – *that's* what's needed."

"*Your* way of thinking usually leads to us getting interrogated by the police."

"But I always get us out of it, don't I? Now look. We're going to head over to Hal's. Hal's always got something to drink kicking around. We'll have a few drinks, and we'll come up with something."

"Shit," said Nick. "I don't want to go over there. I don't want to see anybody at all right now."

"The guy's got an electric dick, and he's still a pussy. Listen, what else are you going to do? I know you like to stay in bed and fondle it all day, but that's out, right?"

Nick sighed. Hugh was right. "Alright. But I don't see how getting drunk is going to solve anything."

"I told you," said Hugh. "My mind works *better* when it's got a little fuel in it. You'll see. Let's go."

They headed over to Hal's. Hal's mother was dead, and his father was a serious alcoholic who was always either off somewhere getting drunk, or at home, too drunk to care what his son was doing. The kind of guy who got up in the morning and started drinking for breakfast. Nick didn't know how he was still alive, or how he still had a house.

Hal greeted them at the door. "Hugh!" he said. "And you've brought your boyfriend!"

"Suck it, Hal," said Hugh.

"Oh, no need to be rude now. Come on in boys, come on in. We were just studying the effects of gravity with Chris' new beer bong. You should see him, he's a fucking artist. He can do two at once in three seconds. That's the record to beat."

They walked into the living room, and Chris was on the couch, holding his stomach. "Oh shit," he moaned, "my fucking stomach."

"Nick!" said Hal. "You're up! I'm going to poor this fine American beverage in through the top there and you just hold your thumb over the tube there until you're ready. When you're ready, you just put it to your lips and open your mouth, you really have to open your *throat*, and let it all in there, just like you do for Hugh's cock."

Nick followed the instructions, and the beer rushed down his throat, and then it was in his stomach in a matter of seconds. He felt the effects right away. Well, it was something to do.

Hugh followed suit. "Not bad, boys, not bad," said Hal. "Chris! Your turn."

"Oooooh," said Chris. "My stomach. Oh fuck."

"You're up buddy!"

Hal poured the beer in, Chris put his lips to the tube, and in one tremendous gulp, it was gone. Chris burped. "No more two at a time," he said. "One's alright. No more two at a time."

They each did another. Nick was starting to feel a little better.

Chapter nineteen

Mikhail and Henderson got back in the car. "Well, what do you think?" asked Mikhail, backing out of the driveway.

"About what?"

"Her. Johnston."

"What about her? She was at the lab the night of Huskfield's murder. You don't think she had something to do with it?"

Mikhail finished backing out of the driveway and stopped. "Look," he said. "At her car."

"So?"

"That's what – six, maybe seven inches of snow? Where are the other five inches? And why is there snow *under* the car?"

Henderson was a good man, but a little slow. Finally, he got it. "She went somewhere. During the blizzard."

Mikhail put it in drive and they headed down the street. "That's right. She went somewhere during the blizzard, when everything was closed and the roads weren't plowed. And she's now, what? Conducting experiments in her apartment the day after she found her colleague with his guts spilling on the floor?"

"So… what? What's it all mean?"

"Somebody cut off Wilkins' head, Henderson. I think it was Johnston."

"But… why?"

"I have no fucking idea," said Mikhail. "Which is why I'm going home. It's been a brutal night, a brutal morning. We all need some rest, we need to go home to our wives and eat a good meal. I might even try to get a few hours of sleep. Then we'll come back and take a look at it with fresh eyes."

They drove back to the station and each went to his own car. Mikhail drove home. Marie was waiting for him, in the kitchen. Even though it was afternoon, she had cooked him a huge breakfast. Bacon, omelets, toast, and homefries. God it felt good to be home. He walked over to her and kissed her on the lips.

She laughed. "Just in time," she said. "I was starting to worry that I was going to eat it all myself." She patted her belly. "I could, you know."

He smiled. The longer he lived in Clairmont, Maine, the less he could believe that it was the same place where she was raised. How could this sleepy town, dark and dreary for most of the year, turn out such a piece of bright perfection? At first, he couldn't understand why she'd wanted to move back. She had just finished her medical degree at Drexel and instead of getting a job at one of the hospitals there, she begged him to move to Clairmont. Meanwhile, he had been doing quite well for himself in the Philly PD.

Their arrival in Clairmont hadn't done anything to clear up his confusion. "Nothing's happening here," he'd said.

"And that's just why I like it. You can't see it, but all of those days going and looking at dead bodies was starting to affect you."

"Right," he'd said. "The only thing dead here is the culture. There's nothing happening, and there's nothing to do."

But slowly, it had grown on him. Here, people understood that they were responsible for their own lives, because they had to work hard just to heat their homes. And they didn't want to cause trouble for themselves, because it was trouble enough just to make it on a daily basis. He'd discovered a wonderful character in the men on the force. At first, they appeared gruff and unsophisticated, maybe even stupid. And it was true enough that they wouldn't be winning any genius awards, but they were smart enough in their own fashion. They knew how things worked, and they knew how to make things work. Above all, they were good people – prejudices born of ignorance aside. Some of the cops he'd worked with in Philly were more corrupt than the people they were putting away.

He sat down and devoured the food. He felt it filling him, giving him strength. Then he got the sudden urge to go to bed, but not to sleep. He got up and took Marie by the hand, leading her into the bedroom.

"Now?" she said, laughing.

As an answer, he turned around and kissed her on her full red lips, and he pressed against her, the hardness against the softness.

Chapter twenty

Sarah scanned the parking lot for cars. Nobody was there. Some police investigation. Did their incompetence surprise her? Not at all. But truth be told, there was nothing there that would help them. She had the head in the trunk, and the notebook on her lap. Not that that Duvlosky prick would know what to do with any of it, were it sitting in *his* lap.

She had the lab to herself. Perfect. She brought the

head into Jack's old lab room and cut into it. When she removed the brain, it finally stopped snapping its teeth. She looked. Ho boy! What a mess. That shouldn't look like that, nor should that. It was dripping in green ooze. She had thought it would be white. She checked the notes again, and sure enough, on the very last page was the evidence that it would be green. How could she have missed that?

She set the brain in an empty five gallon bucket and filled it with lye from Jack's closet of chemicals, and water from the sink. She tossed what was left of the head in there as well. The saw. She'd almost forgotten the saw. It was still in her trunk. She would deal with it later.

She took a look in the closet. Yes. Everything she needed was right there. But standing there, looking at all of the carefully labeled buckets and containers, her heart sank. The whole substance consisted of at least a hundred processes, each one following the last. It would take at least a year, probably two, to complete them all. It was the hard truth that she had been ignoring the entire time.

And had she given any thought to how she would go about creating an entire army of them? She had not. She would need to devise some magnificent delivery method. She couldn't very well go around injecting it into the brain of a thousand women, ten thousand – a million of them, if she had her way. Perhaps inhalation would do the trick? But that was a problem for down the road. And what a long road it was starting to look like.

Her faith in the idea wavered. She looked at the notebook again. There was still the option of a more personal victory against men. She could use Jack's research to cure Alzheimer's. But there was something about that that seemed hollow. It would be a lie, plain and simple. She couldn't live with it.

And then she pictured her army. Ten thousand women ripping the dicks off of a hundred thousand men. She laughed. Jack, you magnificent bastard! She knew he hadn't intended *this*. He had made a mistake, somewhere. She didn't know where exactly it was, but she didn't have to. It was enough for her that she was able to grasp the basic existence of the substance, to understand what it did, when he had failed to do that. This was now *her* work.

Her faith was restored. Her energy was restored. She felt more energized than she had ever felt before. It didn't matter if it took a hundred years. It would be the coming together of all her passions. True, the sex passion had been perverted, but then it had been perverted in her own life as well. It had been perverted by men.

She started up the burner and began her work.

Chapter twenty one

Mikhail awoke and looked at the clock. 9:32 PM, it said. It was exactly 24 hours since Johnston had been awakened by Huskfield's call for his intern. If indeed that's what had happened. Marie was next to him, reading a book.

"Shit," he said, "why didn't you wake me?"

She put down the book and looked at him. "You needed sleep, honey."

He sat up. "What I *need* is to solve this case. And I can't do it in my sleep, can I, honey?"

"And you can't solve it when you're tired, either."

He reached down and got his shirt from the floor. He reached in the pack, pulled out a cigarette, and stuck it in his mouth.

"You see? If anything, you needed *more* sleep. Your mind isn't working."

Mikhail looked at her. "Huh?"

She nodded at the cigarette. "I'm not going to get on you about quitting. Not now. I know you need it just now."

Oh Christ. Had he really forgotten? Even just for a second? "Shit Marie, I'm sorry," he said, putting the cigarette behind his ear. "You're right. I needed the sleep. And you're right that I need more. But... the sooner we get this over with, the better. Right?"

"Right," said Marie. "So I guess you're going to just leave me here tonight? Nothing I can do to convince you to stay, is there? Not even for a little bit?" She pretended to yawn and stretched her arms above her head. Of course, she was wearing his favorite nightie, the one where you could see just the faintest hint of the flesh beneath it. He was hard.

He laughed. "Christ, Marie. This is serious."

"That's exactly why you should have a little fun. So the seriousness of it all doesn't bury you."

He smiled. "I have to go," he said. "Do you really want me to leave this in Clayton's hand? Shit, how about *Sweeny?*"

"No," she admitted. "They'd burn the town down, either on purpose or by accident. Sweeny *did* burn down a quarter of Clairmont Jr. High."

He laughed and got out of bed. "You never told me that," he said, putting on his pants.

"Our little town has a very deep and rich history," she said, laughing.

"It's written in the bricks of John's Doughnut Shop," he said. "I mean, the bricks that replaced the ones Henderson shattered when he drove into the side of the building, drunk."

"Poor Henderson," she said. "He just wants everybody to like him."

"Henderson the Tender Hen," he said. He was dressed. He didn't want to leave, but he had to. This was what he was good at, it was his first glimpse of true action since he'd moved there. Marie would still be there when he finished the thing.

"It's going to be a late night," he said, walking to the

door. "There's no reason *you* shouldn't get your sleep."

"Don't you worry about us," she said. "The only reason we're still awake now is because we couldn't sleep through the awful smell of your farts."

He smiled. "Bye honey. I love you. And it's not my fault you fed me all that stuff."

"Mikhail…" she said. She hardly ever said his name. Only when she was angry, or when she wanted to say something very important.

"Yeah?"

"Just… be safe, okay?"

"There's nothing to worry about, honey. Everything's done and over with. It's just a matter of working out the story. I'm just going to be in my office, trying to write a story. That's all."

"I love you so much," she said.

"I love you, honey," he said. He left.

Mikhail got in his car and drove to the station. The folder was sitting there on his desk. Okay. What was he missing? What was the story?

He read over the poorly-written reports that his men had scrawled in their notebooks over the scattered bodies of Phillips, Rogers, and Miller. He looked at the photographs. There was one thing that all of the repots, all of the photos agreed on. Each man had had his penis torn from his body, just as Huskfield had his bitten off.

He looked at the photos of Wilkins' body. There was a bullet wound in her thigh. That was one of the places he might have shot her, to disable her if she had proven an immediate and dangerous threat. There were eight knife wounds in her abdomen, where somebody had repeatedly stabbed her. There were bruises all over her body.

He was sure that Miller and the others had encountered Wilkins in the woods. He was certain that they had inflicted her with the wounds he was now looking at. He imagined the scenario, of first trying to use reason and authority with her, and then when she didn't respond to that, to disable her with a taser. But maybe the taser hadn't worked on her. Maybe they didn't have access to their tasers. The next step would be to fire a non-lethal shot. And if that didn't work? Then anything went.

The story was in perfect line with all of the images. But it was of course impossible. And where did Johnston fit into it all? He was, again, certain that she had been the one who had cut off Wilkins' head. Everything was laid out for him in the most obvious, logical fashion. And yet it didn't make any sense.

His story rested basically on the fact that Sarah Wilkins was somehow some kind of an invincible being who ripped penises off of men, and the only way to kill her was to cut off her head.

Marie had been more right than he had realized. He *did* need more sleep. But it was almost dawn. The station would be filling up again soon. The reporters would be wanting answers. His men would be wanting answers. The town would be wanting answers.

"Okay," he said aloud, and started again from the beginning.

Chapter twenty two

"Where the *fuck* we going?" asked Nick. He was drunk.

"Not going home to Fran's sweet tits, that's what you're hoping," said Hugh. He was drunk too. Too drunk to drive. They had been walking along the dark road for what seemed like miles and miles.

"It's *dark*. Can't see where the fuck I'm going."

"Don't worry about that. You did good enlisting old Hugh. We're gonna take care that dick of yours."

"Yeah?"

"Yeah. And it's good you got old Hugh around.

THE ELECTRIC BONER

You're such a goddamn *pussy*. That's what your goddamn problem is."

"Yeah? I thought it was my goddamn *electric boner*."

"You got a lot of problems, I guess."

"Yeah?"

"Yeah. You just sit around and wait for shit to happen. You can't do that. You got to *make* shit happen."

"Way I see it, that's just the problem," said Nick.

"Oh yeah?"

"Yeah. Too many goddamn assholes walking around, grabbing at shit, cause *they* want it. They want it now, fuck everybody else. They make the world shit."

"You think someone's gonna come around, give you a free handjob? Give you shit in a nice little box with a nice little ribbon? Fuck that. You gotta be prot... you gotta be *proactive* or those assholes are just gonna wipe their *asses* with you."

"You're saying it's kill or be killed?"

"You're goddamn right it is."

"Why can't it be don't kill and don't be killed?"

"Because it's not. Shit. You got to stop thinking like a pussy. I don't know why it's not like that. It's just not."

"Why can't we just *make* it like that?"

"You go ahead and try. They'll kill you before you get a chance to analyze the goddamn data."

"How are you so sure? What bad ever happened to *you?*"

"For starters, I ended up with you as a goddamn best friend."

"I knew it," said Nick.

"What?"

"You *wanted* to touch my dick."

"Oh, shut the fuck up. Look, we're almost there."

"Almost *where?* I can't see where the *fuck* we're going."

"It's because you don't open your goddamn eyes. You got this world in your head, and it's got nothing to do with the world in front of your eyes."

"You're right," said Nick. "That's just it."

"You're goddamn right I'm right. Now shut up. Now look. You see that goddamn fence? We're gonna climb *over* the fence. Don't know why they bothered putting the fucking thing there. All you got to do is *climb* it."

"Where the fuck *are* we? What's on the other side?"

"On the other side of this fence is the cure for your dick."

"It *is?*"

"Sure it is. We just gotta reach out and *take* it."

Chapter twenty three

Someone was banging at the front door. The police? It couldn't be. Surely they hadn't been so incompetent as to leave without a way back in. Though on review, maybe they had been. Sarah moved down the dark hallway. She'd left the lights out. It was the prudent thing to do, and it was also the thrilling thing to do. It brought her back to last night, when her new and true life had begun. She wasn't above a bit of nostalgia.

She made it to the lobby, and saw two teenage boys, slapping their hands against the plate glass door, illuminated by the parking lot lights. She almost laughed. This town held many surprises – there was no limit to its idiocy.

"You with the goddamn Prius," she heard one of them shouting through the glass. "Open up!"

"No one here after all," said the other one in a loud voice. They were drunk. Little asshole pricks in training. "Let's go."

"Tell us about the green toxic shit, or we'll break the goddamn door down!" shouted the bigger one.

Say what? Sarah stepped out of the shadows and

walked to the door. "What did you say?" she yelled through the glass.

"Said I'm gonna break this goddamn *door* down!"

Sarah unlocked the door and pushed it open. "What was that about the… green… toxic shit?" she asked.

"Right," said the big one. "We know all about it."

"We saw your friend," said the little one. He looked frightened, but was trying not to. How cute. "The dead guy."

"And we saw the green toxic shit," added the big one.

Sarah smiled. "Where?" she asked. "Where did you see this?"

"You gotta tell us how to *reverse* it," said the big one. He reminded her of Duvlosky.

"Reverse it?" she said. "What do you mean by that? 'Reverse it'?"

"Shit," said the big one. "Let's get out of here. This chick don't know what she's talking about. Probably the goddamn cleaning lady. Come back when they got someone competent here."

Sarah quelled the urge to strangle him. At least for now. "I can help you… reverse it," she said, "but I need for you to take me to where you saw it."

The boys looked at each other. "Tell us first," said the little one.

"You can trust me, boys," she said as sweetly as she could muster, though she knew it wasn't very sweet at all. "I just want to help you. I could tell you how the substance functions, but it would be much easier for me to *show* you. Unless you hold a PhD in chemistry?"

"We know all about the goddamn periodic table," said the big one. She would kill him first. "Don't worry about us." He turned to his friend. "What you think, man?"

The little one shrugged his shoulders. "Don't really like her, but why not? Maybe she can help my dick." And maybe she would kill *him* first.

"You want me to help your dick?" she said, forcing the words out, hoping that her smile didn't look too much like a grimace. "I can do that, if that's what you want. Now take me to where you saw the substance, and we'll do that afterwards."

"Shit," said the big one. "Let's do it. Told you, buddy. We're gonna get that dick of yours *all* taken care of."

She stepped outside and locked up the lab. A few snowflakes were starting to fall. "We'll take my car," she said. She led them to the Prius and they got in the back. "Where to?"

"Head into town," said the little one. "Then keep going a bit."

The snow was picking up. She drove slowly toward town.

"So... what is this shit anyway?" asked the big one.

"You'll see," she said. "If you're not lying to me about it. If this isn't your idea of a prank."

"Don't worry about us, lady. We saw it. A fucking *ocean* of the shit." An ocean?

"How come you don't know where it is?" asked the little one, suddenly.

"What's that now?" asked Sarah. Definitely, the little one first.

"How come you know *what* it is, but not *where* it is?"

Sarah sighed. "You must have heard about Doctor Huskfield's terrible murder? On the news?"

"Yeah. So?"

"I'm afraid it was on account of this substance. You see, we work primarily doing research for the government. This substance... what do you mean, you saw an *ocean* of it?"

"A goddamn tub of it, who gives a shit? Go on," said the big one.

"Yes," she said. "That makes more sense then. You see, the substance is part of a very sensitive government project. A project that a group of terrorists has been very interested in. As a precaution, Doctor Huskfield moved the substance out of the lab. Would that he had taken the same precautions with his own life! You see, that Wilkins turned out to work for the terrorists."

"Shit," they said together. Idiots.

"So you are doing your nation a great service by taking me to the substance. I'm afraid that toward the end Doctor Huskfield had grown so paranoid that he didn't tell anybody where he had moved it."

"Turn up here," said the little one.

Sarah turned right at the old fish factory.

"There, that little shack right there."

Sarah parked and they got out. She left the headlights on, illuminating the shack.

"Shit," said the big one. "It's locked. Wasn't locked before."

It didn't matter. Either the substance was in there, or it wasn't. Either way, the boys had out-lived their usefulness. Did they want her to help their dicks? The only want to help a dick was to cut it off. She reached into her pocket and wrapped her hand around the switchblade.

"Hold on a sec," said the big one. He walked back to the car and opened the driver side door.

"What are you doing?" said Sarah.

"Just hold on to your panties lady." He reached in the car. "Goddamn Prius. Where is the fucking thing?" Then the trunk popped open. He walked over to it.

"What do you think you're *doing?*"

"Shit lady. You got a Sawzall in here? But I got a better way." He reached in and grabbed the wrench for the tires. "Step aside, ladies," he said. He walked over to the door. In one quick and sure motion, full of strength, he brought the wrench down on the padlock. The padlock and the plate it was attached to flew to the ground.

She squeezed the knife tighter. The boy - even drunk - was stronger and faster than she had anticipated. The little one wouldn't be any trouble. The big one had to go first. Why didn't he put down that damn wrench?

"Here we go, ladies," he said, and kicked open the door.

Chapter twenty four

"You first," said Nick to the woman, gesturing to the open door. He didn't trust her. Her story had been ridiculous, the most obvious lie he had ever heard. Even with the beer crashing around in his head, he understood that. He didn't think Hugh understood.

"No," she said, "it's time for your reward. You've taken me here, you've earned it. But you'll have to wait out here. I don't want you watching. You'll be next, don't worry."

"What the fuck you talking about lady?" said Hugh.

"You first," she said, turning to him. "I'm going to help *your* dick first. Go on in."

"My dick don't need helping. It's *his* dick that's fucked up."

"What's that hand doing in your pocket?" asked Nick.

"It's snowing and it's cold," she said. "Don't you want to warm up?" she asked, looking at Hugh. "Let's go in there and warm up."

Nick saw a wave of comprehension pass over Hugh's face. But he had a feeling that Hugh was comprehending the wrong thing. "You want to *fuck*, lady? Shit, why didn't you say so?" He tossed the wrench to the ground and smiled.

"Hold on," said Nick. "First, cure me."

"Shit. That's right," said Hugh. "Not going to work if he's still got an electric boner."

"A *what?*" she said. The snow was beginning to blow hard, but Nick thought he saw her eyeball pop out of its socket and hang by a bloody string down the front of her face. When he blinked, her face was back to normal.

"Mike," said Nick. Hugh didn't get it. He was looking the scientist lady up and down, evaluating her. "*Mike*," he said again.

"The fuck?" said Hugh. "Who the…."

"Mike, *listen* to me."

Hugh looked at him. "Yeah?" he said.

"What do you do when you see Mandy Perkins coming down the hall with another love letter for you?"

Hugh squinted and looked at him. "Shit. Really?"

"What are you *talking* about?" said the scientist lady.

Nick gave him a quick nod. "Fuck," said Hugh. "Alright."

They ran. "Hey! You little *shits!*" shrieked the scientist lady.

When they made it back to the main road, Nick could just barely see the headlights, still pointing at the shack. They stopped to catch their breaths.

"Goddammit. Just tell me it wasn't cause she wanted me first," said Hugh.

"She was full of shit. I just… I got this feeling that she was going to kill us."

Hugh laughed. "That little scientist lady? Kill *me*?"

"You really think she was going to take you in there and fuck you? You really think her story wasn't bullshit? You really think she could have fixed my dick? You saw her when you said I had an electric boner. She didn't know what the fuck you were talking about." He could still feel the beer dancing around in there, but Nick felt more clear-headed than he had in a long time.

"Shit," said Hugh, after a minute. "You're right. The bitch was lying to us."

"Let's walk right downtown where there's lots of lights and then call a cab."

They headed downtown in silence. "She wasn't even that hot," said Hugh finally. "I was just gonna do it for *you*."

"Uh huh," said Nick. His clear-headedness left him, and all at once he felt his tiredness. "Let's just go home and we'll figure it out tomorrow," he said.

They made it downtown and called the cab. It came and drove them home. First Hugh, then Nick. Nick staggered into his house.

"It's four in the morning," said Fran, who was sitting on the living room couch.

"Shit mom, not now."

"Why didn't you call to let me know where you were?"

Suddenly, it all came crashing down on him. It was all *him*. Everything that was wrong was his fault. The world seemed like scrambled eggs because *he* was scrambled eggs. He was nothing. He would never have Lucy. He would never have anything except for an electric boner, and that was his fault too. All he was good for was jerking off, and now he couldn't even do that. He started bawling like a baby.

"I'm sorry mom. I'm so sorry. I wish I could be better, but I don't think I can be. I don't know why, I just can't."

She stood up. "Nick, what's wrong?"

He wrapped his arms around her and sobbed into her neck.

"It's okay, honey," she said, hugging him. "You're a good boy. Sometimes the good ones start to feel like they're bad, but it's not true. It's not true at all. You're the best thing in the world. If you weren't, I wouldn't love you more than life itself, more than you'd think it was possible to love something."

It was like waking up from a nightmare and realizing that everything was okay.

"I love you, mom," he said. "I'm glad you're here."

Then he went up to his room and collapsed on his bed.

When he woke up, he felt normal again. He felt so

normal and like everything was just the way it was supposed to be that he reached down and wrapped his hand around his cock. He would have cursed, but his tongue was between his teeth.

Chapter twenty five

The sun was pouring into his office, hurting his head. Mikhail closed the folder in disgust. Was this really all that he could come up with? This theory that Wilkins had single-handedly dismembered Huskfield as well as three of his own, fully trained men? Maybe "fully trained," was a bit of a stretch, but still. In a sense, it all added up, and every instinct told him it was true, but still. It didn't add up at all. How was it possible?

Johnston was the key. He needed to talk to her. This time, he wouldn't be so nice. He would bring her in and have a little chat. Proper procedure be damned. Somehow, he felt that the circumstances didn't call for proper procedure.

He finished his fifth cup of coffee, then buzzed Denise. "Get Henderson out of bed. When he gets here, send him straight in."

He wasn't counting on Henderson for much – or for anything, if truth be told – but Mikhail had done his first year with Henderson showing him around. When Mikhail had been promoted to Lieutenant last year, he had sensed that Henderson felt somehow betrayed. So he had gone out of his way to make Henderson feel that he was an important part of the department. But he wasn't, really. He was mostly just a body.

Christ. Such cynicism. Marie was right. The years of looking at dead bodies in Philly had changed him. But it was just that cynicism that helped to solve cases. His men had lived their entire lives in Clairmont, Maine, or somewhere nearby. They had lived a life sheltered from the world at large. And the world at large was ugly, brutal, murderous. And so it was up to him and his cynicism to put away this bit of ugliness that had breached their peaceful town, and restore it to its innocence.

The calls from the press had stopped. They seemed happy enough with the story that Wilkins had been an embittered employee who had picked up a nasty drug habit. The drugs had made her dangerous, and she had taken advantage of the blizzard to stalk the officers hunting her through the woods and somehow kill them. Finally, the drugs had taken their toll, and she had died of exposure just outside of Finnegan's Pub. A couple of crisp hundred dollar bills had bought a confirmation from Mickey MacDaniels. Not to mention all of the free publicity.

He looked out the window, and just as the last of the snowflakes fell, there was a knock at his door. "Yeah?" The door opened and there was Henderson.

"Good to see you," said Mikhail. "Did you get a good night's sleep?"

"Sure did," said Henderson. "And I thought about what you said, Lt, about that Johnston woman. I think you're right. It *had* to be Johnston that killed Wilkins. What I don't get is: why did she cut off her head? And *why* did she do it?"

"That's just why I called you in here, Henderson. We're going to go find that out. Let's go."

They headed out of the station. The plow truck was just clearing the lot. This one wasn't like the other one. The weathermen had seen it coming, and it had only dropped a few inches. If it hadn't been for the string of murders, Mikhail knew, the whole town would be talking about the strange weather.

They got in the car and Mikhail drove to Johnston's house. Her car wasn't there. They went up and knocked on her door anyway. "Let's try the lab," said Mikhail. "They reopened it this morning."

They got back in the car and drove along. "What do you think, Lt?" asked Henderson. "After thinking it over. What do you think about it all?"

Well, Wilkins was the subject of a nefarious scientific experiment. Something that turned her into a killing machine, with a specialty in brutal castration. It also made her body invincible. Unless, of course, you cut off her head. That's why Johnston had done it, either to stop the experiment, or to keep it under wraps.

"Probably drugs," said Mikhail. "The lot of them. Drugs and a sex triangle."

Henderson seemed extremely satisfied with that. "That's what it always is, ain't it, Lt?"

Until now. "That's what it always is," he said.

They pulled into the lab. The parking lot was nearly full. "I don't see her car," said Mikhail.

Henderson opened his mouth, but before any words came out of it, they got the call.

Chapter twenty six

Hugh's old man, the sadistic fuck, was beating on his door.

"Up and at 'em buddy boy! There's a shovel been calling your name."

Hugh wanted to say, "I've got something for you to shovel," but it came out as an anguished moan. He was badly hungover - on the verge, he felt, of death. He was sick and the world was spinning and he had to get out of his nice warm bed to go shovel the goddamn walkway.

There was nothing for it. The old man wasn't such a bad guy, but, Christ was he obnoxious. He was a devout believer in the virtue of hard work. As if work itself were some kind of thing to attain to. Such utter and complete horseshit. Another four or five hours' sleep - that was something to attain to. That was something that would bring some measure of happiness.

Still, there was something satisfying about pushing through the pain to do something that you didn't want to do, if for no other purpose than to show yourself that you could do it. And yeah, prove to the old man that you could do it if you gave half a fuck.

It seemed important to establish that you really don't give a fuck, and that you're not just pretending to not give a fuck as cover for something else. He didn't know why, or how that was even possible, but it was.

"Shit, Pop!" he finally managed. "I'm awake. I think I have the flu, but don't let that bother you!"

The old man laughed. "The flu, is it? I think I had that when I conceived you."

Hugh was too sick to figure out if that was a brag or a put-down or both. "If there's coffee, I'll shovel," he said. "If not, wake me when the world's over."

He made it out of bed and into the bathroom. He turned on the faucet and vomited, as quietly as he could. Then he pissed into it all, flushed it away and brushed his teeth. In the kitchen, his mother was cooking bacon while the old man added wood to the stove. Hugh got a cup of coffee and drank it standing next to the fire while his parents spoke words that might have been Chinese for all he knew or cared.

Then he figured, might as well get it over with, and bundled up, grabbed the shovel, and went outside. A rational family might have hired someone to plow the driveway with a truck. But Hugh's old man was self-sufficient. Sure. He could just have his son do it. Hugh supposed he should feel honored that his father considered him an extension of his self.

But he didn't. He felt cold and sick. He dug in with the shovel. His body seemed to say, "This is impossible, can't be done." And yet he dug in again, got a load, and threw it away. Again and again. Soon he began to try to piece together the last night. He remembered Nick coming in and asking him to touch his dick. He remembered feeling a mess of emotions about that, which there was no way to sort out now. Fuck it. Maybe Hugh was a little gay? He didn't think so, but it was possible.

Then he began thinking about the scientist bitch. How she lied to him. How she used him. He didn't like that. He threw another load over his shoulder. He was sweating. But he was almost done. And maybe, if he was very lucky, he'd be able to go back to sleep when he was done.

Then he saw it. Across the street at the Duvloskys'. No doubt about it. It was that scientist bitch's Prius. Maybe he wouldn't go back to sleep after all. Life had become interesting.

Chapter twenty seven

"He's not? Well, that's strange. When I called the number he gave me, he told me to meet him here - that he was just around the corner. But come to think of it, I heard sirens on the way over. Maybe something happened that he had to attend to."

She was a beautiful little thing, all tits and a perfectly formed face. No doubt her husband was very proud of his prize, and no doubt she was proud of her strapping, heroic husband, valiantly fighting nonexistent crime in this little shithole town.

"Oh, but let me explain who I am! I'm Sarah Johnston and I was working at the lab the same night that Dr. Huskfield was so tragically murdered. Your... husband, I presume, questioned me and told me to contact him if I remembered anything else. It just so happens that I have... not so much remembered, as pieced something together."

The woman relaxed noticeably. "Why don't you come in, Sarah, and wait for Mikhail here? This whole thing has been very stressful on him, which I'm sure is why he asked you here - our nest, as we call it. And I'm sure it's been most stressful on you, as well."

"Thank you..."

"Marie."

"Thank you, Marie. It *has* been terribly stressful for me. Dr. Huskfield was a truly great man. The scientific community - no, the world - has lost something important. I've been trying to figure out *why*. That's what I've been asking myself for the past two days. Why? Why would somebody do this? And then, like a revelation, it came to me. I know what happened."

Marie couldn't have been more visibly interested. No doubt her life was deathly dull. Her biggest excitement of the day was probably discovering a new shit stain on Duvlosky's underwear when she washed them. Sarah was going to enjoy this, on every level. She subtly locked the door behind her back.

Marie led her into the kitchen and motioned to the island. "Please, have a seat. Would you like some coffee? Tea?"

"Coffee would be lovely, thank you."

Marie went about preparing the coffee. She didn't say anything, obviously waiting for Sarah to go on. Sarah didn't want to disappoint.

"You see, Jack... that's what we all called Dr. Huskfield... Jack had been working for years on developing a drug for the military. I'm afraid I couldn't tell you any more than that - not only because that is classified information, but mostly because I simply don't know any more than that. Well, that's not true. I know about his... test subject. Oh, I'm sorry. I shouldn't be saying this. It will disturb you."

"I went to medical school," said Marie. "I've done my share of cutting things up and poking around. There's no need to tiptoe around me."

"The only reason I know about his research in the first place was on account of the night that the test monkey got out. Oh, it's terrible what we do to these animals, but I have to tell myself that we are justified in sacrificing a few animals if it will help millions of human lives. We may figure out all manner of things this way."

"Yes," said Marie. "There's justification, sometimes. But you said this was a drug for military use. How does that help life?"

So, perhaps she was smarter than Sarah predicted. But how smart could she be, if this was the life she had chosen? To be a *wife*. To throw away medical training on account of a man.

"Oh, but the military helps life. It protects us, just the same as your husband does."

Marie laughed. "Until two nights ago, the biggest worry that my husband had was helping the proverbial old lady cross the street. That's quite a bit different from the sort of political intrigue and duplicity that goes on with the United States government. And that's just the way I liked it - that's just why I wanted to move back here, to raise our child here."

Sarah was taken aback by the entirety of this outburst. She was beginning to have doubts, until she remembered Duvlosky and his arrogant, overbearing, masculine manner. "Oh?" she said. "You have a child?"

Marie looked down at the counter, embarrassed, and then looked back at Sarah and smiled. "I'm pregnant," she said. "Two days ago, the night of the murder - that was the end of my first trimester. You're the first person other than our family that I've told."

Sarah wished she hadn't said that, for a variety of reasons. Most immediately, because she didn't know how to respond. "Congratulations," she said, probably a little too coolly.

"Thank you," said Marie. The smell of the coffee was beginning to fill the air. "But please, go on. You were saying about the escaped monkey..."

Sarah smiled. "He gave us all quite the scare. We heard screams coming from Jack's office and when we went to investigate, the monkey was running wildly down the hall. When we found him, Jack's face and clothes had been badly torn.

"He later confided," she continued, "that his experimental drug was going badly. He wouldn't share the details, of course. But I now believe that his death was the direct result of his experiments." She pulled Jack's notebook out of her purse, set it on the counter, and opened to a random page. It was one of his diagrams.

Marie looked at it casually for a moment, and then became very concentrated on it. "That... that's the periaqueductal gray, and it... that's not right at all."

Sarah looked in disbelief at Marie. She could see it, understand it. She knew exactly what she was looking at. Sarah was on the verge of changing her mind. True, she had said too much, she had dug herself a bit of a hole, but nothing she couldn't get out of. Then, the coffee machine began to beep. Marie's head turned like a trained dog. Better yet, a trained monkey. About to be a test monkey.

"Do you like sugar and cream?"

"Please," said Sarah.

Marie turned and went for the cupboard. Sarah already had the syringe in her hand. Just as Marie opened the glass door, Sarah saw herself standing behind Marie in the door's reflection. Then she saw Marie looking at the same reflection.

Sarah stabbed at Marie's neck just as Marie swung around and brought a coffee mug against Sarah's head. The needle missed, but the mug didn't. It shattered against

Sarah's head. Sarah reeled and screamed, "You rotten bitch!"

Sarah lunged again and this time got her, right around the temporal lobe. But Marie got her, too. Marie got her with the broken and jagged handle of the mug, right in the left eyeball.

Chapter twenty eight

"How are we feeling?" asked Fran. "A little hungover? Here, eat this. You'll feel better." She set out a plate of bacon and toast.

"Thanks," said Nick. He felt a little sick, but the bacon smelled good.

"I just want to say... listen, it's okay to have fun with your friends. I can't stop you from doing what you're going to do, and I don't want to. I just want you to understand about drinking. Sometimes it's harmless. A lot of the time it is. But then there's one time when you go overboard, and that's all it takes. You do something stupid. That's what it does, it makes you stupid, even if you're smart."

Nick put a couple of strips of bacon on a piece of toast, folded it half, and took a bite. She went on:

"But that's not even what I'm worried about. What I'm worried about is that you *won't* do something stupid. You'll think that you can handle it. And it'll make you feel good. And so it will seem like this wonderful thing that's always there for you, and has no bad consequences. Like a friend who never lets you down. Do you understand, Nick?"

"Like Grandpa."

"Yes, like Grandpa. And, like Grandpa, it *will* finally let you down, and it will let down everyone who loves you, and by the time you notice it, it will be too late. It will have its hooks in you too deep, and even if it seems like you've wriggled free, the hooks will always be there."

Nick took another bite. He was starting to feel a little better. "This is pretty heavy for a Saturday morning, mom."

Fran laughed. "I just want to get you while the hangover is still fresh." She went over to the sink and started washing some dishes while Nick finished his breakfast in silence. He decided it was best to put off thinking, at least until he had eaten.

The landline rang and Fran answered. "Hello? May I ask who's calling? Oh, yes, he's right here." She handed Nick the phone. "It's Lucy Littleton."

Nick waited until his mom left the room, then said, "Yaw?"

"Hi Nick. It's Lucy."

"Yaw."

"You're the only Sherman in town. I looked you up."

"Yaw."

"Well, I just wanted to see if you were still going to Jake's party tonight."

"Yaw."

"Good! It's just... everybody's freaking out about this scientist getting killed. Jake was getting ready to cancel the party. We had to talk him into it."

The subject of the scientist cut through the fog of Nick's hangover and awakened something in him. Something other than his electric boner, which the first whisper of Lucy's voice had already awakened.

"That scientist... there was something going on with him. This whole thing... it's something big. Something big and terrible, Lucy." It was the most he had said to her since they were twelve years old.

"It was an insane intern, Nick. The world is filled with insane people. This town is filled with them too, but I didn't think you were one."

THE ELECTRIC BONER

"Lucy, I saw..." Nick stopped. He was sure his mother was lurking close by. He could feel her.

"What? You saw what?" asked Lucy.

"I... look, I'll tell you about it later, at the party, alright? I have to go now. Bye, see you tonight."

She was silent for a moment, and then said, "Bye." He hung up. The conversation had not gone well. Inside his pants, the conversation was still going strong. But he couldn't do anything about that either.

He went to his room and called Hugh on his cell phone. There was no answer. He felt restless. It seemed very important that he should talk to Hugh, to talk about what had happened last night. He thought some more about what Hugh had said on the way to the research lab, about him being a pussy. It was nothing new for Hugh to call him that, and he had long ago realized the truth of it. But now the context had somehow changed, and he couldn't quite figure it out. He had the feeling that the stakes had been upped somehow. It obviously had something to do with the electric boner, with the green toxic shit, but it was just a feeling that something hugely important was happening - something that concerned more than his dick, more than the murdered scientist. It was all related, but related in the way parts of an atom were related to a solid mass.

Suddenly, he grew terrified, as if a legion of dripping, hellish fiends would burst forth from his closet. Dripping with green slime. Now he saw them. They didn't burst forth at all. The door creaked open and first one stepped out, then a second, then a third. They were the size of a small child, bald and naked, jagged bones showing through pale skin, without sexual organs. One of them opened its mouth to reveal a worm-like tongue rubbing itself along bare and black gums. Then a pointed tooth, a fang, emerged through the gums, tearing through, dripping with black blood. Then the creatures began to grow, rapidly, until they towered above him. Teeth broke forth like stalactites from their sick mouths. Claws stretched out of their fingertips. They stood looking at him through black eyes.

As he lost consciousness, Nick was strangely aware of his erection, stronger than ever.

Chapter twenty nine

"What the fuck?" muttered Hugh, and he watched the two women strike at each other through the window. It wasn't the first time he'd looked through that window, but it was the first time he'd seen anything worth seeing. He didn't have any time to gather his thoughts, but an instinct told him that his kind, incredibly hot neighbor needed his help against the scientist bitch.

Then she burst through the door and he had the shovel gripped in both hands like he was poised to take a swing with a baseball bat. His old man had made him play, on through freshman year until Hugh had forsaken practice for smoking weed and hanging out. He liked the game well enough, and had been good enough at it, he just didn't like all of the bullshit that went along with it. He felt the old muscles, still there, still with the knowledge of what to do.

"Hey, bitch!" he said.

She turned and looked at him with her one good eye. Her other one was oozing all over the place. "You... I know you. How can this be? Variables... unaccounted for." She was raving.

"What are you up to you loopy bitch?" said Hugh. "What was in that syringe you stabbed Marie with? That green shit, wasn't it? You tell me right here and now what it is, or I swear to hell that I will knock your head off your shoulders."

She lunged at Hugh with a surprising strength, gathered probably from animal hormones. His cell phone started going off. The sudden sound seemed to confuse her, and the knife glanced across his face.

That was all Hugh needed. He swung, and with a "BITCH!" and a *clunk*, aluminum connected with the back of her head. She dropped face-first in the snow. Hugh inadvertently vomited on her. Then he felt a pang of pity and flipped her over onto her back. She was out, but still breathing. She looked almost beautiful, her face relaxed, with no trace of the haughtiness that had dominated it before. Of course, the gore oozing out of her eyeball didn't help - or maybe it did.

"What now?" asked Hugh aloud. He dropped the shovel and ran into the house through the opened door. Marie was there, on the floor. Her eyes were open, staring at the ceiling. It didn't look good. She was dead, for sure. What a goddamn shame. To lose all that goodness of body and soul. She had always been kind to Hugh. More than that, he had sensed her goodness. And he had, of course, jerked off relentlessly to the image of her body.

He called 911. "I'm at the Duvlosky house. It's bad here. I think Misses Duvlosky is dead. This scientist lady attacked her. I got her with a shovel. I mean, I knocked the scientist lady out. She's outside right now. You've got to get over here."

He hung up. Now what? He'd better keep an eye on the scientist... lady. It was hard to feel anger against somebody who was such a bloody defeated mess. Even if she had killed Marie. But Duvlosky would take care of her. He wondered if he'd kill her. Maybe he shouldn't have been so explicit on the phone. It would make it harder for Duvlosky to kill her. Maybe he wouldn't want to after all. Hugh would want to. Hugh would kill her if it had been his wife.

Maybe best to go let the parents know what's going on first. He took one last look at Marie, and then headed to the door. Then he heard her cough.

Chapter thirty

Nick awoke on the floor of his room. He knew he must have only been out a moment, or Fran would have checked on him and made some kind of a fuss. He looked at the closet door. It was closed.

So maybe what it came down to was that he had gone insane. But he didn't feel that way. And would he know if he had gone insane? How did you tell? His assessment of his vision was that it was insane. But if he understood that, then didn't that make him perfectly reasonable? And yet, another part of him felt as though the vision had happened just exactly as it was supposed to happen. It was real, and it wasn't real.

He lay stretched out for some time until his mother did finally come to check on him. "Nick?"

"Just getting ready to go for a walk, mom." He'd decided to walk over to Hugh's. It was a good two miles, and Hugh might not be there, but he needed to clear his head. His room felt immensely small, and the vision of those... creatures was floating around in his brain, just behind his eyes.

Nick got ready and headed out. It was a clear day, bright with snow. He felt invigorated at once. In fact, he felt more simply alive than he could recall ever having felt. He noticed everything - six goldfinches in the branches of a naked oak tree; a silver Honda Civic with the front left tire nearly threadbare; the way the power lines drooped and hummed; the cracks in the street; the total absence of wind.

He reached in his pocket for a cigarette, got one, and lit it up. He felt the drug touch his chest warmly, intensely. It spread out into his arms. He blew out the smoke and watched it dance lazily in the still air. He did not think, so much as sense his surroundings.

He walked this way for a mile, until he came upon the corpse of a squirrel, run over by a car. The body seemed to sit in a pool of a pure black liquid. The pool began spreading, branching off, streams separating from the main pool and sometimes meeting back up, and finally becoming swallowed up again as the pool became larger and larger. Nick stood watching it and soon it was at his feet. He took a step back without thinking. Then he noticed that his face was soaked in tears. He stepped directly into the black liquid and kept walking.

He saw the police car from quite a ways off. The flashing lights hurt his eyes. Still he walked in an abstract haze, acutely aware of everything around him, and yet somehow not aware of it, as though in a trance - or better, as though looking through someone else's eyes.

He saw the green car parked in the driveway. He knew that car. Then he saw two bodies in the snow outside the house. The snow was red. A figure stood in the open doorway and slowly crossed over the threshold. Nick walked toward it all.

Chapter thirty one

Hugh turned around and saw her slowly get to her feet. "Ummm... Marie? I thought.... are you okay?" She looked at him and he saw her eyes and they were the same as they had been, open and staring, lifeless. He shuddered and his head began to spin.

Then she slowly lifted her blouse over her head. "Oh my God," said Hugh. Still staring directly at him, she unhooked her bra and let it fall to the floor. Then Hugh was the one staring, at two perfect, plump breasts. He got a hard-on. "Jesus, shit, mercy." She gave a strange, mechanical smile and took a step toward him.

Hugh couldn't think, only stand there as a mess of conflicting and intense impressions fought for control of his body. He watched himself reach out his arm as she extended a breast to it. Then he had it in his hand. It was beautiful, and he felt a deep and primal satisfaction and hunger for more.

This was exactly like his fantasies. And yet, something made him withdraw his hand. Reason trickled back into his brain. First of all, in the fantasies, she wasn't married. Standing there in their house, Hugh felt Duvlosky's presence. It wasn't right to bang another man's girl. That wasn't being pussy, that was being a man. Maybe if the guy was a real dick and had it coming, that'd be a different story. But Duvlosky was a stand-up guy. He'd turned his head the other way more than once when the smell of Hugh's joint passed it by.

As his reason returned, so returned his sensibilities. This *wasn't* Marie. The body was there, God yes, in all of its glory. But the warmth and the grace were gone, dead. Without those, the body was just meat. He still had a hard-on, yes, but that too was just meat. And he could beat that off later, once things here were properly sorted out. A man had responsibilities beyond his dick.

Then she was reaching for him. He took a step back and she lunged, grabbing the front of his jacket. With an overpowering strength, she yanked him toward her and then grabbed his dick with her other hand. "Ohhh... fuck," he said, as his resolve wavered again. Maybe just a quickie and then sort things out afterward. But he looked up into those eyes again; he thought of Duvlosky again.

He grabbed at the wrist holding his member. That was the number one priority. He grabbed with both hands and squeezed at the center of her wrist, hoping she would release it. It wouldn't do to yank it off. Despite anything that may happen, he had a great fondness for it. But it was no use - she held on tight. Then her lips were on his and they were warm and he knew that he had lost. He was going to do it after all.

The sound of the sirens made him snap his head back, and once again his resolve returned. "Shit Marie," he said sadly, "I'm sorry about this." He got her face with a quick right jab. He was weak and tired, but felt the strength in the blow, felt her nose shatter, heard it, watched her head bounce back. She let go of his dick then.

Then she was on her knees and grabbed his leg. With her other hand, she unzipped his pants. "Ooooh shit," said Hugh.

Chapter thirty two

Duvlosky passed the stop sign at 70 mph. "Look," said Henderson, "maybe we ought to let Jacobs take this one." Duvlosky didn't respond. He hadn't said a word since the call came in. "I'm sure it's nothing, Lt. Dispatch said it sounded like a kid. Probably just a prank. We've been getting bullshit like this all day..." Duvlosky sped through another intersection. "I'm serious now! You're going to kill somebody."

"Maybe I will," said Duvlosky. Henderson looked at him. His jaw was clenched tighter than a chicken's asshole. There was no talking to Duvlosky. Henderson lit up a cigarette. Who cared about *him* and *his* wife? Why worry about making *her* a widow? If they made it out of this alive, Henderson was going to have a little talk with the chief. Maybe Henderson would get that promotion after all, the one he'd been passed over for last year in favor of the young hotshot coming up from some city in Pennsylvania.

But Henderson's fears were unfounded. They made it, alive, without killing anybody else. They got out of the car and saw the body on the lawn. Duvlosky pulled his firearm and approached it.

It was Sarah Johnston. Somebody had done a number on her eye. She was out. "Check on her," said Duvlosky, then walked into the house like some kind of hotshot. Henderson checked her pulse. She was alive. He radioed dispatch. "I need an ambulance at 327 High Street. Female, approximately 40 years old, with a serious eye wound and possibly other injuries."

Then he heard gunshots. He radioed dispatch again. "Gunshots fired at 327 High Street. Send backup." He drew his firearm and cautiously entered through the open door.

In the kitchen, he saw a teenage boy huddled in a corner on the floor with his pants down to his ankles. Henderson recognized him as Frank MacMillian's boy. A bit of a punk, but really not a bad kid. The kid stood and pulled his pants up.

Henderson turned and saw Duvlosky pointing his gun at his wife. She was bleeding from a wound to her shoulder, and bleeding from the nose.

"It's no use sir," said the kid, sniffling. "That's not your wife. Whatever that scientist did to her... she's dead. She's some kind of fucking zombie."

"Lt," said Henderson, his ticker throbbing in his chest. "Instructions?" He had no idea what the hell was going on, except that it was nothing good.

At the sound of his voice, the wife turned and looked at him. Those eyes. Henderson felt weak in the knees. He felt like his heart was going to explode. Then she looked back at Duvlosky and began moving toward him. Duvlosky fired again. The bullet went through the center of her skull. Henderson saw it with his own eyes. She kept approaching.

"The head," said Duvlosky, eerily calm. "Find something to cut off the head."

Henderson was anything but calm. He spotted a serrated knife laying on the kitchen counter. He picked it up with a trembling hand. "Lt.... what is this? What's going on? That's Marie!"

"Give me that knife. Now you and the kid grab her. Hold her tight. Be careful, she's stronger than you think."

Henderson looked at the kid and nodded. He didn't know what the hell, but he knew how to take an order. They each grabbed at an arm. She let out a terrible sound, inhuman, like a dying rabbit. Then the kid was flying through the air, and smashing against the kitchen cabinets. She turned and looked at Henderson. Her eyes were death. Henderson pissed himself. Then she picked him up by the shoulders. He felt his feet leave the ground. Then he was *flying* through the air, backwards. It was very strange. He saw the knife poke out of the front of her throat. Then he heard a loud crash and felt something enter the back of his skull and then he was outside and then he was dead.

Chapter thirty three

Nick and Officer Duvlosky reached the scientist lady at the same time. Duvlosky was cradling a severed head against his chest with his left hand and had a gun pointing at the scientist's head in his right.

"Don't do it, sir," said Nick. Duvlosky's hand was shaking. His face was dripping with blood and tears. "She can help." They stood there like that for some time. They heard approaching sirens. Duvlosky dropped his gun in the snow and hugged the severed head with both arms. Nick saw now that it was Marie Duvlosky's head.

Nick felt his stomach tighten in pity. Tears filled his eyes. Why did things like this have to happen? Why couldn't life be good and go on gently forever? Why did we get a taste of ambrosia and a mouthful of shit? The sirens were getting closer.

Duvlosky stopped sobbing and looked at Nick. "Your friend..."

"Hugh? Is he alright?"

"He's alright. He's inside."

Nick nodded and then began walking toward the house. The sirens were almost upon them. He stopped at the doorway and said, "Sir, we need to talk. I can tell you what caused this, I can show it to you. I'm sure she's moved it, but I have a picture on my phone."

Duvlosky nodded. "Better go check on your friend."

Nick found Hugh sprawled out on the kitchen floor, staring up at the ceiling. "You okay?"

"Well, I got about the worst case of blue balls there's ever been. Other than that, I'm great. I mean, also besides being traumatized for life in about eight different ways." In other words, he was okay. "Listen buddy, my hands are shaking something terrible. I've been laying here trying to roll a joint, but the shit just keeps spilling all over the floor. Mind helping me out here?"

Nick heard the sirened vehicle pull in. He heard voices, a mess of voices, shouting. Among them he recognized Hugh's parents.

"Your parents are worried about you."

"Yeah, they were great, huh? Where were they when the zombie bitch was trying to rip my dick off? Listen, about that joint."

"The cops are here. They'll be in in a minute."

"Fuck em. They got bigger things to worry about. Now Nick, I've already smashed two faces in today... both of them prettier than yours. If you don't roll me that joint..."

Nick laughed. "Here's the proof that marijuana is an addictive drug. You just... well, I don't know *what* you just saw or did, but I know it involves at least two dead bodies."

"Can you think of a better time to take a break from reality?"

"I guess not," conceded Nick. He knelt down and gathered up the bits of weed and rolled them into a joint. He put it in Hugh's mouth and lit it for him.

"The last of the California shit," said Hugh. "You'd better take a hit, too. Right about now, I'd welcome your thinky-ass thoughts on the situation."

Nick took a hit. "I can smell it. The green toxic shit. Whatever happened here, the shit was involved."

"'Involved' is one way to put. Another way to put it is that that... *bitch* jammed a needle of it into poor sweet Marie's head, thereby turning poor sweet Marie into a zombie bitch intent on alternately sucking me off and killing me."

"You're saying the green toxic shit turns people into... what, zombies? That give you blowjobs?"

"I'm not saying it, I said it. I saw it. She was dead, and then she was up grabbing at my dick, and then she was throwing people out of windows. The only way to kill her was to cut off her head. Duvlosky somehow knew that. Poor guy. Did you see him out there? Did he kill the scientist bitch?"

"He wanted to, but he didn't. This is all insane, Hugh. This is the same stuff that turned my dick into a lightning rod. And it also turned Mrs. Duvlosky into a... zombie?"

"I don't believe it, and I'm the one who saw it happen, all of it. Well, I didn't see you jerking it, but that isn't difficult to buy."

Then Duvlosky entered. Mercifully, he had left the head outside.

"Alright," he said. "We've got five minutes. Let's talk. And, Jesus Christ, pass that joint over here."

PART III

Chapter thirty four

Four strokes, quick and light, to flatten the back, and the blade was ready. Zack Ellis wiped off the sludge from the waterstone on his pants and brought the chisel back to the bench. There was nothing like a freshly honed edge. The smooth and effortless cutting action was like poetry. It transformed the tedious process into something more akin to music - the wood was the violin, the chisel the bow, and he was the musician, coaxing forth the harmony of form, the flourishing melodies of details.

After chopping to the line, he held the board up to the light and worked away at any last obstructions in the corners. Then he pressed it together with its mating piece and he had it, a perfect dovetailed corner, no gaps, tight and strong even without glue. He was getting better. It was a matter of being patient, keeping a sure hand and a clear head focused on the work. That, and having sharp tools sensitive to the pull of the grain.

He swept off the bench and could hear the wind beginning to pick up. The sheets of metal roofing that covered his piles of lumber outside started first rattling, then banging heavily against the stacks. Then the lights went out. The sky had darkened, he saw through the window. It was dark, too dark to work. The wind was building. He heard a massive crashing sound and went outside to have a look.

The wind was blowing so heavy that he had to fight it a little. He made it to the back of the shop and saw that one of the metal sheets had blown off of one of the lumber piles. It was nowhere to be seen. Standing in the midst of his piles, he heard the rush of the wind, the creaking and rattling and banging of the remaining metal sheets. The snow from the ground and the top of the stacks was shooting through the air, stinging his exposed face, making it difficult to see. He realized that he was in danger. The metal had sharp edges. If one could blow off even beneath the weight of the cement blocks holding it down, then another could just as easily. And it could take his head off too.

He turned to go back into the shop and all at once the wind stopped. There wasn't even the slightest breeze. It was as calm as it had been that morning. The sky was still covered by a layer of dark clouds, darker than he had ever seen. It was disquieting. Zack shuddered. Then he laughed. Afraid of the dark and a little wind?

He saw the missing metal sheet, blown just to the edge of the woods. Some kind of storm was coming. He'd better go get it, and cover the stack again. It would be a tragedy to lose all that good cherry, to lose all the magic contained beneath the rough sawn surface, all of that color and the infinite variations of grain, because he was too cold and lazy to keep it from getting wet. It had been drying long enough that letting it get wet at this point would mean that it would surely cup and twist and crack like some thing tormented by unknown stresses and forces. It would be, yes, a tragedy.

He had to trudge through a foot of snow to get to it. He wasn't dressed for such foolishness. From deep in the woods, he heard a loud snap. He made a note to check on it when conditions were better. After all, that fallen tree might someday make a piece of fine furniture. Finally, he reached the metal sheet. He wasn't looking forward to carrying it back, but it had to be done.

He grabbed a corner and lifted it. Christ, he should have at least got a pair of gloves from the shop. This is what happens when you get impatient and rush things: you make it that much harder for yourself to get the job done. As he lifted the sheet, something he saw made him lose all of the strength in his body, and as he dropped the sheet, the edge cut his palm deep, and he sunk amidst the blood-soaked snow.

Chapter thirty five

"Let's cut the bullshit. I'm here and you're here because something like this has never happened before. What do you do when the lieutenant cuts off his wife's head and claims that she was... undead? It would be one thing if it were just my word. But I have a witness. And then there's this. Jonathan Huskfield's notebook, in Sarah Johnston's possession at the time of the incident. And then of course there's the empty syringe, with visible traces of a green substance and what will be proved to be Marie's blood. Finally, remember what happened to Philips, Rogers, and Millers. Remember Wilkins' body. I now believe that her head was removed by Johnston, who was attempting to understand the substance. I believe that she succeeded, though the rest of her motives remain a mystery.

"Our town is already swarming with national reporters. They're going to be asking a lot of questions. It's not your job to answer them. It's not your job to ask questions either, but I understand that you have them. If I had the answers, I would give them to you. Instead, I'm going to give you orders. Those orders are going to help us find the answers to our questions.

"This case has now become the only case that we're concerned with. If someone's speeding, we let them speed. If someone's robbing, we let them rob, at least for now. There are eight of us. We've already lost four to this... thing.

THE ELECTRIC BONER

"Cooper has been assigned to watch over Johnston at the hospital, in case she wakes up. That leaves seven of us. Our first priority is to find this. This photograph was taken by a high school student when he first encountered the green substance. He claims that he saw Huskfield at this shed. Later, he and his friend brought Johnston to the shed, at her insistence. The shed is now empty, with no trace of the substance. We believe that Johnston has somehow relocated it.

"Jacobs and Sweeny. You're on Johnston's place. Search every inch of it. Fuck a warrant. We're not going for a conviction here, we're trying to stop an evil force. Break windows, break doors, tear fabric, do whatever you have to. Clayton and Richaud, you've got Huskfield's house. Same rules apply, but you're looking for anything that might help explain this thing, anything we might have missed on our walk-through, because we weren't looking for it. Check the toaster, check under the rug, check behind the toilet.

"I've given copies of Huskfield's notes to the research lab, along with the traces of the substance from the syringe. They've agreed to do an analysis. They're just as determined to solve this thing as we are. I'm putting Jackson and Jeffries on the lab. It's the only other likely place where Johnston would have stored the substance. I also want these scientists protected, and subtly watched. There's no way to know who else is involved in this, or what anybody's motives are. Let's be a bit more civilized here, but the objective is the same. Get the job done, no matter what.

"As for me. I'll be making rounds checking in with all of you. No rest until this is done. I'll also be dealing with the bullshit. Reporters, maybe some bureaucrats. I'm going to ask you all to deny any knowledge of this green substance. As far as you know, it doesn't exist. You're investigating murders.

"And remember: you have to cut off the head."

Chapter thirty six

"Would you quit worrying about your electric boner? Duvlosky's got it covered. They got the scientist bitch. She'll talk, he'll make her. It's over."

"No. I have this... feeling. It's just beginning."

"That's it."

"I had this... vision. Something bad is coming."

"No more pot for you, ever. You've lost your privileges."

"I'm different now. Whatever happened to me, it's not done happening. I don't know how to describe it. It's like I'm turning into someone else. Or I'm feeling these things I've never felt before, and starting to see things I've never seen. For a while anyway, and then I'm back to myself."

"That happened to me once too, when I didn't jerk off for three days. Once we get your johnson functioning again, you'll be right as rain. You'll see."

"But it's not what's happening to me that has me worried. It's what I'm... sensing. Out there. Coming for us, for all of us."

"Look, I almost just got my dick ripped off by a fucking zombie. I watched a guy cut off his wife's head. And I watched the head go on living after that, until he stabbed it in the brain. Now that's pretty fucked up. But it's over. It happened and there's nothing anybody can do about it, so I'm just going to go on doing what I do and try to forget about it. And yeah, it blows that you have an electric boner, but we're going to sort that out, too, we're going to find the antidote, or whatever. Duvlosky is. Out of all of us, he got the rawest deal, but you don't see him sitting around moaning like a pussy. He's out there doing what needs to be done."

"I'm going to do what needs to be done, too. I can sense that. I just have no idea what it is."

"I'll tell you what you're going to do. First of all, go home and fold up a pillow. Cut a hole in a watermelon. Whatever. Just find something to stick your dick into, and then do it."

"I hadn't considered that."

"Look, I know what I'm talking about. Next, after you mess up Fran's good linen, I want you to take a good rest. Watch some soap operas, read a fashion magazine. Whatever you do to soothe that manic brain of yours. Then, we go to that pussysucker Jake's party."

"You really still want to go to the party, after everything that's happened?"

"Hell no, but we're going. You've been whimpering to go, God knows why, so we're going. If we stay at home fucking pillowcases all night, the scientist bitch wins."

"Alright. But... oh, shit, maybe you're right. Maybe it's just my dick after all."

"I am right, and it is your dick. Now, go find something to stuff it into."

Chapter thirty seven

"Power's out," said Richaud.

"Hey, that's just the sort of detective work that's gonna solve this thing," said Clayton.

"And that's just the sort of attitude that's going to put *your* lights out."

They were on edge, and poking around some dead scientist's house in darkness wasn't improving their moods.

"Christ, look at this," said Clayton, shining his flashlight over the expanse of a painting that took up half of the living room wall. "The guy was a sick fuck, that's not up for debate." The painting depicted a room in what must have been some kind of palace. There was a young and beautiful woman on her knees on a strip of red carpet down the center of a marbled floor. She was naked and had an iron collar around her neck. Coming from the collar was a thick chain, dropping down to the carpet and leading to its opposite end, where there was an ornate golden throne. Sitting in the throne was an old and frail-looking man with a long white beard. He was clad in a purple robe and a golden crown and was holding the other end of the chain in one hand.

"That's what this whole thing is. These assholes screwing with the natural order of things," said Richaud.

"So then you're buying the Lt's story?"

"Well, it makes sense, doesn't it? Huskfield was trying to make sex slaves, and something went wrong. I mean, look at the damn painting."

"I saw it. Christ, let's just do this and get the hell out of here. I'll take the first floor, you take the basement," said Clayton.

"Maybe we should stick together. What if he's got some kind of secret chamber with more of those… things inside?"

"Pull yourself together Richaud. There's no secret chambers full of zombies. Let's just get this over with."

"Fuck you, *you* take the basement."

"Christ, alright, I will."

Richaud watched Clayton disappear down the hallway. He heard the door open, then heard Clayton descend the creaky steps. Oh man: why did they have to be creaky? Then all he heard was silence. He shone his flashlight at the painting again. The old man seemed to cast a shadow, as if he were three dimensional. But it was only the shadows in the painting itself.

Richaud was sure there was a secret opening somewhere. He just wasn't sure if he wanted to find it. But it was his duty to find it. It was his duty to keep his town safe. But how much duty could you perform, with some zombie eating your brains?

He steeled himself and tried to pull the painting from the wall. It wouldn't budge, probably bolted on there. He took out his pocket knife and made a slit down the center of the canvas. As he did so, it seemed as though the old man were looking directly at him. But Jesus, that's the biggest cliché of them all. He laughed, but he wasn't sure if he was amused, or just trying to pretend that he wasn't terrified.

He tore back the canvas and shone his light at the wall. Nothing. Just painted drywall. He knocked on the wall. It sounded normal enough. He laughed again, and this time he was sure it was in relief.

He shone his light around the room. There was nothing much to search. It looked barely lived-in. There was a single wooden chair, a bookcase full of books, a small table, a lamp. Richaud walked over to the bookcase and shone his flashlight over the books. They were mostly scientific books and journals, many of them written by Huskfield himself. Then he saw 120 Days of Sodom by Marquis de Sade. He pulled it out and flipped through the pages. Then he tossed it on the floor and went through the same routine with some of the other books. He pulled the bookcase away from the wall and knocked on it. Nothing unusual.

He walked down the hall and toward the bedroom. The door was closed. He hesitated, took a deep breath, and opened it. It creaked open. He shone his flashlight in. The bedroom was just as sparse as the living room. Just a bed, a dresser, and a closet door. He flipped the covers off the bed. Then he lifted the mattress. Nothing.

He heard Clayton creaking his way back up the stairs. He shone his light over to the dresser. There was a small wooden box on top of it. He went over and tried to open it, but the lid wouldn't come off. He took out his knife again and tried to pry it open. It wouldn't open.

Clayton walked in. "Find anything?" asked Richaud.

"Oh, just a secret chamber full of zombies," said Clayton, laughing.

Richaud scowled. "Nothing here, either. Check the kitchen, then let's get out of here."

"Yes sir, boss sir," said Clayton, still laughing as he walked back through the hall.

Richaud looked at the box again. There was something in there. Something terrible. Maybe he should just leave it and forget he ever saw it. No. His duty. Was he Man or chickenshit? He struck at the lid with the butt of his flashlight. It splintered apart. He realized that he was expecting some kind of evil spirit to fly out of it, and when it didn't, he laughed again.

He shone his flashlight in. There was a small vial in there. He picked it up and shook it. There was a liquid inside. It looked pure black, but maybe it was only the lack of light that made it look like that. It looked blacker than anything he had ever seen. He turned it around and there was a white label with letters and numbers printed neatly on it. It said: "XB15."

Chapter thirty eight

Nick was working with a hair-trigger. Just thinking the name "Lucy" got him hard. Then he had her in his head. They were at the party, each holding a red plastic cup. She took him by the hand and led him to a bedroom. "Oh Nick," she said, "I'm so scared. You're the only one who can save us."

He leaned in and kissed her soft, full lips. At the same time, he folded the pillow in half and placed in the center of the bed. Then she was unbuttoning his pants. Then he was unbuttoning his pants. Then she pressed her palm against it. "I need you, Nick. I need you inside of me.

Everybody's gone insane and you're the only good one left."

Then it was out in the open. Then he put it in the pillow, and slid it in and out, slowly. She had it in her hand and was softly stroking it. "It's beautiful," she said. It felt good. It felt better than anything else had ever felt. Maddening shocks of pleasure stabbed at him, becoming too much to bear. He started thrusting harder. She sat down in the bed and pulled him down by the arms. "Please, Nick, please," she whispered. Then her pants were off.

Now he was really slamming away at the pillow. It was working. It was working better than ever! Now he was working away on top of her, looking into her eyes. He was on the verge of cumming and then her irises went black. Then the blackness spread out to swallow her entire eyeballs. The blackness oozed out her eyes and dripped down her face.

He was fucking the pillow with all of his might. She pulled her lips back and revealed a mouthful of jagged fangs in putrid and rotting gums. "Nicky boy," she hissed, "I'm going to rip your fucking soul out."

Now his face was wet with tears and he knew he was at the point of no return. Two more thrusts and it would be over with. Now the flesh was falling off her face, dripping into blackness, and then there was only blackness and then he was cumming and his head filled with light, his head exploded with lightness as if staring directly at the sun, as if standing inside the sun and looking at the very core and he felt the light spread through his body as it first tightened almost inside itself, and then finally relaxed into an oozing easiness, and then he felt nothing at all and everything was blank, grey, nothingness.

He opened his eyes and looked down at the pillow. There was a hole there as if somebody had taken a cigarette six inches in diameter and put it out in the center of the pillow. He looked down at his fingernails. They looked fine: clean and trimmed.

Chapter thirty nine

Mikhail sat at the desk in his office. The phone wouldn't stop ringing. His *head* wouldn't stop ringing. He didn't know what to do. The worst part was pretending that he did know what to do. It was the show of being brave and in control when in fact you were terrified and helpless. But, something told him, putting on the show was a type of bravery in and of itself. People were looking to him, for answers, for instructions. As if he knew what the hell was going on... as if he hadn't just lopped off Marie's head and then stabbed it in the brain because it wouldn't die.

Something he did know, then and now, was that he lost Marie before he had entered their house to find her... body... on her knees.... He'd seen her eyes and he'd known that he had lost her, forever. The MacMillan boy had confirmed it in between gasps. Johnston had killed her, and then she'd come back to life. Something died in him then, too.

"Can you tell us why you killed your wife?" They'd been asking him that, non-stop, all day. His men, the chief, and the reporters. Endless reporters. Where did they all come from? Reporters from all over the world. He had to be more careful in his answers to them.

"She had terrible things done to her, terrible experiments. She was no longer my wife. She had been transformed into something inhuman, intent on brutality and murder. She would have killed the boy if I had not intervened."

"But why did you cut off her head?"

"Because that was the only way to stop it... her."

"What do you mean by that?"

"I told you... she was the victim of terrible, unnatural experimentation. She was no longer human."

"What kind of experimentation?"

"Well, that's what we're working on finding out - provided we don't have to spend the next month reporting non-stop to the media. Once we know something," he lied, "you'll know it just as soon. There will be a full investigation into my actions, as well as all of the actions that led to my wife's tragic death. Until that time, no further comment."

After hours of this, he had simply stopped answering the phone. Let them get the story from each other. This was the last thing that he needed. There was the Sherman boy, and what he described as his "electric boner." There was still hope for him, to help him - maybe. But if there was hope for him, maybe there had been hope for Marie? Maybe there was a way to cure her?

No. What's done is done. And Marie was done. Her soft touch and sweet laugh were gone. Her good mind and her good heart were gone. Their unborn child would never be born. But he couldn't think about that, either. Every time he started to, he felt sick and incomparably sad, as if life were impossible, as if he were trapped in a tiny room and the walls were evil and unbreakable. As if the next breath would not come, and there was no reason for it to come. Laughter and happiness were tricks, jester masks covering worms and rotting meat.

Finally, he had to get out. He had to do something, not only because it was expected of him, but because if he didn't, he would surely shoot himself in the head. Maybe he would have deserved that. Maybe he should do it after all.

He walked through the office. "Denise. If any reporters call, tell them I've given my statements, and there's no further comment. If anybody else calls, unless they're a Clairmont police officer or someone literally dying, tell them to leave a message."

He headed out and got in his car. Poor Henderson. He'd just liked driving around and talking to everyone in town, catching up on gossip, bullshitting on all manner of subjects, giving teenagers a scare, but in the end letting them off with a wrist slap. And yet, his death was a sort of strange and uneasy vindication for Mikhail. She had killed Henderson. She was dangerous and would have killed again if he hadn't stopped her. "But why did you cut off her head?"

He decided to go to Johnston's apartment first and check in. It was on the way to the lab. There was no need to go to Huskfield's - he didn't expect to find anything useful there - and if he went to the hospital, he was certain that he would kill Johnston. It was only the Sherman boy who had stopped him before - some gentle urging in his eyes.

Mikhail pulled into the driveway and shut off the car. He put his head on the steering wheel and gripped it tight. Here we go again. Time for the show. Did the show ever stop? It had always stopped whenever he saw Marie, and now that she was gone, maybe it would be a good thing to keep the show going for as long as he could. The glimpses he got behind-the-scenes weren't anything to look forward to.

He got out of the car and the door to the apartment opened and there was Jacobs. Jacobs was a good man. He knew how to think and he knew how to see both sides of a story. That's why Mikhail had put him with Sweeny. Sweeny was good at being forceful and direct. They balanced each other out, and together they could cover a lot of ground. Mikhail was certain that there was some vital clue in Johnston's house. After all, she had had a busy few days. She was bound to have gotten careless somewhere along the line.

"Anything?" asked Mikhail.

THE ELECTRIC BONER

"No sir," said Jacobs. "We're almost done with our search."

Sweeny stepped out and lit a cigarette. "Nada Lt," he said. "Well, we found a purple vibrator, but that's about it."

Mikhail felt the heat rush to his face. "No," he said. "There's something here."

"Just that vibrator," said Sweeny. "Jacobs almost fainted when he saw it, you know."

"There's something here goddammit!" shouted Mikhail. Jacobs and Sweeny exchanged glances. They're looking to you, they're scared, but they're not sure if you can lead them. He pulled out a cigarette and lit it. The sky was dark and it was cold.

Chapter forty

"Wow," Carlos was saying. "Wow, wow, wow... wow."

Officer Jackson was staring at him. "Alright, doc. Out with it: whaddya got?"

Carlos looked up from the microscope. He'd just flown in from LA two weeks ago, after having received his PhD in chemistry from Stanford in the spring. He found Maine to be a strange place, and the locals stranger. They amused him to no end. Particularly this Jackson of the jowls and drooping mustache, exuding tiredness, gruff and attempting to give an air of authority, but obviously as lost as if he had just found himself suddenly transported to Thailand - where, Carlos felt safe in assuming, he had never been. But Carlos had been there - he had been all over the world, and he found there were villages in the bush more culturally connected and in tune with the world than Clairmont, Maine was.

Carlos was an idealist. He believed that science held the real and direct key to a better world. That's why he had jumped at the chance to work with the esteemed Dr. Huskfield, whose recent articles had shown such groundbreaking progress in understanding and treating Alzheimer's. When he heard that Dr. Johnston was also conducting research at the Clairmont facility, he couldn't believe his amazing fortune. It turned out that they were both rather unpleasant people - but then what did that matter? It was their work that mattered, and they were two of the brightest stars in America, lighting the way of the future.

Carlos had noted the mood that day, the first day the lab was open after Huskfield's death. Everyone seemed positively delighted. At first Carlos thought it was on account of Huskfield being such a bastard. Then he began to understand. It was that, but it was also that his absence had left an open chair, and those who had put up with him for years felt like they deserved it, along with the subsequent and significant pay bump. It made Carlos sick. When later news of Johnston's disgrace reached the lab, he was sure that they would break out the champagne. Such jubilance over such a tragic loss for science. Very likely, Carlos himself could have risen through the ranks and procured one of the two empty chairs. He was, after all, more gifted, more diligent, and more dedicated than the rest. But the thought hardly entered his mind. Instead, he had resolved to leave Clairmont Maine forever and never look back. That is, until this.

"I'll tell you what I got, chief," said Carlos with a genial smile, "I got about fifty different chemical compounds, each with a striking similarity to a human hormone. Fifty different synthetic hormones, and I'll tell you what's more: they don't seem to be getting along too well." Carlos had tried to explain it so that a third grader could understand. It amused him to see the officer's face twist in confusion.

"So then you got it figured out, kid, do you? That's great."

"Figured out? I'm afraid not. I know what I'm looking at, but it would take months, maybe years of study to begin to understand how it got there, or how it works. There's really no telling how long it would take. It's the most complex chemical puzzle I've ever seen."

Jackson frowned. "Well, keep working."

"Maybe if I could talk to Doctor Johnston..."

"Just keep working. Let us worry about Johnston," Jackson said, fully returned to his gruffness.

"I should at least see Doctor Huskfield's notes. They would go a long way to explaining this," said Carlos, maintaining his smile. His father had taught him that. No matter what they do to you, smile.

Jackson sighed. "Just look at your microscope, kid. You do your job, I'll do mine. I'll be back to check on you soon." Jackson turned to leave.

Carlos bent back over his microscope. "Very well, sir. I should feel lucky you've even let me look at this. When the Feds get here, they'll confiscate it all."

Jackson stopped in his tracks. He frowned. "The Feds?"

"Sure," said Carlos. His back was to Jackson, but he was smiling anyhow. "This is their research facility, after all. Doctors Huskfield and Johnston are their employees... or were. Sarah Wilkins, too. I know you're doing your best to keep this substance out of the news, but how long do you think that will last? And what do you think the government will do once it finds out? Who's to say that this substance wasn't created per their instructions? Considering the dramatic manipulations that it's capable of..."

Jackson had heard enough. "Alright kid, just wait here a minute. I'll see what I can do." He left the room and Carlos studied the substance in fascination. It was like watching a ballet. A violent ballet, but beautiful all the same. It was more godly than anything God had ever created.

A few minutes later, Jackson returned and tossed the photocopied version of the notebook on Carlos' desk. "There ya go. Be quick about it."

Carlos flipped through the pages. "There are pages missing. A lot of them. It goes from page 5 to 10... 13 is missing... 16... 18... 21 through 24... who's seen this?"

"Just yer as-teemed colleeeges," said Jackson.

"Well, my esteemed colleagues are thieves. No doubt there's much in here that could handsomely advance one's career. It would be better if I had the complete original. But, as you said, I'll do my job and you do yours." Carlos smiled. "Thank you, Officer Jackson."

Now Jackson was smiling. "Don't mention it kid. Let me know what you find. I guess I got some bodies to search."

Carlos flipped through the pages again. A lot of it focused on the brain, not his area of expertise. But he had friends from school, friends from his travels that could help him there. One page toward the end had the chemical structure of the green substance laid out crisply and cleanly. That would save a lot of time. Carlos had said the bit about the Feds as a bluff, but the more it sat, the more it made sense. Anyhow, the situation seemed urgent. The police were blatantly holding information back, and they seemed on the edge of their nerves.

Flipping backwards through the pages, Carlos stopped at one with a header of XB15. The green substance had been named XB20. This page also had a clear delineation of chemical structures. In the margins were Huskfield's notes, written in a hand that only a scientist could use, and only a scientist could read.

"Most intriguing yet, also most disastrous. Keep in mind for next project, if this one fails. Many possibilities, after some major overhauls."

Carlos studied these pages intently. The focus was still on the brain and hormonal interplay, but here Huskfield also delved into genetics. Again, not Carlos' specialty, but he knew enough to understand the gist of Huskfield's notes. It seemed that Doctor Huskfield had experimented with trying to change the physical stuff of a human being, of trying to change the outward structure and appearance of a person as well as the inner, chemical structure.

Carlos had to fight to keep himself on task. It was all so overwhelmingly fascinating. It could all be used to create a better world. But for now, his task was the green substance. Somehow, though they were mostly backwards and ignorant, he had grown fond of the people of Clairmont. He just now realized it. Maybe it was that oaf, Jackson, that had finally endeared them to him. After all, it was the human race he wanted to save. That's something you can't do all at once, and this strange little place was as good of a place to start as any.

Chapter forty one

Richaud called Duvlosky's cell. "Richaud here. We've finished our search of Huskfield's house."

"Let me guess," said Duvlosky, "nothing."

"Tell him about the secret chamber full of zombies," said Clayton, laughing.

Richaud flipped him off. "We did find a... substance, sir, in a vial."

"The green substance?" asked Duvlosky.

"Well, this one looks more black than anything. But it's hard to tell, with the power out and all."

"The power's out there? It's not here."

"It's out up and down the road here, as far as I can see. Branches down. Must have been a localized gust of wind or something."

"Well, I'll tell you what," said Duvlosky, "I'm driving from Johnston's place to the lab. Meet me there and we'll see what out scientist friends have to say about your substance."

"10-4," said Richaud and hung up. The sky was covered with dark clouds. He looked back to Huskfield's house. It seemed sinister, somehow. He was sure they'd missed something, but he wasn't about to go back in that place. "Let's get the hell out of here," he said.

"Now," said Clayton, "you're talking sense."

"Duvlosky wants us to take this stuff to the lab."

"I thought we were looking for a green substance?"

"Who knows. Let's roll."

They got in the car. Clayton was driving. Richaud held the vial between his thumb and forefinger and looked at it. Yes, it was black, no doubt about it.

"What do you think it is?" asked Clayton, turning onto Fletcher Rd.

"What do you call a cross between an elephant and a rhinoceros?"

"What?"

"'Ell if I know."

Clayton guffawed. "That's good, Richaud. You had me worried back there, talking about zombies and shit."

Richaud looked out the window. They passed Zack Ellis' house. He liked the Ellises. Zack had made him a gun cabinet when he had helped find the Ellis boy who had been lost in the woods for a day and a night. He liked his town and the people in it, and it made him proud to protect them. He began to feel guilty for not going back inside Huskfield's when every instinct told him that there was something tremendously important in there. Then he felt a tingling in his fingers, where he was holding the vial of the black substance.

"FUCK!" screamed Clayton. Richaud looked up to see the deer flash in front of the windshield. The front left of the car clipped its rear end, making the car veer slightly off the road. Richaud thought he saw the deer spin around and run off into the woods, but it was too dark to tell for sure. The tires caught a patch of ice on the side of the road and that was it. Clayton worked the wheel in tight jerks, but it was no good. They were sliding.

Richaud saw the tree and then he looked over at Clayton's head resting against the air bag. But the head was turned in a way that it wasn't supposed to turn. Then for some reason he looked down at his hand. There was blood dripping down his wrist, and his hand was black. Then everything was black.

Chapter forty two

Zack struggled to his feet. He stood and looked around in a slow circle. There was his shop, there was his truck, there was his driveway, there were his lumber piles, and there was the metal sheet that had blown off, and beyond it, the dark woods. Everything was dark, but the woods were darkness itself. He clenched his cut hand and slowly lifted the metal sheet with his other hand.

It was a male human body. It was difficult to say whose body it was, as the flesh and muscle had been stripped from the head, leaving only a skull with two round eyeballs staring in amazement and a purple tongue sticking out straight and stiff. The rest of the body was covered in winter clothes, a thick brown coat, tan pants, and black rubber boots. Two green swollen hands spread out at its sides.

Zack threw the sheet aside. Judging from the size, the clothes worn by work, and the location of the body, he guessed it was Peterson from down the road. At once he ran through all manner of scenarios as to what could have happened, what could have done that, and nothing fit. The only thing that made any kind of sense was that some human being had done this. Somebody had flayed the skin off this man's face and left him at the edge of the woods on Zack's property.

But if that were true, who would do that to Peterson? True, Zack didn't know him well, but he always seemed low-key and genial enough. But you never knew about people. They carried around entire universes of the untold. In that way, people were like wood, full of hidden colors, and hidden defects.

Or maybe it wasn't Peterson. Lately, there had been a handful of drug-related murders in Maine. Here and there. You heard about someone getting murdered on the news. Later, either through police reports or friends who knew somebody who knew somebody, you heard the whole story, the motives. Drugs were almost always involved. But, Zack had done his share of drugs in the past, and what kind of shit must the person who did this have been on?

It helped to try to work out the problem. It was better than standing there like an idiot. But this wasn't his problem to work out. It was the police's. Zack turned back toward the shop. Then he heard another branch break in the woods. He stopped and listened. Something was coming.

Chapter forty three

Mikhail stopped at the store for a coffee. He needed it. Rather, he needed rest, he needed vast spaces of time to be alone and sort out what had happened. But it didn't work that way. Life didn't stop when you wanted it to, unless…

He noticed the clerk looking at him while trying to make appear that she wasn't looking at him. No doubt she hadn't pretended to not see him when he had been on the TV. And she had always been so friendly with him. Things change. They change slowly all the time without your noticing it, but sometimes they change all at once and then you have to adjust. You have to change along with them, without any map on how to do so. But, somehow, you also have to stay the same. You have to keep your sense of morality through it all, your sense of identity. "Thank you," he said. Adapt, or don't adapt. Those were your choices. He just hadn't decided on what the right choice was.

He got in his car and headed to the lab. Jackson had reported that one of the scientists there was making progress on understanding the green substance. That was good. But what worried Mikhail was that nobody seemed to be any closer to finding the stockpile of the substance. Jackson and Jeffries were searching the lab, Sweeny and Jacobs had searched Johnston's, he himself had searched the shack where the boys had found it, and Richaud and Clayton had even searched Huskfield's, turning up only a black liquid, adding to the mystery instead of solving it.

Where could she have put two hundred gallons of such a dangerous substance? How did she move it from the shack to its current location? In between cutting off Sarah Wilkins' head and arranging it so that Mikhail had to cut off Marie's head? The answer had to be simple, obvious. Why couldn't Mikhail see it?

He reached the lab and Jackson met him in the parking lot. "Sir," said Jackson. "There's the good and the bad in there. I got a kid, Carlos, working on the thing good. The rest of them are louts, not to be trusted. I found half of them with pages from Huskfield's notes stuffed in their pants, their bras, their goddamn undies. The other half of them, I couldn't find at all."

"So we got one good guy in there?"

"And I'm not even sure about him. These goddamn scientists... they talk Russian. But the kid feels right."

"And no sign of the stockpile of the stuff?"

"Jeffries is still going over the place. He's been complaining that it's too big, there's too many nooks and crannies and strange devices and such."

"Richaud and Clayton are headed over. I'll put them on the search. Now, I want to talk to your scientist."

Jackson led Mikhail into the building and through a series of hallways and down one flight of stairs and then another and then another. The entire facility was underground. There was no way of knowing how deep it went from looking at it from the outside. Mikhail had never properly regarded it, even on the night of Huskfield's murder, but now that he was descending the concrete steps, it seemed to him very strange that this place existed in Clairmont, Maine. That made him wonder how weak his knowledge of things really was. How much of the world was unknown to him? Almost all of it, he decided. All he wanted was to know a little more, to know what the substance was that killed his wife, to know where the rest of it was hidden. Then he could rest, or kill himself.

They walked down another flight of stairs. Mikhail remembered that it went ten stories deep. They had searched the floors for Wilkins, but Mikhail had been too focused on the job, too fueled by adrenaline to consider that anything but normal. Now that his focus had began to wander due to the mental and physical spiritual strains he was under, he got the impression that the further down he went, the closer he was getting to Hell. And he was beginning to feel like that was his home, that he belonged there, at the very bottom floor.

For the thousandth time that day, he pulled himself together. The show must go on. "I'm going to get Sweeny and Jacobs in here too. Jeffries is right. This place is massive. This is where we're going to find it." It was, yes, obvious. Why had he wasted any time sending his men anywhere else? Why had he despaired of the search when the search hadn't even begun?

"Here we are," said Jackson. On the fifth floor below grade, Jackson led Mikhail down another hallway, lined with heavy metal doors. He stopped at room 610 and opened it. There was the scientist, studying Huskfield's notebook.

"Kid, this is the Lt, Officer Duvlosky. Lt, this is the kid, Carlos."

Carlos looked at Mikhail, smiled, then looked back at the notes. "You know, Officer Jackson," he said, "it's going to be very difficult for me to do my work with you fellows dropping by every six minutes for a chat."

"Jackson," said Mikhail, "why don't you continue rounding up our fugitive scientists?" Jackson nodded and left the room. "Carlos, I won't take much of your time. I just need to know what you've found."

"Mr. Duvlosky. You have to understand that it is difficult for me to tell the story with only half of the plot. There's something you haven't told me."

Mikhail closed his eyes and rubbed his temples with his thumb and middle finger. It's true that they had left the scientists somewhat in the dark. He saw Huskfield's dismembered body again, bloody and gruesome; he saw Wilkins' beheaded corpse frozen on the ground; he saw his wife, on her knees…

"We've left out the sexual aspect," said Duvlosky. That was the worst part, that it took what he had with Marie, the thing that could give life, and turned it into an instrument of death. "Whatever it is, it makes its… subjects… aggressively sexual."

"We know three effects, then. One: it turns its subjects aggressively sexual, as you now say; two: it turns its subjects aggressively murderous; and three, it allows its subjects to sustain serious injuries and still continue to function in accordance with effects one and two."

"The last one… number three… it's more than that. It's more than we told you. It kills the subject, and then somehow brings her… it back to life. And then the only way to kill it again, as far as we can tell, is to cut off its head and kill the brain."

"You should have told me this, before."

"This can't get out. Can you imagine how people would react?" said Mikhail. But he wondered if he hadn't told the scientists the full story because the full story was too painful. To talk about it was to relive it. It was to look into his dead wife's eyes, to see her reaching with dead hands, intent on killing him and everyone else.

Carlos sighed. "The aggressive behavior, both sexual and murderous are simple enough to understand. One component of the substance is an incredible cocktail of synthetic hormones. These would send impulses to the brain, and consequently the body, and make the subject behave in a way that would be impossible for me to predict, without experimentation. But that experiment has been done for us."

Mikhail felt another stab of pain to think of his wife as an experiment. "What about the other part?"

"That is more difficult to explain. I can tell you that pain is nothing more than impulses to and from the brain. If the brain were hijacked, so to speak, it is possible that the subject would cease to feel pain. Perhaps we are looking at a brain, and consequently a person, that can only work with two impulses: the sexual one, and the one to kill, as part of the fight or flight response. All other feelings, including pain, cease to be felt."

Mikhail tried to process this all. "But we're not just talking about not feeling pain. We're talking about you can't kill them. Blood loss, damage to major organs... how can something go on living like this?"

Carlos frowned. "I don't know," he said. "The body moves because of the brain, but it needs an uninterrupted pathway of blood, nerves, muscle, to and from. I need help on this. I need physicists, brain specialists, nerve specialists... I need a team."

"Can you work with the scientists you have here?"

Carlos smiled again. "I'm afraid this is a bit out of their league. In terms of what's available locally, I would need Doctor Johnston."

The name filled Mikhail with rage. He quelled it. He was beginning to feel like the shooting targets that he trained with. Every time you hit them, they left a hole, and if you kept hitting the center, there was nothing left to hit.

"When – if – she wakes, you can talk to her. Until then Carlos, do your best. I can't thank you enough."

Carlos smiled. "Happy to help." He looked back at the notebook and Mikhail left.

He leaned against the hallway hall and rubbed his head again. What did it matter? What did it matter what the substance was, how it worked? Then he remembered the Sherman boy, Nick. He had forgotten all about him. It was for his sake that Mikhail had to find out what it was, and how to save the boy's penis. He had forgotten to tell Carlos about that, too. It would maybe help him understand the substance, and it would give him a more particular goal to work toward.

He turned back to room 610 and his cell phone rang. How it got reception so far underground was just another mystery. It was Cooper. He answered it. "Yeah?"

"She's awake."

Chapter forty four

It was getting closer. Then Zack could see two yellow dots glowing in the darkness. Eyes. He turned and tramped as quickly as he could through the snow, back toward his shop, occasionally glancing back. The dots were growing larger, the noise closer. Then he turned and saw that a figure had emerged from the woods, of human stature and without yellow glowing eyes.

"Mr. Ellis," said a female voice, imploringly. "Please, wait! It's Claire Peterson. I'm looking for my husband. He went for a walk last night and never came back. You haven't seen him, have you?"

Zack stopped walking. He searched for any sign of the yellow dots. They were gone. Then his heart sank at the task he was faced with. "You better come in the shop, Claire, where it's warm. We need to talk."

Zack backtracked to meet up with her, then held her hand as they made their way to the shop. "It's so dark," said Claire, breathing heavily. "I have a feeling that something terrible happened to Jeffery, in this darkness."

"Let's go inside, Claire," said Zack again, trying to form the words in his mind, "where it's warm."

They reached the door, Zack shoved it open, and they entered. The power was back on, he noted. "Please, sit," he said, indicating his stool. "Just a moment." He walked over to the stove, where the fire was dying. He fed it fresh wood.

Claire hadn't sat down. She was touching a cabinet that Zack had nearly completed in ash, perched atop a stand of white oak with gracefully curved, flowing legs. He was just finishing up the interior drawers, and then it would be done.

"It's beautiful," said Claire. "You know, I've seen your work at the galleries in town, and I've always admired it. More than admired. It's moved me, touched me." She laughed. "But then I look at the price tag and I know I could never afford it."

Zack wrapped a rag around his wounded hand. Claire saw the blood and gasped. "You're hurt!"

"It's nothing," he said. "And I'll be happy to make something for you some time, but I need to tell you something."

"You're an artist," said Claire, as though Zack hadn't spoken. She laughed again. Zack felt his nerves explode.

THE ELECTRIC BONER

"You know, I always wanted to be an artist. I mean, make a living at it."

"Claire, please, I believe that I may know what happened to your husband. I can't be sure, but I'm afraid..."

"I can paint, you know," said Claire. "I put on a show in college once. That was... oh, three thousand years ago. I was studying art at NYU. That's where I met Jeffery. Oh, such a long time ago! You know, sometimes I feel as though I've lived six different lives as six different people, in different times, different places. Really though, it's just the one life, one thing leading to the next, with absolute inevitability."

Zack looked uncomfortably at his shoes. "Claire, your husband is..."

"A selfish slob?" suggested Claire, and laughed once more. "Please, Mr. Ellis, allow an old lady her indulgences. And there is nothing so indulgent as talking about yourself, as thinking about yourself first. Lord knows it's a honey I've tasted little enough of in my long, dull life."

Zack didn't know how to respond. Wasn't she concerned for her husband? Or had she already accepted that he was gone, and this was her way of working through the grief?

"Those days were sweet," she went on, "but of course we were fools. We moved here without graduating, without knowing anybody, without jobs. Only a few dollars here and there from dear old mom and dad until they decided it was time for us to learn our lesson. If we wanted to live free in nature, they would let us find out what it was like. And find out we did.

"There is no such thing as a starving artist. It's a hoax. You can't starve and be anything but a starving person. But for a short while the fantasy persisted for us, and we were able to eat humbly and have a roof over our heads for a time, by selling my paintings and his freelance writing. Such happy times, but we knew that it wasn't sustainable. Then I got pregnant, and that was that. We had to get 'real jobs', as my parents called them. We were trapped, just like everyone else."

Claire laughed again. "Oh dear, I'm boring you. But don't worry, the story is almost over. One day - I remember, it was our sweet little Devin's fifth birthday - the phone rang. It was for me. Somebody was telling me that I had to make a decision fast. I didn't know what he was talking about. 'About the show,' he said. 'What show?' I asked. 'Didn't your husband tell you?' 'Please sir, it's my son's birthday, he's having a party, I really need to know what you're talking about.'

"He explained to me that Elliot Dalton had seen some of my paintings at a friend's house and was enamored by them. That's the word he used: 'enamored.' Do you know who Elliot Dalton is, Zack?"

"No," he confessed.

"At the time, nobody did. Now he is one of the most renowned art critics in the United States, and the owner of the Yarnford Gallery in New York City. My work was to be in their third official show. But it never happened, Zack. Do you know why?"

Zack had a good enough guess. "No," he said. He got some masking tape from a shelf and began wrapping the rag on his hand with it. "Tell me," he said, putting the tape down on the workbench. He kept his good hand on the bench, slowly rubbing the maple top.

"When I asked Jeffery about it that night, he confessed that he had purposely not told me about the call. 'Why?' I asked him. 'They said they needed twenty painting,' Jeffery said. 'You don't have twenty painting. You haven't painted in five years.'

"'But I could make twenty paintings. I can. I just need a few months off from work.'

"About that, he simply said, 'No,' and that was the end of the discussion. And that was the end of my dream. Later, of course, when Dalton became a name, dear old

THE ELECTRIC BONER

Jeffery encouraged me to seek him out again. But Dalton knew how to hold a grudge, and the early years of his rejections had left him with little taste for it. He remembered me, and he remembered that I had refused to be in his show.

"That's the end of the story, Zack. From there on out, it has been the terrible grind, the senseless and menial jobs to pay the bills. An idiot son who just barely graduated high school and is now following his father's glorious footsteps as a flooring installer. I made a painting a few years ago, you know, of a..."

"Misses Peterson," said Zack. "Your husband is dead."

Claire laughed. "It that what you've been so worried about? I only made him faceless as he made me faceless. But I'm not going to do that to you. I'm going to teach you what it's like to live a free and natural life by cutting off those precious hands of yours."

Chapter forty five

Nick stretched out on his bed and looked at the clock. 6:15. Hugh would be there in 45 minutes to pick him up for the party. Lucy would be there. She had called him to make sure he was coming. He had to go, he had to talk to her, to impress her somehow. He looked at the pillow by his feet, with a hole seared through its center. He could show her that.

He liked it there, lying in bed, staring up at the ceiling – he always had. He liked his mind, liked letting things pass through it. It was better than television, better than reading a book, better than going bowling. He liked to think about himself, to examine what sort of thing he was, to examine what sorts of things other people were, to wonder about something that had happened during the day, to try to imagine what other people thought about the same occurrence. It was good to work towards the truth.

When he was little, say six years old, he used to think about how everybody in the world was going to die. He thought about his mother dying and it made him sad and afraid. He thought about himself dying and it made him afraid, but he couldn't imagine it, it was almost like it wasn't true. It was certain that everybody else would die, but him? How could that possibly be? How could he stop seeing things and hearing things and smelling them, touching them, thinking about them? He didn't believe in Heaven like some of his other friends. He believed that death was nothingness, that things simply stopped. And he knew that he was being ridiculous, but he still somehow felt that he was the exception.

He used to think about going on living when everybody else was dead and he felt like crying. But he didn't cry. He knew that his mother wouldn't want him to be sad. Even though she would be dead, it was somehow important – what she would have wanted. And thinking about that, he felt brave. Being brave meant being afraid, but doing a thing anyhow.

Now, ten years later, the thoughts were still there as they always had been. It wasn't something that changed. Everybody was still going to die and he was still sad about it. He closed his eyes and watched the movie of his mind. Everything had become so vivid since that morning. He saw a pit and then a green hand rose up out of it and clutched the rim. Then there was a second hand, and a third, and soon there was a sea of green hands, thousands of them, clawing at the rim. He knew that if he looked into the pit, he would see his friends, he would see Hugh, he would see his mother at the bottom of it, torn apart.

He opened his eyes. Death and love. These were the things he had thought about since he could remember thinking. Important themes. His thoughts on death were always sober, with the hard edge of a truth that you didn't

THE ELECTRIC BONER

want to be true. His thoughts on love could be that way, when thinking about his mother for example, but often they were silly thoughts – fantasies, really.

For years, Lucy had been at the center of them. When falling asleep, he liked to imagine that she had been captured by someone, ninjas or monsters or spies or something. And he had to fight through them all to get her, to rescue her. Of all those who set out to rescue her, he was the only one who could. The outcome of such a rescue used to be that she would kiss him on the cheek and ask him to be her boyfriend; through the years, the reward had grown more graphic.

That's all my visions have been, he thought. Whatever this green shit is, it's just intensified whatever kind of ridiculous fantasies I've carried around since I was a boy. It's intensified my fear of death, and conflated it all. That's all it is, some kind of chemical intensification of whatever's already up there.

He looked at the pillow: that, though, is real. He felt better for the physical release of his sexual tension and the mental release of the tension about his visions, but there was still the matter of his electric boner, and whatever the hell it shot out of it to burn that hole in the pillow.

What if it never went away? What if he never got to use it, for real, on a girl? He thought back to when it was normal. He had blown it then, unable to talk to a girl, to even look at her without feeling red and ashamed. If he had known what would happen, would he have been bolder? He felt bold now, when it was too late. He felt bold at night, when he was alone, when feeling bold was useless. Whenever it counted, his boldness was nowhere to be found.

Still, something had happened today, with Lucy, on the phone. A surge of boldness real and immediate, and he felt that if they had been alone together in a room, he would have opened up to her, and talked to her as himself for hours. For through his cowardice, he had always felt a certain confidence all the same. He felt that Lucy was in his reach, if only he could reach out and touch her. And now that he felt ready to reach out and touch her, tonight, at the party, he had a different fear. Where once he had been sure of the touch, but afraid to reach, it was now the other way around.

Time passed in these reflections, and he heard the rattle of the Jetta come to a clattering halt in the driveway. It was time once again to leave his head and enter the world. He'd done the work of convincing Fran to let him go out, and now all he had to do was do it and see what happened.

He threw the spent pillow into his closet and went downstairs. Hugh was in the living room talking to Fran.

"Don't you worry, ma'am, we're going to behave ourselves like perfect angles. Look, here he is. Positively glowing, too, I'd say."

"Right," said Nick. "All ready."

"We wouldn't be going at all, Fran, but our boy here has such a crush on Lucy Littleton. Isn't he adorable, our little boy, all grown up?"

Fran laughed. "Little Lucy? Our boy has good taste. She's a cute one."

"Goddammit, Hugh."

"Yes, I was sitting around thinking, why on Earth does Nick want to go to this silly party? Then it came to me at once. You should see how his sweet little face gets all red whenever she's around."

"For the love of everything that's good and nice, Hugh, please let's just go."

"Don't forget to call and check in at least once tonight," said Fran.

"Fine, fine, yes, alright. I'll see you later mom."

Fran laughed. "And say 'hi' to Lucy for me."

Nick was out the door. It was pitch black out, and cold. He climbed in through the back of the Jetta and waited for Hugh to finish schmoozing with his mother.

Hugh came out, got in the driver's seat and started up his chariot. He reached under the seat, brought out two bottles of beer, handed one to Nick, and said, "Let's do this."

Chapter forty six

Sarah Johnston awoke. She tried to open her eyes, but only one of them opened. She was in a hospital. There was a man leaning against the door jamb, watching her. He made a call on his phone and she closed her eye again and tried to piece together what had happened. There was a tremendous noise in her head.

In jagged flashes, it came back to her. The Duvlosky woman stabbing her in the eye, the boy hitting her head with a shovel. She opened her eye again and lifted her head. She was strapped to the bed.

So this is how it all ended. This is what failure looked like, a true and final failure of the highest degree. It was almost peaceful. She could finally rest. She could sit back and relax and be a slob just like everybody else. She snickered. Is this what she had been afraid of? It was nice. Just let go of everything, let somebody else sort it out. She closed her eye. She could finally sleep.

A hand grabbed her shoulder roughly and squeezed it. "Wake up, bitch."

"Just a few more minutes, pop. I already did all my homework for the week."

"You better start talking before Duvlosky gets here."

She snapped open her eye. "Oh, just leave me alone."

"Where is the substance?"

"The what?"

The man slapped her across the face. "The substance! Tell me where you stashed it, or Duvlosky won't get a chance to kill you himself."

Blood dripped into her mouth. She looked at him. The slap had fully awakened her, brought her back to herself. "I don't know what you're talking about," she said. "What substance? The last thing I remember, I had gone to Officer Duvlosky's house to report something that might be pertinent to Doctor Huskfield's murder. He wasn't there, but his wife was. She made me coffee, and then all at once became maddened and attacked me. She stabbed me in the... my God, my eye! Is it gone?"

The man backed away from her and grew thoughtful. She could see his little monkey brain grinding away on its inadequate gears. "You're lying," he said at last. "We've got you and you're going away for a long time. Make it easier for yourself and tell me where the substance is."

"I assure you, I have no idea what you're talking about. If for some absurd reason you think I've committed some kind of a crime, I would ask to see my lawyer. She can be on the next flight from New York."

"Whatever kind of evil shit you did to Marie... well, it would be a shame if you passed away before we could make that call to your lawyer. But, say the word, give the location, and I'll drive down there myself and pick her up."

"That sounded an awful lot like a threat, officer. And yet, here I am, completely unaware of committing any sort of crime or knowing the whereabouts of any substance or even what substance you are referring to."

The officer walked back over to the door jamb and leaned back against it. "Fine," he said. "Your way it is. Deal with Duvlosky."

That was how men operated. By threats of power without any real power to back it. She closed her eye again. There was a way out of this. There had to be. There was always a solution. A physical escape was impossible. She had to use her mind. That wouldn't be a problem, outwitting these monkeys. But right at the moment, it was difficult to keep her mind focused. They had drugged her with something, to ease her pain. That was nice, she thought. How thoughtful. She was beginning to drift off again.

Then she heard a voice. Someone said, "Cooper, why don't you take a smoke break?" Then she heard the door closing. She felt something pressed against the side of her head and opened her eye.

"You killed me wife," said Duvlosky. "If you don't tell me where the substance is, I'm going to kill you."

Sarah smiled. "Go ahead," she said. "Good luck trying to explain that. How is your story about the dead rising up and giving handjobs working out for you?"

She heard the gun cock. Gun cock, she thought. It made her laugh.

"Go to Hell," he said, and she felt the nozzle slide from her temple toward her forehead and then, with the side of the nozzle resting on her forehead, he fired. The noise was tremendous. She felt the gun slide back to her temple and heard the faint click through the ringing as he cocked it again. She was no longer amused. She felt the strength leave her body. She shit herself, and could smell it. She felt the warmth of tears on one side of her face. She didn't want to die.

"The lab," she said. "It's in the lab, in room 110, where you found Huskfield. It's in the closet where he kept his chemicals, in 40 or so black five gallon buckets with white lids, among all of the other buckets."

He kept the gun there for what felt like a lifetime. "Please," she pleaded, "I did what you asked. Don't kill me."

Slowly, he pulled the gun away. "You're not done yet," he said. "You've got one more job to do. You've got to talk to our friend Carlos, and after that you can fuck yourself in prison for all I care, but I won't kill you."

Chapter forty seven

Zack's chisel was in his hand and when he saw the flash of yellow in her eyes, he brought it down with all of his strength. He felt it respond to her flesh, go through it, and then it was in the maple bench top.

Claire looked at her hand, attached to the benchtop through the chisel and laughed. "Oh," she said, "this is going to be fun!" She pulled her hand back, perpendicular to the chisel, and Zack watched as the hand was torn in half. He jumped back and made a quick assessment. There were worse places to fight it out than his shop, for several different reasons. He reached for the framing hammer hanging on its hook and then he had it.

"You must be pretty happy here, in your warm little shop tucked away in the woods, creating your little masterpieces," said Claire as her face first began to droop and wrinkle away from her head, and then tighten back up, so that she looked ten years younger. Zack watched as the two halves of her hand rejoined each other, and the wound disappeared as though nothing had happened. "It must be nice, marrying into money like you did. It must be nice having a wife who loves you and supports your dreams. Enjoy it while it lasts. It's not going to last very long, I assure you." She pulled back her lips, and instead of teeth there were long yellow jagged fangs.

Zack swung with the claw of the hammer and it stuck in the side of her head. She grabbed the handle, pulled it out and laughed. Then he had his drawknife in hand. It was good to have everything organized like that. He knew where everything was, and when he went for it, it was right there.

"What's so goddamn funny, Claire?" he asked, landing the drawknife in her throat, while plotting out his next moves. Awl, then that file which he never got around to making a handle for, then the chisel again and out the door.

"You are," she said in a voice filling with fluid. Blood began dripping out of her mouth. "You think your happiness is going to last forever. You think your dumb luck is your own doing."

Come on now, just come a little closer. "I'm sorry you had a shitty life, Claire, I truly am. But I won't let you make my life shitty, too. You'll have to find another outlet. The world has its fill of ugliness, it's beauty we're wanting." Perfect. He pegged her hand with the awl to the 2 by 6 cleat on the wall which held his clamps. "Give painting another shot," he said, spinning around her. He grabbed the file with the sharp handle from under the bench and then it was in her other hand, pinning that back to the bench. He yanked the chisel free, ducked between her legs and drove it through her left foot, attaching that to the plywood floor.

He was almost out the door as Claire pulled her hand free of the awl. He didn't stick around for the rest of the show. He got in his truck and sped down the driveway, to his house. He ran in the house. Sylvia was in the kitchen, making pasta. He grabbed her arm. "In the fucking truck! NOW!" he said. "Thomas! WHERE IS THOMAS!?"

"Upstairs," said Sylvia. "Zack..."

"Get in the truck and lock the doors until I come out. If you see Claire Peterson before I come out, DRIVE."

Sylvia ran outside. Zack ran upstairs. Thomas was sitting in his chair, watching television. Zack grabbed him with his good hand and slung him over his shoulder. He ran back down the stairs and out the door. Sylvia unlocked the door and then they were all in the truck. "GO!"

Sylvia stepped on it. As they approached the shop, they saw two yellow dots glowing in the darkness. "Keep going, baby," said Zack. "You're doing great. If you hit something, just keep going straight. Everything's going to be okay."

Thomas started crying. "It's okay, Tommy," said Zack. "Papa's got you."

Sylvia was crying too, silently. They made it out of the driveway and onto the road. In the rearview, Zack saw those yellow dots, watching them.

Chapter forty eight

Jackson got the call. He was chasing down one of the scientists like an angry parent hunting his obnoxious child.

"Jackson, it's in room 110, in the supply closet, in 40 or so black five gallon buckets. Go there and check it out, but for Christ's sake, don't touch anything. I'm going to have Jeffries herd everyone together and get them out of there. Then I'll be along to figure out what to do about it, and send someone with Carlos to the hospital to have a chat with Johnston. Until I get there, your job is to secure room 110, and make sure no one gets near the substance. We're almost there, Jackson. It's almost done."

Jackson hung up and watched the scientist turn the corner. Let Jeffries deal with her. Jeffries was going to have a hell of a time rounding them up. Jackson turned around and headed back through the hall. The door to the stairway opened and someone came out of it and plowed right into him, slamming him against the wall.

It was Sweeny. "Sweeny, watch where you're going! Christ, you almost smashed my head in."

"Sorry, bud. We just got here, and got the call from Duvlosky. The shit's going down, huh?"

"There's nothing going down, Sweeny. Just calm down and do your job and it'll all be over soon," said Jacobs, who had emerged from the stairway, calm and composed as he always was. Nothing rattled the guy, even when he had the flu.

"You guys heard from Clayton and Richaud?" asked Jackson. "Nobody can get ahold of 'em."

"Naw," said Sweeny.

"Well, good luck chasing all of 'em down," said Jackson. "Who knew scientists could be such punks? Running around with their secret pages stuffed in their buttcracks."

He headed up the stairs to the ground floor. From somewhere, he could hear Jeffries shouting: "For fuck's sake, just STOP! We're not gonna arrest you, we just need to get everybody OUT of here!"

Jackson made it to room 110. The door was locked. He banged on it. "Open up! This is the police. You need to let me in, and then evacuate the building." He heard noises coming from inside, but got no response. "You need to understand," he said, "nothing's going to happen to you, unless you don't open this goddamn door." No response. "This is your final warning, before I break the goddamn door down." No response. He looked at the door. It was metal, in a metal jamb. Nothing the Jaws of Life couldn't handle.

He went outside and made it to his car. It was pitch black. From the woods, he could hear the coyotes yowling. He decided that whoever was behind that door was going to come out of it with a broken nose. He opened up the trunk, but as he did so, remembered that he hadn't actually been on duty, so he wouldn't have the Jaws. "Goddammit." Who had them? Goddamn Clayton and Richaud. Where were they?

Jackson grabbed the car jack and lugged it inside. "Hey buddy," he said through the door. "I'm coming in." He swung it back and smashed it against the strike side of the door. It dented the door and the jamb gave way a little. He caught his breath and swung it again. The jamb gave a little more. Again and again, until he couldn't feel his arms or shoulders. He was dripping with sweat as he made the final swing and the side jamb flew off the stud. He dropped the jack, pulled his firearm, and swung the door open.

Inside, there was a scientist standing over several tubes of chemicals. He put his hands in the air. "I surrender!" he said.

"You little asshole," said Jackson. "Stay where you are." He stalked toward the scientist and, with his gun in one hand, reached for his cuffs with his other.

"Listen," said the scientist. "You don't understand. The research in these notes... I could cure Alzheimer's disease. I just need you to leave me be."

"You can think about that tonight in jail... but I'm gonna need those notes, too. Don't worry, we're gonna have Carlos take a good look at them."

"You idiot! How can you not understand how huge this is?"

"Now put your hands behind your back."

The scientist slowly lowered his hands. But they never made it behind his back. Instead, he grabbed one of the tubes and flung it at Jackson. It splashed against his face and then he felt it burning. His face felt like it was on fire. He screamed and grabbed out for the scientist. He couldn't see anything, but he got the fucker by the neck.

He took all of the searing pain in his face and tried to transfer it through his grip into the scientist's throat. He could hear strangled gasps and gurgles. He felt the man flail about, grabbing at his hand, but it was no use. Jackson was full of fury, and much stronger. He heard glass breaking and then there was an explosion and then he couldn't hear anything at all.

Chapter forty nine

They passed the research lab, where they had drunkenly knocked on the door the night before. To get to Jake's place, you took the road that cut through the woods, then headed back in the direction of town until it dead-ended, so that you were just on the other side of the woods from the lab.

"Look, they're in there now, working up a cure for that sick cock of yours," said Hugh.

"Yeah," said Nick. He was trying not to hope. Better to get used to the disappointment as soon as possible, so you can forget it and go on focusing on other things. But, despite his logic, he was hoping anyway. It was hard not to.

They arrived at Jake's. Cars were parked haphazardly in the driveway, on the side of the road, even some on the cobblestone walkway leading to the house. Jake himself was on the lawn, standing in a foot of snow, trying to mitigate the situation.

"You can't park there! My parents will kill me!" he was pleading with Hal, who wasn't paying him much mind, and was one of the ones who had parked on the cobblestone, cracking it and crushing it beneath the weight of his truck.

"Shit," said Hal to Chris, who already looked wasted. "I didn't know they had curbside service here."

"Please move!"

"The damage is done, my friend," said Hal, smiling. "I'll be back in the spring to re-landscape. Until then, try to enjoy yourself. It is your party after all."

Somebody knocked over the mailbox post and Jake went running to them, beyond exasperated.

"Looky here," said Hal as Nick and Hugh walked up the path, around the truck, to the front door. "The cavalry's arrived. Good, I was starting to think me and Chris were going to have to drink all this shit ourselves." He held up a 1.75 l bottle of cheap vodka. "Chris says he's going to put some of this in the beer bong later and chug it down. I think it's going to be one of those kinds of nights."

"Good," said Hugh, reaching the door.

"Yeah," said Hal, "I heard about the shit that went down today. Rough. That good sweet pussy gone forever."

"Let's not talk about that right now," said Nick.

Hal turned around to say something to him, but then saw Chris, pissing into a flowerpot on the front porch and laughed.

"You guys are fucking animals," said Nick, but he couldn't keep himself from chuckling.

"Why thank you, sir," said Hal, pulling out a cigarette, lighting it, and walking into the house.

Nick, Hugh, and Chris followed him in, and they heard Jake yell, "Hey!! You can't smoke in there! I'M SERIOUS!!" just before Chris slammed the door shut and killed his voice.

"Poor bastard," said Hugh. "He probably he thought was gathering everybody together for a chess tournament."

Nick looked around. A quarter of the high school was there, plus as many people again who had recently graduated, or had dropped out recently or long ago. And it was only 7. The party was just getting started. He scanned the bodies for Lucy, but couldn't find her.

"Hey," said Hugh. "There's Silas. I'm going to see if he wants to burn down Rome. You with?"

"Nah," said Nick.

"We're in," said Hal. They all walked off toward Silas, who was talking to three girls, making them laugh.

Nick watched. Here he was again, an awkward stranger in a sea of happy, secure people. "Where's the keg?" he asked somebody. Nick didn't recognize him.

"Over there, brother," he said, pointing to the kitchen.

Nick walked over to it, filled up a cup, and found a corner to stand in. He started drinking. It made him feel good, but it still didn't help him be bold. By the time he was drunk enough to be bold, he was too drunk to be coherent, or do anything. It was just another case of not

THE ELECTRIC BONER

having the means, but being sure of the end; or having the means, but losing sight of the goal.

Where was Lucy? He was glad she wasn't there. He felt small and alone. He closed his eyes and listened to the din of voices. Such incoherence, but so insistent. No one voice could be heard, no one voice mattered. He opened his eyes and the blur of laughing faces was much the same. Shit. Why had he come?

He stood in his corner, and Lyla walked over to him. When he saw her approach, all thought left his head, he felt everything leave him. Goddammit.

"Hi!" said Lyla. She was wearing a pink mini-skirt, showing off her long, gorgeous legs. Her beasts were on the verge of exploding out of her tight-fitting pink shirt. It made Nick's head spin. He took a good swallow of beer and managed a "Hi."

"What are you doing here standing all alone?" she asked.

"Observing," he said.

"Oh yeah? What do you see?"

He searched his mind for something clever to say. It was blank. "People," he said.

"Oh. Well, have fun," she said, and walked off.

As soon as she was gone, the rejoinders began rushing into Nick's head like the crashing tide. That had been an easy one, and he'd blown it. But it was alright. Lyla was beautiful, but she had a cruelness to her. Then of course, there was the fact that he had an electric boner, which made everything a moot point.

He began feeling like a moot point himself, standing there in his corner. He felt like people were looking at him, wondering what was wrong with him. But, he told himself, it's not true. They're too concerned with themselves to notice you.

He finished his beer and got another one, wavering between extreme confidence and a desire to crawl inside of himself and stay there forever. He went back into his corner and looked again at the crowd. They all seemed to be waiting for something to happen. There were those who waited for things to happen, those who made things happen, and those who hoped that nothing ever happened. Nick had always felt himself in the last category, but now he realized that he too was waiting for something to happen. And he was sure that it would.

Chapter fifty

Sylvia slammed on the brakes. Officer Richaud was standing in the center of the road, his car wrapped around a tree on the side of the road. Sylvia screamed.

"He needs our help," said Zack. He rolled down his window. "Officer Richaud! Are you okay? What happened?"

Richaud staggered toward the car and braced himself against the hood. Up close, they could see the blood dripping down his face. "Goddamn deer..." he gasped. "Radio... need to call it in. Send help."

Zack looked ahead to where the police car was. The truck's headlights shone around a figure in the driver's seat, with his head against the airbag. Even from this distance, Zack could tell that he was dead.

"Come on!" said Zack. "Get in." This was the man who had helped find their Thomas, when he and Sylvia had been out of their minds with terror.

Richaud fell out of sight. Then they could see his hand grab the hood as he tried to pull himself to his feet. "Stay here," said Zack. He jumped out of the truck and went over to Richaud. Richaud was in bad shape. Zack saw a shard of clean white bone protruding from his right shoulder.

"It's okay," he said. "We'll get you to the hospital."

"Thank... you," said Richaud. Zack dipped under his good shoulder and helped him to his feet.

"Tommy," said Zack. "Mr. Richaud's hurt real bad. We need to give him a ride. You sit on my lap now. Don't worry that he's all red. He's going to be okay. We all are." Zack got in the truck and little Thomas crawled on his lap. "Can you make it in?" he asked Richaud.

"I think so." Richaud grabbed the handle above the window and hauled himself in.

"Your station isn't answering the phone. 911 is just a recorded voice. We've had some trouble too. We're going to bring you to the hospital, and then we're going to the station to let them know what happened." Zack closed the door for Richaud. Richaud closed his eyes and his head started to nod. Zack shook him by the shoulder, the bad one. "Stay with us now, officer!"

Then in the rearview mirror, he saw the yellow orbs. How could she be so fast? "Sylvia, GO!!!"

Sylvia started driving. Her tears had dried up and her face was blank. Zack had tried to begin explaining what had happened, but she seemed somewhere far off. He didn't want her driving, but there was no other choice. Before, they had to get away fast, and now, he had to stay with Richaud, to keep him awake until they could get to the hospital. But she was doing a good job driving. She had stopped just in time to not hit Richaud, without losing control of the truck, which would have been difficult for anyone.

They drove along, through the darkness, until they made it to town. Zack had to keep squeezing Richaud's shoulder. Thomas never stopped sobbing. "Almost there, buddy. Everything's going to be okay." Town was full of life. Everybody had come out, it seemed, to go to dinner, go to a movie, go for drinks.

They passed town and were almost to the hospital. Richaud was groaning wildly. He was trying to say something.

"What's that?" asked Zack.

Suddenly, Richaud lifted his bloody head, looked at Zack, and said, "I'm taking Tommy back to the dark forest."

Before the words registered in Zack's brain, Richaud had his hand over Thomas' face. Sylvia screamed. Then Zack saw Richaud's eyes – they were glowing yellow. He had his pocket knife in one of those eyes in an instant. Then he reached over, opened the door, and gave Richaud, who was laughing wildly, a kick onto the speeding pavement.

He watched as the yellow orbs disappeared behind them, then looked at his son. Thomas's face was smeared with the blood from Richaud's hand. But the blood looked black. "Tommy, are you okay?"

Tommy looked up at his dad. "I don't belong to you, you know," he said in his ten-year old voice. "You should have let me finish my show." And then he had Zack's esophagus in his hand. Zack heard his wife scream, then he saw his son's eyes turn bright yellow, then he died in pure and total terror.

Chapter fifty one

Carlos heard the explosion from upstairs. Then he heard screams. Then he saw the green smoke seeping through the air vents. He grabbed his respirator mask from the closet and drew it over his face. He watched as the room filled with green air. He ran to the door and flung it open. The hallway was filling with green, too.

He looked back at the table where the traces of the green substance were in the glass slide, under the microscope, which were next to Dr. Huskfield's notes. Then he heard another scream and ran down the hallway, to the stairway. He had been holding his breath, but when he could hold it no longer, he gasped for air three times. He stopped running and waited. Nothing happened. The respirator was working.

He ran into the stairwell. The air was green everywhere. He saw Mitchell Kleinfield lying motionless on the landing and ran past him. The screams grew louder and more frequent, and then they began to grow less frequent, and then they stopped.

Carlos had reached the ground level. He swung open the door and rushed into the hallway. Directly in front of him was Officer Jackson. He was standing between Carlos and the exit, between Carlos and the fresh air. His face was badly burnt and his eyes were dead. He reached for Carlos, for his crotch. Carlos turned and saw Claudia Jenkins. She began reaching for his crotch as well. Then a hand was reaching over her shoulder, reaching directly for his nipple. Carlos grabbed that hand, and then a hand grabbed his buttocks. A finger was poking at his anus. Then Claudia had his testicles in her grip. He had gone out for a drink with her once, but she was such a bore. Now she held his manhood. Then another hand reached and pulled off his respirator. He held his breath for as long as he could, even as Claudia squeezed tighter and tighter, and began to twist. Then he could take it no longer and breathed it all in.

Chapter fifty two

She stood watching the taillights disappear into the night. She didn't know what she was doing there. She didn't know who she was. She tried to remember. She remembered being in a house. It was a man's house. She was standing next to him, they were looking at something. It was a painting. In the painting, there was a naked young woman on her knees chained to a collar held by an old, wrinkled man sitting on a throne.

"It's beautiful, Claire," said the man whose house they were in. That must be her. Claire.

"You really like it, Jack?" she asked. "I was afraid I couldn't do it, that I wouldn't remember how to do it. But I did." She was happy. That made her afraid that it would go away again. It always went away.

"Let's have some good red and look at it all night," he said.

"I love you," she said.

He laughed. "What? How could you love me? I'm ugly and I'm mean. I like to tie you up and blindfold you and fuck you in the ass. How could you love that?"

"Jeffrey hasn't fucked me in two years," she said. "I'm old and starting to wrinkle. I'm starting to sag. This has all been like the opening of a flower for me, after a long hard winter."

"Speaking of long and hard," he said, smiling.

She laughed.

Then it was later. She was in his house again. He was yelling at her. "How many times do I have to tell you, you crazy bitch? *Leave me alone!*"

She was crying. She wasn't happy any more. It had gone away like it always went away. "Good God, Claire, don't make me take out a fucking restraining order on you. You still have a family, you know. Go to them. Try to make things right. I don't know. All I know is that you have to leave me alone. I don't have time for this. Go."

He turned his back on her and was looking in his closet. She picked something up from the table and left.

Claire stood in the darkness, and tried to remember what it was she had taken. It was all so long ago. It was as if it had happened to someone else.

She remembered. It was a small container that held a black liquid. Yes. Jack had told her about it. It was very important, and it was the culmination of his life's work. But it had turned into a failure. *That's* why he was upset, why he didn't have the time for her any more. She was a distraction, he had said – a distraction that caused him to make mistakes.

She had taken it and she was going to drink it, to kill herself. But when she'd gotten home, she changed her mind. She could still make things work with Jack.

Then it was years later. She was still unhappy. She was watching television. A man was sitting in a chair on the other side of the room. He was watching it as well.

"Shit," he said. "Can you believe it? His intern? I guess the prick finally pissed off the wrong person."

"Shut up," she said. "God, I hate you."

"What the fuck did *I* ever do, Claire? Christ. I'm so sick of your bullshit."

"Nothing," she said. "That's just what you've done. *Nothing.*"

She went to the bedroom. She still had it. It was all she had. There was no reason to live any more, no reason to drag it out. She dug to the bottom of the dresser and got it out. She opened the container and poured the black liquid down her throat.

Then she was peeling the face off of a man. Who was he? She couldn't remember. Then she was standing on a road, in the darkness and the coldness. Who was *she*? She couldn't remember. Then she remembered. She was the coldness. She was the darkness.

BOOK II: THE COMING

PART I

Chapter one

Lucy was putting on make-up. No. Little Lucy Lillian Littleton was putting on just a little bit of make-up. Just so. Some of them painted it on in Van Gogh gobs, faces that were not their own. Lucy wondered what it would be like if her face were not her own. Would her insides also not be her own? What made a person a person? Lucy thought a person was on the inside, but she liked to look pretty all the same. Pretty little Lucy Lil. She smiled into the mirror, her lips just a little redder than they really were. Lucy enhanced, but Lucy nonetheless, through and through. Then she stuck out her tongue at herself. She was going to have *fun* tonight. Damn right she was. She was going to have a few drinks, maybe get a little high. Lucy letting loose.

She put on the finishing touches, then went to her room to wait for Viki. Viki was always late. You could be giving away a million dollars, and Viki would be late. Lucy couldn't understand it. There wasn't a second to waste. Why waste a second? Didn't Viki realize that they were all going to die some day? Someday, the seconds would all be useless. But for now, they were there, waiting to be filled. *Wanting* to be filled. And if you didn't fill them, they floated past you, empty.

Lucy put on some music. She was going to dance tonight. There wasn't any doubt about that. She knew it would drive the boys crazy, but that's not why she did it. She did it because it felt *good* to dance. When you were dancing, the seconds became so full that they felt like they were going to burst open. If the boys wanted to watch her, then let them. That was their prerogative. If that's how they chose to fill their seconds, who was she to tell them they were wrong?

Oh, but the subject of boys wasn't quite as clear cut as all that. Not clear cut at all. In fact, it was the fuzziest thing there was. There was Jake, there was Steve, there was Eric, there was Nick, and even his smart-ass friend, Hugh. She didn't mind a smart-ass. They all had different names and different faces and they talked different and they had different lives. They had different strengths and weakness. And, she imagined, they all kissed different. She imagined it. She imagined kissing Steve, with his black stubble. It would probably hurt. Viki said he had a big one. She'd heard it from Sam.

But she thought she wanted to kiss Nick most of all. She couldn't even really tell you why. When it came to kissing, logic had a way of flying out the window. There was nothing logical about it. What was the point of pressing your lips up against a boy's lips, of letting him stick his tongue in your mouth? Maybe it didn't have a point, except that it felt good.

But Nick was so *shy*. What did she have to do? Hit him over the head with a frying pan? She had just about. If he couldn't the hint, there was nothing she could do about it. It would have to be someone else.

Finally, after ten million years, Viki arrived. And she *still* wasn't ready. She was sitting in her car, putting on lipstick. Lucy said bye to her parents, assured them that she would be a good little girl, the very model of Puritan behavior, and got in the car.

"I thought maybe a rift had opened up in the space-time continuum, and you'd got swallowed up," said Lucy.

"Relax, you dork," said Viki. "You *never* want to be the first one at a party. It makes you look desperate."

"I *am* desperate," said Lucy. "Desperate to *dance*."

Viki laughed. "You really *are* a dork, but you're a sweet dork, so I'll forgive you."

They drove to the party. Viki went through town, even though it was the longer route. That was alright with Lucy. She liked to look at all of the people and wonder about their lives. So many different people, so many different histories, so many different futures. She noticed that Viki wasn't looking around. Viki did it so all the people could look at *her*. That was alright, too. It was just another difference, that's all.

"What the fuck is *that?*" said Viki, as they were stopped at the traffic signal. She pointed at the moon. A green mist was rising toward it in the distance. Lucy shuddered.

"Must be a fire," she said.

"A fire with *green* smoke?"

"I don't know," said Lucy, as the traffic light turned green. "It looks like it's coming from right around where we're going. Maybe we'll pass it."

"It's probably all the pot smoke coming from the party," said Viki. They laughed.

Chapter two

Fran swirled the wine around in the bottom of her glass. Something was troubling Nick. Something had been troubling him before he'd witnessed the horrible scene at the Duvlosky's. In fact, he seemed *better* after that, and that's what worried her the most.

Why didn't he talk to her? The more she tried to get him to talk, the less he talked. But that's how she had been when she was a teenager. That's how teenagers are, she reminded herself. But that's also how Tom had been, and he had been a grown man. Not much of a man, to walk out on his family when the responsibilities had grown too much for him. No, Nick wasn't like that. He was a good boy. He held the goodness in him. But Tom had held the goodness in him, too. He had just been so *fragile* that when he broke, it all spilled out of him. Nick was fragile too.

She took a swallow of wine. What could she do? Get too close, and he would go running. But do nothing? Let him suffer? She couldn't bear it. She had to do *something*. She would figure it out. She was used to that – to figuring out things on her own. She had made some missteps, but they had only taught her important lessons. That's how you figured out where the path was – by getting your feet wet.

She put on Sibelius. Her extravagant sound system was one of the few indulgences she had allowed herself after the inheritance. That money was life itself. It wasn't to be touched, except for the necessities. When she was gone, it would be there, waiting for Nick, so that he could live the life he wanted to live. But she didn't want him to get a taste of luxury, a taste of the power of money. It was the struggle that built character, and it would do him good to get out in the world and find his own path. She never wanted him to leave, but she loved him too much to keep him from doing that.

The music began its soft ascent, its slow building of tension. She thought of the other night, when Nick had come home and burst into tears. The memory stabbed her heart. She saw him then, his core exposed, and it was the most beautiful thing she had ever seen. But he was so *fragile*. She was afraid that he was going to break, finally, in her embrace.

The tension in the music grew thicker. Soon would be the climax, the release of all the tension. She didn't know the symphony very well. She didn't know if it would be a happy release, like an orgasm, or a mad release, like an explosion, with the pieces scattering in the air and trickling back down to the Earth.

She poured another glass, leaned back on the couch

and closed her eyes. The violins were swelling, something vey urgent was going on, something very important was about to happen. The horns joined in, at first solid blasts of a heavy sharpness over the fluidity of the strings. Then the blasts became drawn out, turning into wails. There was uncertainty. Which way would it go? To a coming together or a falling apart?

Right when she was about to find out, the CD started skipping. She had bought an eight thousand dollar sound system, and a 99 cent bargain CD to go in it. She laughed and clicked it off. Nick had transferred all of her CDs onto the computer for her, and had shown her a half dozen times how to hook the thing up to the stereo and bring up the files. She still didn't have any idea of how to do it. She laughed again.

Well, she had better figure out something else for entertainment tonight. Nick was always telling her to get out of the house, but she never really wanted to. She knew well enough what was out there. Still though, she didn't want her social skills to atrophy. Once Nick left home, she would find herself with a lot of free time on her hands. She'd better start practicing now.

She walked over to the phone and called Lisa MacMillan. "Lisa! This is Fran. I know this is out-of-the-blue, but how about we go into town and grab a drink?"

"I don't know Fran, it's so enthralling here, watching Frank sit on the couch drinking beer and yelling at the Celtics. But I suppose I could tear myself away for a drink or two. What are you thinking, Finnegan's?"

"Oh no, too rowdy for this old girl. Let's do the Silver Fox. An hour from now?"

"It's a date."

She hung up and smiled. See? That was easy. She got ready and headed into town.

Chapter three

Mikhail saw the smoke from a distance. Green smoke. He felt the muscles in his neck tighten and picked up the radio. "Jackson, this is Duvlosky. Respond." No response. "Jackson, come in." He flipped the dial. "Sweeny, this is Duvlosky. Are you there? Sweeny?"

As he approached the lab, the smoke grew closer. He turned down the road and then he was right on top of it, in the parking lot. He saw it billowing out the front door, rising to the sky. As he got closer, he saw that the glass on the door had been shattered. He saw a path tramped in the field, plowed in the snow, as though a herd of cattle had wandered through. Then it split off, and there were two smaller paths, each heading into the woods, one going North, and one going East, toward town.

At first, all he could do was sit in his car looking from one to the other: door, to smoke, to path, to path. Then suddenly the thought came to him: how much can one man endure? Was there a point where mercy came into play? When a man's suffering became all there was inside him, shouldn't there be the mercy of sudden death? Everything shuts down, and that's it.

He tried to think how many scientists there had been in that building. It was impossible to say, but if he had to guess, around a hundred. The kid, Carlos, was one of them, with his bright smile. And how many of his men? Jackson and Jeffries, Jacobs and Sweeny. Had Richaud and Clayton ever made it?

He tried for the twentieth time. "Richaud, Richaud, come in, come in, for the love of Christ *come in*." For a response, he got dead air. Then, just to hear a voice, he radioed Cooper.

"Cooper, this is Duvlosky, come in."

"This is Cooper."

So he had at least *one* man left. "Report."

"All's normal here, sir. I mean, except for the god-awful stench of shit. She's been whining for me to change her diapers. What do you think?"

"Let her sit in her own shit for a while," said Mikhail. That, and Cooper's voice, was all he had going for him. "As long as you can stand it, anyway."

"10-4. Anything else?"

"No, no. Just checking in," said Mikhail and hung up the radio. He pulled out his gun and set in on the seat next to him. He looked at it. Five minutes, he told himself. Make your decision in five minutes, and that's that.

Nothing. The question answered itself before he could even ask it. What did he have to live for? Nothing. "Nothing I can do to convince you to stay, is there?" she had said, stretching out in his favorite nightie. God *damn* it. Her smile and her warmth spread out in his mind. For a moment, he felt that he could touch her, if he just reached out his hand. But when he did, he got only the cold dashboard.

He felt the tears streaming down his face. It would be so *easy*. And what did he know? Maybe there *was* an afterlife? Maybe he would get to see her again, for real, and touch her, smell her sweetness. Then everything would be good again. Maybe she would still be pregnant. Maybe their little kid would already be there, waiting for him. Would it be a boy or a girl? He wanted a girl. He wanted to stun the world, to fill it with brightness, with another Marie.

He *had* wanted a girl. Now he had nothing.

Suppose he didn't do it? What else could he do? With the lab destroyed, with Carlos gone, what hope was there for the Sherman boy? And what could he possibly do against a hundred of them – in two different directions? *It...* the one he had faced before... it had taken three of them to destroy it. A mob of fifty would tear a man to bits in a matter of seconds. So it was a choice between dying in terror at *their* hands, or dying alone by his own hand.

Two paths.

One of them went North. Dimly, he wondered why. He couldn't say. The other one went East, to destroy the town with absolute certainty, the town that Marie had loved so much.

The five minutes were up. He reached for his gun.

Chapter four

"Have mercy," said Sarah.

"Mercy?" said the man, Cooper. "Say that again to me. Say that fucking word again to me."

Sarah sighed, and then instantly regretted doing so. Letting out that much air meant she'd have to take that much more back in. She felt like crying again, but she would be damned if she was going to let this Cooper get the satisfaction.

"I *cooperated* with you," she said. "I told you where the substance is."

"In fact, say one more fucking word at all to me."

Sarah didn't respond. The drugs were starting to wear off, and she was beginning to feel the pain in her eye. And then a different sort of pain started to trickle into her head. My god, she thought, what have I done? It surprised her. She had always felt the rightness of her actions, the rightness of her life, and that it was the world that was bad. Now, with the smell of her own shit seeping into her nose, with the warm wet feeling between her legs, it was difficult to feel important. And once she stopped feeling important, she began to review what she had done from a different, humbler perspective. She had killed the Duvlosky woman, had used her as a lab rat. And she had planned to kill many more. As many as she could.

She deserved to sit in her own shit. She deserved a lot worse than that. And she would get it. "I'm sorry," she said in a whisper.

THE ELECTRIC BONER

"*Sorry,*" he said. He walked over to her. "What did I say? I said *one more fucking word.*" He lifted up the back of his hand, and Sarah saw the glint of a gold wedding ring for a moment, until it was against her face. She felt an explosion of pain and closed her eye.

When she opened it again, it was full of hatred. She *was* right. This is what men were. They weren't content to just have you strapped helplessly to a bed, sitting in a pool of you own shit. They had to hit you, too.

She smiled. "I'm sorry I didn't kill your whore of a wife, too," she said.

He got her again, and this time, doubled back and got her with the palm of his hand, too. She felt the blood drip from her mouth. She had never known so much pain. Then she heard a scream. For a moment, she wondered if she had let it out. But she was biting down on her lip.

Cooper turned his head. "What the fuck was that?" he muttered. Then she heard another scream, coming from outside the door.

Cooper walked over to the door and opened it. "Behave yourself," he said. Then he shouted to someone outside. "Hey! You! Come here. I need you to keep an eye on this woman." When he said "an eye," he turned his head into the room and smiled at her. "Don't let her out of the straps. And for Christ's sake, clean up her shit, would you be so kind?" Then he was gone.

A woman in a nurse's uniform walked in and shut the door behind her. Sarah heard another scream.

"What's going on out there?" Sarah asked.

"We get screams like that all the time," said the nurse. "Nothing to worry about. Now, you poor dear, let's get you cleaned up." Sarah watched in disbelief as the nurse undid the straps. "I don't take my orders from *him,*" she said. "Besides, how are we supposed to freshen you up if we can't even get at you?" she laughed.

Sarah smiled. She liked her. She wondered if she were stronger, would she try to overpower the nurse and escape? No, she thought. She's nice. Let her do her job. Do you think she *likes* cleaning up your shit?

When the straps were off, Sarah's arms lifted involuntarily, from the strain she had put on them, trying futility to break free. "Let's start by getting that messy old thing off of you," said the nurse. She helped Sarah sit up, then helped her lift the smock off.

"Let's clean you up and get you a new bed, too," said the nurse smiling. Then Sarah heard another scream.

The nurse stopped smiling. "That *is* a lot of screaming," she said. "Usually it stops after a minute, after the drugs are administered."

Then she heard a man, maybe Cooper, shouting. "Stop right there! That's far enough! What the FUCK-?"

Then she heard gunshots. The nurse's eyes opened wide. They heard more gunshots, and then another scream. Then everything was quiet. Then somebody was turning the door knob.

Chapter five

Mandy Perkins had found him. Nick didn't mind that she was a bit chubby - alright, more than a bit chubby. It wasn't the fat on her body that was the problem; it was the fat on her *personality*. She got up right in your face and talked, *loudly*. If you moved your head a bit, she'd move *hers* so that finally there was nothing else in the world except the sights and sounds of Many Perkins.

But just now, she seemed lovely to him, her voice like music. He was sick of standing in the corner by himself. The three cups of beer that he'd drank, rather than making him feel good, had only left him with a headache. He'd switched to water. He was drinking water by himself, considering calling a cab, when she exploded into his view. There had been no warning sign, she was just *there*. For such a big girl, she had some serious stealth.

"Nicky boy!" she said. She looked and sounded a little drunk. "Whatcha doin' here all by yourself?"

"Just thinking," he said.

"Watcha thinkin' about?"

"You."

"*Me?*"

"Sure," he said. "What is it you want out of life, Mandy?"

For a moment, she was quiet, thinking. "I don't know," she said. "Nothing. I just want to have a good time. I want to go to college and have a good time there and then get out and find a good job and a good man and settle down into a good life."

"That sounds nice, Mandy. I hope it works out for you. I'm sure it will."

"What do *you* want out of life, Nick?"

"I don't know what I want. Sometimes I look around and everything makes me so sad and all I want is for the sadness to go away, but I don't know what to do about it."

"That *is* sad."

Nick laughed. "I guess what I want is to be more like *you*."

"I get sad, too," said Mandy.

"But you never act like you're sad. Sometimes I walk around all day looking at my shoes."

"You can't wallow in it. You have to try to pretend that it's not there. You have to start doing other stuff. Then it just goes away before you know it, at least for a while. Ice cream helps, too."

Nick smiled. "Aren't you afraid that you're just pushing it all down, and some day it's all going to explode at once? Repression, they call it."

"Every day's a new day. I don't know what it will be like tomorrow. All I care about it what it's like *now*. And honestly, Nick, you're kind of a bummer right now."

Nick laughed. "Sorry. You get back to the party. But I

liked our talk. We should talk again some time. Go have fun. I'll be alright."

Nick looked at her face and it was like he was seeing it for the first time. It was nice. He had been wrong in his judgments about her. No, not wrong. He didn't like people demanding his attention. Rather, he had been *incomplete* in his judgment. He had pronounced a sentence, while only knowing a handful of words. But once made, a judgment was a judgment, regardless of how it was reached. That's why it was best to not judge anything at all, until you absolutely had to.

"Try to have a little fun," she said. Then she turned and walked off.

The conversation had refreshed him. She was right. Dwelling on shit didn't help anything. Here he was, and everyone was having a good time, so why shouldn't he? The faces came into focus. He began to comprehend them as distinct people. There was Mike Cunning. On Thursday, Ricksclyde had kicked him out of class for not reading *Huckleberry Finn*. There but for the grace of God could have gone Nick.

Things could always be worse. Even the electric boner. Maybe Duvlosky would find the cure. Maybe it would go away on its own. And if it didn't? Then he would just take it one day at a time. There were worse things that could happen to a person. And he'd seen a few of them that afternoon.

From his corner, he had a clear view of the door. He watched the stream of people coming, filling the house. Soon there wouldn't be much room to move. Then he saw the door open and Lucy walked in behind Viki. She was wearing a puffy purple jacket, and a white hat with flaps over the ears.

Nick got the sudden feeling that the world was going to end, tonight. Then he asked himself, So what if it does? Do you want to spend your last moments huddled in the corner, wondering what might have been? He walked toward her.

Chapter six

Dennis Calvin stretched out his legs and changed the channel. Christ, what a crazy day. He was glad it was finally over. Jessica was passed out on the other side of the couch, with a half-full gin-and-tonic on the side table next to her snoring head. What did he have to do? Stop bringing the shit into the house altogether?

He sipped his own drink. Tomorrow. He'd have The Talk with her again tomorrow. And she'd listen, and say, "You're right, baby, you're right," and she'd knock it off for a few days, and then start back in. "Oh, just one drink. I know I went on a binge there, but I think I can do it if I just cut back." Same old bullshit. But he'd deal with that tomorrow. He'd dealt with enough shit for tonight.

He wasn't even going to let himself think about whom he'd replace Duvlosky with. That, too, could wait until tomorrow. For tonight, he was just going to have a goddamn drink and watch the goddamn Celtics lose. He wasn't even going to think about Henderson.

Let Duvlosky run things for the night. If he wanted to call in the whole goddamn force and have them waste their time on his ghost story, then let him. It would be his last night. Then... goddammit! This wasn't how things were supposed to be. None of it was.

He took another drink and watched the Celtics miss an easy one. Then he took another look at Jessica. God, that snoring. It was so *stupid*. Just when he thought it had stopped, just when he let himself hope that there'd be a minute or two of peace, she'd open her big mouth and there it would be again, that terrible crackling sound, like a knife stabbing him in a brain. Like the shard of glass that had stabbed Henderson in the brain. Or so said Duvlosky.

What if he just left? What if he just said, "Fuck it," and picked up and moved to a different state, started a different life? He was no prince charming, he knew that, but in a big city, there were a lot of different women, with a lot of different tastes. Maybe he'd head down to Florida and find some old rich widow. His dick was getting harder to find by the day, but he figured he could still put the old boy to work.

Christ, it was too depressing. Watching the Celtics get their asses handed to them, again. He flipped through the channels. Hey, now that's interesting. It was one of those late night reality sex shows. There was a guy up there, uglier than him, with a bigger belly on him, harrier… and he was getting some solid puss. Why not old Dennis?

He looked over to Jessica. The goddamn apocalypse wouldn't wake her now. He unzipped his pants and pulled out his dick. He gave it a good tug. Christ, he remembered when just a short skirt gave him a hard-on. Now it was like he had to fill out paper work, send it off, and wait for the reply.

There were some good, solid tits on the screen now. He was tugging away. Goddammit! It was still limp. He grabbed it in one hand and smacked it with the other. Then he spat on his hand and started rubbing it all over. It was no good.

Broken. Everything broken.

He chugged his drink. Fuck that. He was going to make it *work*. He started pulling angrily on it. It didn't feel good at all. It hurt. But he wasn't going to give up. Not Dennis Calvin. He could give up on Jessica, on the Force, on this goddamn town, but not his *dick*.

He felt the tears coming down his face, but he couldn't turn back now. He yanked it, slapped it, spat on it. It sat there through it all like a dead fish. Then he looked at Jessica again. *She* had done this to him.

His cell phone went off. What the *fuck!* Who the fuck was calling him *now?* He tucked his tired dick back into his pants and looked at the phone. It was Duvlosky. Good. The fucker would pay, *now!* With his goddamn half-cocked story about why he murdered his wife. In the back of his mind, a funny thought occurred to Dennis. He could understand why Duvlosky had done it. Jessica had once been almost as beautiful as Marie. Maybe Duvlosky had somehow caught a glimpse of his future, and got out while the going was good. That just made Dennis more pissed. He flipped open the phone.

"Chief?" said Duvlosky.

"I'm not your goddamn Chief any more, Duvlosky. You're fired. You got that? You ain't a Clairmont police office no more. Go fuck yourself."

"Listen to me, Dennis. I need every cop in the state of Maine. I need every goddamn-"

"Go fuck yourself," said Dennis, and hung up. He felt a little better.

Chapter seven

"It's bedlam," said Lucy, taking it in. She almost had to shout, just to hear herself.

"Good," said Viki. "About time something happened in this town."

Lucy saw Eric Brown, standing on the kitchen counter, making some kind of a speech. Somebody pantsed him. She crossed him off the list. She spotted Jake Canter, passed out on a chair in the living room. Somebody had scribbled all sorts of nasties on his face. Poor guy. Off the list, and probably grounded for the rest of his life to boot.

Then she mentally tore up the list all together. It was too trite, to begin with, and in the second place, this wasn't what she had in mind. Not at all. It was so impersonal here, and everybody was wasted. Why waste a kiss? Still, she could dance. If she could just find a bit of space. And if the music weren't such thud-thudding crap. Alas.

"Let's get a drinkie," said Viki. "And *party!*"

Lucy shrugged. Lucy kept an open mind. Never prejudge. Somebody was puking on the couch. Maybe that was a blessing in disguise. Maybe Jake's parents were tired of the couch and wanted a new one, but couldn't justify it. Maybe she could learn to understand the ways of the thump-thumpery and enjoy herself all the same. Why be a snob?

"Let's get a drinkie," agreed Lucy.

Then came a face, a sweet face from the crowd of bodies. It was Nick Sherman's face. There was a smile on it like somebody was poking him in the back and telling him to smile, or else. It was cute.

"Lucy," he said. Then he nodded. "Viki. It's good to see you two."

"Are you our escort?" said Viki. "I think we're going to need one in this jungle." Then she added, "Is Hugh here, too?" Viki wasn't a second-waster, after all. Not where it counted, for her.

"He's around here somewhere. And I'd be happy to escort you two. Where are we headed? The keg or the hard stuff?"

"Better make it the hard stuff," said Viki. "It smells like several things died here."

"The hard stuff, Nick," said Lucy.

"I was afraid you were going to say that," said Nick. "That means we're going straight to the belly of the beast." His face had relaxed during all this, and his smile become more natural. Nick had become *charming*, which Lucy always knew he was, except around her, when he became as interesting and dynamic as a crushed plastic cup on the side of the road.

Oh, the night was starting to look good again, and full of possibility. That's what you get for being open-minded. Things are *never* what you want them to be, but sometimes they're just exactly what you want them to be for all that, if you can be a little flexible and learn how to look. And Lucy had about 10 years worth of ballet shoes in a box somewhere to prove that she *was* flexible.

Nick led them, heroically, through the throng. They rubbed elbows with one fellow who seemed to be asleep on his feet. Everybody had her own talent. That's what made the world interesting. The world became all the more interesting when they finally made it to the kitchen.

Eric was still speechifying on the counter, apparently oblivious to the fact that his pants were around his ankles.

"…I'll tell you what's more, guys. Lissen to me. The fuckin thing runs *deep*. Who you think's controllin this country? You think it's the fuckin *pressident?* The pressident's a product, just like that fuckin' hat you got on there, Justin. Hey, Justin! You *lissenin'* to me? I said yer fuckin hat's a fuckin' *product.*"

"Shut the fuck up," said Justin. "You sound like a fucking rooster shitting out of its mouth instead of its asshole." But he took off his hat anyway, and looked inside it, as if it held some sort of vital answer.

Nick plucked a rum bottle from beside Eric's foot. Lucy noticed that Eric only had one shoe on. Where the other shoe was, Lucy supposed that Eric himself did not know. Maybe nobody knew, or would ever know. Nick mixed them each a drink, rum and coke with ice.

"I feel so bad for Jake," he said. "He'll need to hire a crew to clean up before his parents get back. I was thinking about setting up a donation jar, but I'm afraid all of the money would be gone, and it would be full of bodily fluids by the end of the night."

Lucy laughed. My goodness. Nick was charming the pants right off her. She liked it. Where had he been hiding all these years? She took a drink. Just a sip. It was spicy and burnt the back of her throat a little bit, but it wasn't too bad. Not bad at all. She felt a bit of warmth spread through her body.

"So," she said, "what do you folks do for fun around here?"

"I think you're asking the wrong guy," said Nick. "I've just been standing in the corner over there drinking water." Viki gave Lucy a look, and Lucy saw Nick catch that look. Then he smiled. "But Hugh's somewhere smoking up. We can try to find him, if that's what you want."

"Are you going to smoke?" asked Lucy.

"No," said Nick. "It makes me too... withdrawn. I'd have to find a bed to crawl under somewhere."

"Well, I'm sure Viki..." but when Lucy turned, she saw that Viki was gone. She was already across the room, talking to Mike of the black stubble. Viki moved like a cheetah. "Forget it," said Lucy. She took another sip, then suddenly remembered something. "What were you going to say, earlier today, on the phone? You were saying that you saw something?"

The smile left his face, and suddenly it became very serious. Not shy, but serious. "It's nothing. It's something I thought was important, but it's not."

Lucy had never been more interested in her life. "Now you *have* to tell me."

"No," he said with finality, like the period at the end of a sentence. "That ended at the Duvlosky house today. I was there, you know. And it's not something I want to talk about, not just now." Then he smiled. His whole face lit up. It was a beautiful face. She wanted to kiss it. She wanted to kiss it more than anything else in the world, like the way the apple fell on Newton's head, with that kind of force. "Let's talk about something else," he said. "Like Ricksclyde. How can you *stand* him? Every time I see him, I picture a turtle. An ancient turtle, ten thousand years old, crawling slowly forever on."

She smiled and stepped closer to him. She pressed her body against his. She felt his warmth. It was like coming in from the cold and standing next to a warm fire.

She cupped her hand over her mouth and stood on her tiptoes, to reach his ears. She felt the warmth of her own breath as she whispered, loudly so he could hear, "He's hot."

Nick looked at her, and for a second their faces were inches apart. She looked at his eyes, looking intently into her eyes. For a second, that's all there was. Then she couldn't bear it any more, it was like some kind of mad torture, she didn't know what to do. Little Lucy didn't know what to do. She stepped away from him and he laughed.

"No fair," he said, "I saw him first. Besides, you'd give him a heart attack."

"Never underestimate Dick's Bride," she said, laughing.

"Ha! I never thought I'd hear you say that."

"Yeah?" she said. She had regained some of herself. She was aware of her surroundings again. The world came flooding back in. "And what did you think you'd hear me say?"

"I don't know. Lucy, I... I..." his smile disappeared again. His face was beautiful. There was a soft ache in it, somehow. She felt herself grow weak, she felt herself bursting with hope.

"Yes? Yes? You what?"

Then his face changed. All of the color fled from it, like a flock of birds when you approach. The warmth fled, too. It was cold. Lucy shivered.

"They're coming, Lucy," he said. "They're almost here."

Chapter eight

Fran ordered a Pinot Grigio. Lisa ordered the same.
"So," said Lisa. "What's new?"

"I'm worried about Nick," said Fran.

"You're *always* worried about Nick. You always have been. That's not new at all. Though after what the boys saw today…"

"It's not that," said Fran. "There's a change going on with him. I don't know what it is."

"Let me guess. He's sick all the time, asking for you to pick up some more Kleenex?"

Fran laughed. "No. That started a few years ago."

"Does the boy have a girlfriend?"

"Not that I know of."

"The boy needs a girlfriend. Someone to keep him on his toes, that's all."

"I've done just fine without a man around," said Fran.

"I know you have, dear. God bless you. You're the envy of the entire PTA." Lisa lifted her glass. "That deserves a toast."

Fran clinked glasses, then they both had a drink. "What about you, Lisa? It seems like a lifetime ago since we did this, had a drink."

"Nothing new with me," said Lisa. "Frank falls asleep on the couch a little earlier every night. Hugh has a different girlfriend every week. Other than that, things stay the same. And that's good. I like it like that. I've had my fun."

"And I think *that* deserves a toast," said Fran. They clinked glasses again.

Then a woman walked up to them. "Excuse me," she said. "I don't mean to intrude. No, that's a lie. Intruding is my job. I'm Felicia Jones, reporter for the National Star. I'm off the clock, I swear it, but you're Lisa MacMillan aren't you?"

Lisa looked at her. "Yeah. I remember you. You were there this afternoon. What more can I say to you?"

Felicia smiled. "It's like I said. I'm just a stranger in this town of yours, here for the night, feeling a little bored.

Would it bother you if I had a glass with you?"

"Fran?"

"Fine with me."

"Have a seat."

"I'm Fran."

"Nice to meet you," said Felicia, taking a seat. "You'll excuse me for saying so, but this is a strange town you live in."

"What's so strange about it?" asked Lisa.

"Well, it's just so *quiet*. I walked here from my hotel, and I didn't hear a sound, except for the occasional distant passing car. In DC, the noise *never* stops. It's a constant hum, sometimes loud, sometimes dim, but always *there*. I think this is the first time I've heard actual silence in years."

"That's just why we like it," said Fran.

"But it hasn't been so quiet for the last couple of days, has it?"

Lisa turned to face Felicia. "I thought you were off the clock?"

Felicia laughed. "I am. Just making conversation. I was just at the other bar there, Finnegan's. It's all they were talking about. And yet, here you are – it happened right across the street from you, with your son right in the middle of it, and you're acting as if nothing happened."

Lisa turned back to the bar. "What happened? Something that's not our business. Right, Fran? Tell her what our business is."

Fran laughed. "Right now, it's trying to make the most out of two glasses of cheap, stale wine."

"Don't you think there's something more to the story than what the police are saying?"

"Look, lady," said Lisa. "I think our friendship is at the end of the line. Time to get off."

"You can't blame a girl for trying."

"Of course I can," said Lisa.

Felicia's phone rang. She looked at it, then picked it

up. "Felicia Jones, National Star.... Officer Duvlosky?... What? What did you just say?... Listen, is this some kind of joke?.... Alright. Jesus. I get it. You people want me out of your town. You don't take kindly to strangers. Fine. I'm gone tomorrow.... What? No. You want to make a fool of me. Goodbye, Officer Duvlosky." She hung up.

"What was that?" asked Fran.

"Oh, you can take your town and shove it for all I care."

"Was that Mikhail Duvlosky?" asked Lisa. "What did he say?"

"Now you're interested in the news? What did he say? Only that there were a hundred zombies loose, half of them headed in a bee line for town, and that I should alert the press. Some joke."

"It's not a joke," said Lisa. "The poor man's out of his head with grief."

Fran finished off her glass of wine. "Why are we avoiding the truth?" she asked.

"What's that?" said Lisa.

"The truth is, Officer Duvlosky cut off his wife's head today. While your son watched. While Officer Henderson was thrown out of a window and killed. While that woman lay out in the snow with her eye poked out."

"Yes," said Felicia. "That's true so far. It's the why and the how where everything starts to get murky."

"Lisa, would your boy lie to you?"

Lisa laughed. "Hugh tells a thousand lies a day."

"But about something like this. Something that mattered."

Lisa frowned. "I don't know. I don't think so. I don't see why he would."

"And that's just it. We don't want to face the truth. We're stuck between two uncomfortable possibilities, and we don't want to acknowledge either one as being true. Either Mikhail killed his wife in cold blood, as well as Henderson, while your son watched, or he didn't. If he didn't, if Hugh and Mikhail are telling the truth, then Marie really *was* the victim of some kind of unnatural experimentation, and the only way to stop her murderous behavior was to cut off her head."

"The truth," said Felicia, "often lies somewhere in between the two extremes."

"Where's the middle ground?" asked Fran.

"I don't know, but I know that Duvlosky, and your son, Lisa, weren't telling the whole story. I've heard enough untruth in my life to know it when I hear it."

"And what did Mikhail say, just now?" asked Fran.

"He said that there was some kind of substance that turned people into sex-obsessed monsters, intent on killing. He said that the substance was unleashed somehow in the research lab just out of town. He said there are now a hundred zombies roaming the woods, half of them about to enter town, and the other half going in a different direction, he didn't know where. He said to alert the presses and evacuate the town. He said the only way to kill them was to cut off their heads."

"Out of his mind with grief," said Lisa.

"That may be," said Fran. "But is there anything in his story that doesn't fit with the other story?"

"No," admitted Felicia.

"And if it's a hoax, or he's gone insane, but you do what he says, what's the worst that can happen?"

"I'll lose my job," said Felicia. "And I'll never be able to get another job as a reporter."

"But what if he's telling it true? What if there were a mob of zombie killers descending on this town as we speak, and you did nothing, when you could have so clearly done something?"

For a moment, there was silence. Everybody in the bar was listening. Yes, thought Fran, this is why she liked Clairmont. It allowed you some moments of silence.

"God damn it," said Felicia. "After this, no more small towns. If there *is* an 'after this'."

She picked up her phone and made a call.

Chapter nine

Sarah watched though her one good eye as the door opened. A little boy was standing there, drenched in blood.

"Oh honey!" said the nurse. "Are you okay?"

"I feel sick," said the boy. "My tummy hurts."

"Your tummy? Are you sure that's all?"

"My tummy hurts. I'm hungry."

"How did you get here?" asked the nurse.

"My tummy hurts, and I'm not going to let you stick any needles in me. They hurt."

"Can you wait a minute, dear?" the nurse asked Sarah. Sarah nodded. What are a few more minutes of shit if it helps a little boy? She almost laughed. What would that boy grow into? Just another man. But seeing him there, innocent and covered in blood, she couldn't help but feel a surge of tenderness in her. Tenderness? What was that? She didn't know it, but she knew she felt it. If she made it out of all of this, she would take another look at Jack's notes. Even if it was from prison. She would do what she could.

"Sometimes," said the nurse to the boy, "we *have* to get you with the needle. But it's only to make you feel better in the end, honey."

"I don't want it," said the boy.

The nurse laughed. "You're hungry, you say? When was the last time you ate?"

"Just now," said the boy.

"And you're still hungry? Hmmm... that might be cause for the needle after all. Who brought you here? Can I talk to your parents?"

"I ate my parents," said the boy. "No, that's a lie."

"I should hope so!" said the nurse.

"I only ate part of them."

"Which part?"

"This is boring," said the boy. Then he tilted his head back and opened his mouth. Long yellow jagged teeth emerged – no, grew – out of his black gums. The nurse screamed. Sarah shit herself all over again. The boy lowered his head and Sarah saw that his eyes were *glowing* yellow.

He moved with a quickness too quick for Sarah's eye. Then his teeth were in the nurse's leg. She screamed and Sarah screamed too. Then the boy was climbing up the nurse's body, and then he was at her throat, biting into it with his fangs, tearing away flesh and organs.

They fell to the ground together. The nurse was dead. "Owie!" said the boy, as his ass hit the floor. Then he stood up. "Cyclops," he said.

"Please," said Sarah. He walked toward her. As he did so, the stench overpowered her. It smelled like a rotting corpse, but not quite. She had spent the last few hours hoping to smell something other than her own feces. Now she was praying in earnest, for the first time, to God, for the return of that smell. Anything other than *this*.

"I don't like Cyclops," said the boy. "I liked the lady with a lot of snake heads and the one who could sing nice, but the cyclops was always *stupid*. That was all he was. Was dumb."

"Please," said Sarah. "I don't like the Cyclops either."

The boy laughed. He stepped closer. That *smell*. "Good," he said. "I like you. We just have to make one little change, right?"

"R… right," said Sarah.

The boy slid his small hand over Sarah's face. Sarah's arms *might* have been strong enough to respond, but nothing else about her was. He brought his other hand up to her eye and wiggled his little pink fingers around. Then he stopped wiggling them and held them still, spread apart as they were. Then he brought all of them together, in a fist, except for his index finger. He turned his hand around then, so that the fist was facing him, and it looked like he was presenting something to Sarah. It was a single finger, the index finger, the universal sign for "number one."

Then a yellow claw grew out of that finger. Sarah watched it. It grew longer than the finger itself.

"I don't like Cyclops," he said.

"Please," said Sarah.

Then the claw began to change its angle, slowly, from ninety degrees to zero. Then it began to approach her eyeball. It stopped right before it reached her eye. She saw a yellow point at the end of a long, crooked claw. That was the last thing she ever saw.

Chapter ten

"And the fox and the chicken got married and lived together happily ever after." Benjamin Clemmings looked down and saw that Jason was asleep. Thank God. He closed the book and set it on the nightstand. Then he kissed his son on the forehead and walked quietly downstairs. He got a beer and sat down on the couch next to Linda.

"Jesus Christ, honey, where do you find this shit? The chicken and the fox get married?"

"This is the new generation, honey. It's not like it was when we grew up. Jason needs to learn tolerance. He needs to learn that people are all the same, no matter what they look like, or what stereotypes there are about them."

"But what happens when our little chicken comes face to face with the fox? I liked our stories better, when a fox was a fox, and just wanted to trick people so he could eat shit that wasn't his."

Linda laughed. "God forbid he should turn out like *you*, thinking everyone's out to get him all the time."

THE ELECTRIC BONER

Ben smiled. "Sometimes that pays off." He looked at the TV screen. Somebody was creeping around in the shadows. You just saw the eyes, and then the glint off the knife. She didn't mind watching people get stabbed to death, but she had a problem with the fox eating the chicken? Oh, let it go. She was right, anyway. What kind of a horror show would Jason turn out to be, if it were up to Ben alone to raise him? And what kind of a horror show would he himself be, if it weren't for Linda?

The desert flashed through his mind. The hot, white, lonely desert. The bombed villages, the bodies lying on the side of the road. It was good that it did that sometimes, that it all came suddenly back to him, as if for a moment, he were back in Afghanistan, sweating balls and wondering if this step would be the last step he ever took. It reminded him of what a good thing he had here, in Jefferson, Maine, with his wife and son.

Let Jason read all of the sissy stories he wanted. In fact, the more, the better. Let the boy grow up to be gentle, let the boy grow up to love peace, and to love making peace. Let the boy grow up to be anything but the image of his father.

Then the man on the screen was raising the knife. Then you could see his face. Ben didn't know who the hell he was supposed to be, but judging from Linda's gasp, somebody important. Just as the knife was coming down, the screen went black.

"Come *on*," said Linda. "What the hell?"

Then Cal King, the Channel 5 news anchor, came on the screen. "Ladies and gentlemen, I bring you urgent, breaking news. The town of Clairmont is ordered to evacuate immediately. I repeat, all people currently in Clairmont must immediately leave. As yet, we are unable to say exactly *why*. But we are told that there is a massive and immediate threat to the lives of all those in Clairmont. I repeat…"

"What is this?" said Linda.

Ben felt the rush of adrenalin, the one he knew so well. The one he felt every time he'd entered a house, not knowing what would be there – not knowing if some crazy motherfucking extremist would be waiting around the corner to blow his head off.

Cal King went on. "All law enforcement officers everywhere are urged to make their way to downtown Clairmont and provide assistance. And they are advised that the only way to stop them is to cut off their heads. Wait… what? Bruce, what the hell is this? Are you fu…" The screen went black again. Then the whole thing started over, in a loop. "Ladies and gentlemen…"

Ben stood up. "I have to go," he said.

"What?" said Linda. "Since when are you a law enforcement officer? And just what the *hell* is going on?"

"I don't know," said Ben. "But people need my help." He laughed. "I guess the fox got loose."

"You *can't* go, Ben. I'm scared. I need you here."

"We're twenty miles from Clairmont, Linda. I'm going to go there and see what's happening. I'll call you and let you know. If there's any danger, I want you to take Jason and drive somewhere far away from here. Go to your parents' in Virginia."

"*Please* don't go Ben. I'm so scared. I love you so much."

"I love you too, Linda. I love you more than anything. But I have to go. They need me."

Linda was crying. Ben sat down and put his arm around her. He kissed the side of her head. Then he stood up. "Everything's going to be okay, baby. I can handle myself. Bye."

He turned around and walked out to the garage. "Cut off their heads," Cal King had said. He could do that. But was there any reason why he shouldn't bring guns, too? He couldn't think of one. Better brings the guns. A lot of them, too, just in case.

Chapter eleven

Dennis leapt off the couch, spilling his drink. "God*dammit!*" he roared. Jessica snorted, lifted her head for a second, then flipped over and resumed snoring. He watched the screen as Cal King started over for the third time. "Ladies and gentleman…"

His phone rang and he answered it. "*What?*"

"Calvin. This is Glenn up in Jefferson. What the hell is going on over there?"

"Major fuck-up, Glenn. My fuck-up for hiring Duvlosky in the first place."

"What? What's going on?"

"I just fired the asshole, and this must be his way of getting back at me. Well, we'll see about all that. Don't you worry, I'm going to straighten this all out."

"So you *don't* need our assistance?"

"No, no. It's just a goddamn hoax, Glenn. Appreciate the call though."

"Thank Christ," said Glenn. "And make sure Duvlosky pays for getting me out of bed, the sick fuck."

"Will do," said Dennis and hung up. Oh, Duvlosky was going to pay alright. He was going to pay out of his stupid asshole. Before, Dennis was just going to let him retire gracefully and leave it at that. Then Duvlosky had agitated him, had interrupted him *just before* he was about to get a hard-on. So he fired him, and he would have been content to leave it at that. After all, Dennis was a good guy, and Duvlosky *did* have a story about his wife, as ridiculous as it was. Best to just let the whole thing go away quietly.

But now. Now Duvlosky was going to jail. Then he was going to prison, for the long haul. But all of that would be *after* he got his brains sorted out once and for all by Dennis' fists. Dennis was going to add twenty years to

Duvlosky's life in one fell swoop.

He got dressed, got in his car, and radioed the station. "Denise, this is The Chief. Can you tell me where Duvlosky is?"

"Dennis," said Denise, "Dennis, what's going on? I'm scared."

"It's nothing to worry about, dear. Have you heard from Duvlosky?"

"He said... he said... oh God..."

"Nevermind what he said, dear, he's lost his mind. Can you just tell me where he is?"

"He's headed to town... to try and..."

Dennis flipped off the radio. Town it was. His head pounded with rage. He tore out of his driveway and down the road. He turned left on Fletcher Rd. and sped on.

He saw it just in time, two eyes reflecting in his headlights. He slammed on the brakes. Goddamn deer. He was going to *kill* that goddamn deer. He pulled off to the side of the road. No. No time. The goddamn thing was probably half to Canada by now anyway. He'd come back for the fucker, once he was done with Duvlosky. He'd track it all the way to Canada if he had to, and blow out its stupid brains.

He started the car and pulled back onto the road. Then he saw it again, in the rearview. Oh, that was it! He'd given it a chance. Old Dennis wasn't a bad guy, but he had his limits. Why couldn't they understand that? Why did they keep pushing him? He gave them chance after chance after chance, and they just gobbled it all up. No more chances. It was reckoning time. For Jessica, for Duvlosky, and for this *goddamn deer*. He spun the car around.

"What the *fuck?*" he said. There was a woman standing there, in the middle of the road. Good thing for her Old Dennis was there. Christ, what was she *doing*? He got out of the car and approached her.

"Ma'am... what are you doing here out in the dark, wandering around in the middle of the road? You're gonna

THE ELECTRIC BONER

get yourself killed."

"I forgot who I was," she said, "but now I remember."

"Claire? Claire Peterson? What happened? Did you hit your head? Have a bit too much to drink? Come on now, I'll take you home."

She smiled. "Oh, but I am home, Officer. It's you who needs to go home."

"Jesus Christ, Mrs. Peterson. You're drunk out of your mind. I *really* don't have time for this, but you're gonna get yourself run over if you don't come with me."

"You fat slob. You don't get it, do you? It's you who's coming with me."

The fury returned. Fat slob? It was reckoning time for Claire Peterson, too. "Maybe I never saw you," he said. "Maybe I never saw you til I drove into work in the morning and found your dead body in that ditch over there. How would you like that, you stupid bitch?"

"You poor fat slob," she said, "in your Big Boy Cop Uniform. Does that make you feel like a Big Boy? Or aren't you just a frightened little boy?"

That was it. The matter was settled. He walked over to her. The first time he slapped her, it was for the fat slob remark. When her head turned back around, it was Duvlosky's face he saw, and he slapped that one, too, a little harder. Then it was Jessica's face, not like it was when he'd first seen it, young and radiant, but as it was now, old, wrinkled, used-up. He slapped her with all his might. Then, strangely, he saw a deer head. Why not? He slapped that one too. He slapped them all, again and again. It was The Reckoning of Dennis Calvin.

Finally, he had to stop and catch his breath. How was she still standing? She turned her bloodied face and smiled. "Are you quite done? Good. Now it's *your* turn."

She grabbed his right hand and he almost laughed. Did she think she could take on Dennis Calvin, Chief of Police, Full of Fury? "The show's just getting started," he said.

"Indeed," she said. He felt a sudden pain in his wrist, incredible, and looked down in shock to see five long claws going into it at different points and coming out on the other side. He screamed, and she pulled. She pulled his *hand off*. He reached for his gun with his left hand, but she grabbed it and slapped his other hand into it. He stood there holding his own severed hand, the strings of veins dripping blood. "I'm going to kill you," he growled.

"Are you?" she said. She laughed, and he saw a mouth full of yellow fangs. "How unkind, Officer. That makes *me* feel unkind. I *was* going to kill you, but I think I'm not, now. Now I'm going to leave you in that ditch over there, to think about what you've done. I imagine it's going to be a long, dreadful night. Especially after I take your car. And your legs."

She lunged and sunk her fangs in just above his knee. Then that was it: Dennis was out of the game. When he woke up in the ditch, his legs were gone. For a second, he didn't feel anything at all. "It wasn't supposed to be like this," he muttered to himself. "Goddamn deer." Then he felt it. He felt the pain, and it was worse than anything that had ever come before it and he knew that he had blown it, Old Dennis Calvin had blown the whole thing.

Chapter twelve

Fran's face went white and her eyes grew large. "Felicia…"

"You'd better go," said Felicia, almost laughing. "You don't want this mob of zombies getting a hold of you, do you?" That was good, she thought, "her face went white" and all that. That could be the opening line.

"Yes," said Lisa. "Let's get *out* of here, Fran."

"What did you say again?" said Fran. "You said that

half of them were coming to town. Where is the other half going?"

"Duvlosky didn't know. They were headed North, he said." Felicia couldn't imagine what could possibly be *North* of here. Trees, trees, and more trees, maybe a few inbred potato farmers.

"*Nick,*" gasped Fran. Oh, that's good. She could add a mother-son element to the story.

"My God," said Lisa. "You're right. The Canter's place. The boys."

"We have to go," said Fran. "We have to save them."

"I couldn't convince you to record your trip on video, could I?"

"Oh, shut up," said Lisa.

The two ladies ran out the door. Felicia reached over and got their wine glasses and poured them all together. No sense wasting it. And no sense wasting the story, either. It might be the last one she ever wrote. It *would* be a good one, she had to admit. And why be so negative? Once she lost her job, she could finally finish up her novel.

She downed the wine and stood up. "I guess you better go, too," she said to the bartender. She paid and left. Down the street, she could see a mob of people standing outside of Finnegan's. That's where the story was, where the people were.

Pandemonium broke loose in Finnegan's, where the townsfolk had gathered to drink and talk, to let loose and relax after a hard week of work. Little had they known that their peaceful, happy night would end in terror and confusion.

Okay, so it was a little exaggerated. They looked more like a herd of cows chewing grass than anything. And, when she had been there before, she had seen a fist fight break out and tumble out the door, so the bit about a "peaceful, happy" night was a bit of a lie.

She watched as people got in their cars and left. She walked down the hill and entered the bar. It was still half full.

"Buncha bullshit," a man was saying. He was drunk and loud. "I come here the last twenty years, every Saturday, and it's gonna take a goddamn *bulldozer* drag me offa this barstool tonight."

"Either that, or we just wait for you to *fall* off like you usually do," someone rejoined. That got some laughs. But Felicia wasn't amused. This wasn't what she'd hoped for, not at all. She was hoping to see at least one body, trampled in the mad rush for the door. But the place was just the same as she'd left it, only there were half as many people, and they were twice as drunk.

How could she have fallen for it? Those two bitches had egged her on. She sat down next to the man who had boasted about the bulldozer and ordered a double vodka. A drink to the death of her career. "Hey," she said to the man. "Aren't you *frightened?*"

"Pete Glovens ain't never been scareda *nothin,*" he said.

"Yeah, cept for that wifea his," said somebody else.

"Aren't you even *curious* about that?" she asked, pointing up to the TV, where the local doofus was still going on.

"Gonna take a goddamn *bulldozer* drag me offa this barstool," he said again. Oh Christ.

"The zombies are coming," Felicia said, as a final attempt to get a rise out of him, to get *something* out of this rotten situation.

"Let 'em come," said the esteemed Mr. Glovens, shrugging. "I'll knock their goddamn heads off, they try anything with me."

Felicia slammed her drink down and ordered another. Then she heard it. First a soft thud, barely distinguishable over the drunken slur of voices. Then another one, a little louder. She turned and looked. She saw a mass of faces looking in the window. Their eyes were dead.

Chapter thirteen

"You're scaring me."

The vision receded before Nick's eyes and he was looking at Lucy again. He felt like crying, but that would be the worst thing in the world that could happen. "I'm sorry," he mumbled. All of the momentum that had been building in him was gone. He was back to being scrambled eggs.

"Sorry about what, Nick? Are you okay? What's going on?"

He wanted to vanish, to close his eyes, and when they opened again, he would be in his bed, alone. That's where he belonged. "I'm sorry," he said again.

She scowled at him. He'd never seen her scowl before. It was somehow just as beautiful as her smile. Everything about her was beautiful.

"No sir," she said. "Something just happened to you, and you're going to tell me what it is. Unless...." She looked down at the floor and her face grew red. My God, that was most beautiful of all. "It's okay," she said. "It's okay if you've got a boner, I don't mind."

Suddenly, the life rushed back into him. He felt the laughter forming in his stomach, warm and ready to burst. He laughed. "If only you knew, Lucy," he said.

"Tell me," she said. "Then I'll know."

"It's a long story, and not one I can tell here, in front of all of these people."

"Then let's find a room somewhere, off by ourselves," said Lucy. Or had she? Was this happening? Or was this just another fantasy? Nick didn't think he could tell any more. Maybe the best thing to do was to act like it *was* a fantasy. Then he could do what he wanted, without letting himself get in his own way.

"Okay," he said.

Then the house erupted in shouting. "Holy shit!" somebody yelled. Nick turned and looked into the living room. A circle of bodies had formed. "She's gonna do it!"

"What's that?" said Nick.

"Who cares?" said Lucy. "Some kind of idiocy. Let's go."

She took his hand. He felt dizzy. He felt a rush of warmth, a rush of happiness.

"She's sucking him off! You guys, come look! She's sucking him off!"

He followed Lucy through the crowd, away from the crowd. They were at the foot of the stairs now.

"Let's go upstairs," she said.

This couldn't be happening. But he felt her hand, and it was real.

"Okay," he said.

Then the shouting turned into screaming. Something was flying through the air. It landed at their feet. Then Lucy dropped his hand and started screaming. No, he thought. No, what's happening? He looked down. It was somebody's dick.

PART II

Chapter fourteen

Hugh looked down at his dick in her hand. Oh God. He was a goner, he knew that, unless he did something fast.

"Stop," he said. "Let me do you now."

Lyla giggled. He pushed her down onto the bed and undid her jeans. He rubbed her pussy through her underwear and could feel that it was wet. Then he pulled those off and slid his finger in and wiggled it. She moaned.

The clit, he remembered. Go for the clit. He pulled out his finger and stuck his head down there. The clit, sure, but where was the damn thing? He started licking around the outside. It was wet and tart. He liked it. She started moaning louder.

"Yes," she said, "lick it, Hugh, lick my pussy."

Then he found it. Or he thought he did. Was that it? That little bump there? He touched it with the tip of his tongue. She screamed. Yep. That was it. He started flicking his tongue at it. Like that? Is that how you do it?

"Oh FUCK!" screamed Lyla. "Don't stop! Keep doing that!"

That's how you do it, alright. He pressed on it with his tongue and started moving it around in a circle. He kept switching it up – up and down, to circle, to side to side. His tongue was starting to get tired. Then she closed her thighs around his head, and even with his ears covered, he heard her scream the loudest one yet. Then she grabbed him by the hair and pulled him away.

"I came," she said, breathless. "Nobody's ever made

me cum before. Now it's your turn."

She bent down and put it in her mouth. "Holy mother of sweet fucking Christ," he said. It felt so *good*. He watched her head bobbing up and down on his dick. It didn't take long. There was no stopping it now. "I'm gonna cum," he said, and touched the side of her head. He expected her to pull her head away, like Viki had, but she didn't. She just kept sucking away.

He came in her mouth and she swallowed it all. His head was tingling with pleasure, both of his heads. "Lyla," he said, "I love you."

She gave it a kiss and then lifted up her head. "Oh, relax," she said. "It's just a blowjob. But I've got to say, Hugh. You've got some skills. We should do this again some time."

"Let me give you my phone number. Let me give you my e-mail address, my home address, my fucking social security number. Any time you want."

Lyla laughed. "I'll keep that in mind," she said, pulling up her pants. Then she opened the door and left, leaving him in his bliss.

He lay there looking up at the ceiling, replaying it in his head. Then he started to think about Nick. The poor fucker. What if his dick never got better? What if he was never able to feel what Hugh had just felt, the great glory of it all? No. They would find the cure. They had to.

He decided he'd better get up and go find Nick. He was probably in a corner somewhere, crying into his beer. It was too bad. Nick was the best guy that Hugh knew, and he didn't even know it himself. He pulled up his pants and headed downstairs.

There, at the bottom of the steps, was the man himself, standing next to Lucy. Good for him. But then he saw that Lucy was crying. Goddammit, Nick. What the fuck is wrong with you? What did you do now? Probably told her about your electric boner. Idiot.

He looked out over the railing at the party. At first it

THE ELECTRIC BONER

didn't make any sense. Had someone dosed him? Had he dropped acid and forgotten about it? The kitchen was full of scientists, getting it on with his classmates. They were all slobbering over each other, feeling each other up. In the living room, people were screaming. He couldn't see what was going on there from the stairs.

Then he saw a cop, the asshole one, Sweeny his name was, making out with Viki. What the *fuck* was going on? Then he caught a glimpse of Sweeny's eyes. They were just like Marie's had been, dead and staring.

"Nick!" he shouted. "Is this what I think it is?"

Nick turned around and nodded. Lucy was hugging him now, sobbing into his chest.

"Come *on*," said Hugh. "Upstairs! Let's jump out a window and get the *fuck* out of here."

"No," said Nick.

"*What* did you just say? You want to *stay* here?"

"We can't just leave them."

"They're already dead," said Hugh.

"What's going on?" sobbed Lucy. "What's happening?"

"You go," said Nick. "Take Lucy."

Then the screams started in the kitchen. It was happening.

"Fuck that," said Hugh. "You're coming with us. Do I have to knock out that stupid head of yours?"

"No," said Nick. "This is it. This is what I have to do, it's what's been coming."

"Jesus Christ," said Hugh. "You've lost your goddamn mind."

Lucy lifted her head. "If he's staying, then I'm staying."

"Shit," said Hugh. "Shit."

"EVERYBODY!" shouted Nick. "Find something sharp. You have to *cut off their heads*."

"Shit," said Hugh, walking down the steps. "Shit."

Chapter fifteen

"Shit," said Mikhail. "Shit."

He stopped at the top of the hill and looked down at the mob of them gathered outside Finnegan's. Christ, he just hoped that somebody was coming. Now even Cooper wasn't answering his radio. There was only the chance that a department from another town, maybe Jefferson, had got the broadcast and were on their way. But he couldn't wait until then. The street was still lined with cars. There were still people in there, people too proud or stupid, or both, to heed the broadcast. If he couldn't save Marie, he could still save the town that she loved. But it didn't look good.

He looked down at the axe he had picked up at Willie's Hardware. He'd had to smash the window to get in, but Willie would forgive him, if either of them were still alive at the end of this. "Marie," he said to the axe. "Your name is Marie, and we're going to cut off as many of these fuckers' heads as we can, right baby? My good sweet baby?"

There was nothing left to say after that. He'd made his decision, and all that was left to do was to follow it through to the end. He took his foot off the brake and accelerated down the hill. He saw them banging their hands against the window of Finnegan's. He saw the glass shatter. One of them stepped in.

He was up to 45mph. There was a break in the line of parked cars, and he squeezed in and up onto the sidewalk. The passenger side mirror hit a light post and went flying away, disappearing into the night. Now he was up to 55 and almost there.

There was a bench ahead of him on the sidewalk. He smashed into it and it broke apart. A piece of metal hit the windshield and shattered it. A shower of glass rained down into the car. He closed his eyes and felt it splatter against his face, the small bits of glass, stinging him like wasps. He opened his eyes again and felt the rush of the cold wind coming into his face.

Then he was there. He aimed straight for the center of the mob and plowed into it. There was a flurry of bodies flying through the air. He felt the thud of one under his car. Then the car stopped moving, held up by the weight of 25 bodies in front of it. A hand was reaching in, through the open windshield. Mikhail felt dizzy, everything was blurry, but he saw it coming. He pulled his knife out and stuck it into the hand, pinning it to the dashboard.

As things came into focus, he saw that the hand was attached to Carlos, the smiling kid from the lab. Carlos was no longer smiling, and was no longer Carlos. It moved its head closer, dead eyes looking at Mikhail, and began licking its lips. Mikhail reached for Marie and brought her back as best he could while still strapped into his seat. She stuck in Carlos' neck and he let her go. "Sorry, kid," he said, and he grabbed Carlos' hair with both hands and slammed down, wedging the axe further in. There was a spray of blood and a horrific screech, the same one that his wife had made, and then he yanked the head back up and slammed it down again, and again, and again, until, on the last time, the head came off the body, gushing. Marie slid down to the floor of the car and Mikhail threw the head, still screeching, back into the mob, which had begun to reassemble outside. They were crawling on the hood now.

Mikhail unbuckled, picked up Marie, opened the door, rolled out of the car, and retreated a few steps. He glanced inside Finnegan's which was alive, and dying, with screams and bottles and tables and bodies crashing and thudding to the ground. Half of them had crawled in through the broken window. He saw old Pete Glovens in there, a regular at the drunk tank. One of the things had his face gripped in one hand and was squeezing, while the other hand squeezed below the belt. Then, with a quick twist, it snapped Pete's neck, and let him fall to the ground.

Mikhail turned his back to the pub and faced the mob outside. They were approaching him. He lifted Marie with both hands and swung wildly. A head flew. But it was no good. A hand was around his right wrist before he could bring the axe back up. He kicked out and got the thing in the knees and it let loose its grip. He brought Marie up on a backswing and just grazed the neck.

He was tired. Blood and sweat dripped down into his eyes. He wiped it away and then he saw it. Jackson. His face had been burned, but Mikhail could still see the dead eyes glaring at him. "Jesus Christ," he muttered. He leaped and swung. Jackson's head dropped to the ground, still glaring at him with dead eyes. Another head came flying from the pub window behind him and landed next to Jackson's. It was Willie Wentworth. There would be no need to reimburse him for the axe.

Mikhail brought Marie up for another swing, but it was no use. It was over. A hand had him by the shoulder, and then another one by the leg. Then he was on his back, staring up at four of them. One of them tore his pants down and then they flipped him on his stomach.

He closed his eyes as they shoved his face into the pavement and spread him open.

Chapter sixteen

Lucy didn't know what was going on, but she saw somebody – no, some*thing* – that looked exactly like Officer Sweeney twisting Viki's hair around his – *its* fist. She decided to do something about that. She didn't know what she was going to do, and before she could think it out, she was on her way, running toward her screaming friend.

Nick was yelling at her. "Lucy! Wait! Stop!"

THE ELECTRIC BONER

The Sweeney-Thing looked at her with terrible eyes, eyes that lacked all life, eyes that were everything ugly. It grinned and yanked down with its hand, and then Viki was on her knees, screaming, in total terror. Lucy was in total terror too, she figured, but it didn't do anybody any good, and so she leaped, just like she had been trained to leap in ballet class, only this time, instead of having her arms lifted gracefully above her head, they were out in front of her.

She dug her thumbs into the Sweeney-Thing's eyes as she collided with its body, latching on to its torso with her legs, wrapping her legs around it, and jamming her thumbs in deep. They kept going further in until she was sure that she'd hit brain, and she heard a terrible screech, as of ten thousand tires on ten thousand roads to Hell and then there were two hands at her throat, choking her. She plunged her thumbs in until they were down to the second knuckle and they wouldn't go any further and then, when she was sure that she was going to die, she pulled outward with all of her strength, and the Sweeney-Thing's head tore apart in two.

She fell to the ground gasping. Viki, Hugh, and Nick were all standing over her, staring down. Nick offered his hand and pulled her up.

"Holy shit," said Hugh. "Remind me not to piss you off."

"What now?" asked Lucy. She felt light-headed and sick and ready to collapse.

"Christ," said Hugh, "I say we just let her go at them. Did you *see* that shit, Nick? She *tore his head apart.*"

Jake Canter's head rolled past their feet, eyes open, tongue out. He would never be on anybody's list now.

"The kitchen," said Nick. "Knives, forks, pans, anything."

"What?!" said Viki. "You want to fight these fucking things?"

One of them reached into Mike Cunning's chest and pulled his heart out. Hugh looked around. "We're in it now. They're by the stairs, doors, windows, everywhere. We're fucked. Might as well cut off some heads."

There was a path to the kitchen and they made their way carefully, carefully, like Lucy's cat Jazz whenever the front door opened and he wasn't sure if it was danger, but here and now, they were quite sure it was danger. Eric Brown was still standing on the counter, with his pants around his ankles, but now one of the things was grabbing at his leg. She saw Eric grab a pot from the rack overhead and swing it at the thing's head. Then the thing yanked on Eric's legs and Eric fell and she saw his head hit the counter as the thing dragged him down to the ground.

As they got closer, the bodies got thicker. Lucy saw an arm reaching out for Nick.

"Nick! 9 o'clock!"

Nick turned and looked at her. "What? Lucy, I don't care what time it is."

"Your *right*, Nick, turn *right*!"

Nick turned to see it just in time. He leapt back, out of the way. For someone who wasn't on any of the teams, he was pretty athletic. But then there was another one behind him. "Behind you!" she screamed. She saw Hugh come up around the thing and sweep-kick its legs, knocking it over. Then she felt a hand grab her shoulder and spin her around. It was a scientist lady-thing. It mauled one of her breasts and she screamed in terror. She heard Nick yell her name. He plowed into the thing and tried to tackle it, but it wouldn't let her go. Then she felt a splash of warmth against her face and saw the thing's head come off its neck.

Hal Prescott was standing there, holding a samurai sword. "That's for Chris, you sick fuck," he said.

"Holy shit," said Hugh. "Nice."

"You like that?" said Hal. "It was hanging in the hallway. Not bad, right?"

Nick was still hugging the torso, like a grotesque teddy bear. He let it go and it slumped to the ground.

"Anybody know what the fuck's going on?" said Hal. He pulled out a cigarette and lit it.

"Yeah," said Nick. "We got about fifty more heads to cut off."

"Sounds good to me," said Hal.

"Stick with us," said Hugh. "We're going to duck into the kitchen there and grab what we can in the way of fine cutlery."

"Have fun doing that," said Hal. "I've got other fish to fry, like that bitch over there that got Hannah." He walked off.

"Let's go," said Nick. They walked carefully, carefully to the kitchen. Lucy could see Eric on the floor now. He was still alive, but the thing was doing something nasty to *his* thing. Lucy grabbed a rolling pin from a shelf and swung it at the thing's head. It was no good. The thing tore into Eric. Then it turned, looked at Lucy and stood up.

Nick grabbed it by the hair with both hands. It got hold of Nick's arms. Then Hugh was there, with a big knife in his hand. He started sawing away at the thing's neck. Blood was gushing. The thing didn't seem to know what to do. It kept grabbing one of them, then the other. It made that horrible shrieking sound.

"Goddammit," said Hugh. "I can't cut through the bone."

"You got everything else, though?" said Nick.

"I think so."

Nick gave the head a quick twist. Lucy heard something snap, and then Nick was holding the head and the body fell to the ground. Nick dropped the head.

"No problem," said Hugh, out of breath. "*Only* fifty, you said?"

Lucy looked around. Hal got another one with his sword, but there were two more right behind him. There were bodies everywhere, and body parts. Hope, thought Lucy. As long as you have hope, you're alright. Then she watched as the two things grabbed Hal, each by an arm. They pulled in opposite directions, and then his arms were torn from his body and he was screaming.

Hope, thought Lucy, hope.

Chapter seventeen

Ben Clemmings crested the hill and there it was. He knew a slaughter when he saw one. He *felt* it, felt the rush as he prepared for action. No, it wasn't a rush, it was a calm. And it wasn't a calm like the pills the doctor gave him made him feel, it was a calm like suddenly the rest of the world had fallen away and everything was still and there was only one thing left and he knew exactly what to do about it. The only thing he had to figure out was who was doing the slaughtering, and who was getting slaughtered.

As he got closer, he got his answer. Whatever the mob was, it wasn't human. They didn't move like humans. When he got even closer, he saw the eyes. He'd seen those eyes hundreds of times before, in the skulls of his dear friends and the Enemy alike. Only, those bodies didn't move. Those bodies would never move again, of their own accord.

But there was one there, swinging an axe, who wasn't like the rest. He was human, Ben could see. And he was tired and alone. Then he lost his axe and they had him. Ben slammed the car to a halt and jumped out of it. He had his Beretta in hand and aimed at the head of one of the ones who was holding the man. It had been a while since he'd fired it, but it felt just like it always had, like it were an extension of himself. He got his target. Then he got the next one.

They let go of the man then, but they didn't drop. Some of them turned and looked at him, and then started walking toward him. He saw the man, who he now realized was a police officer, spin around and break free of the mob.

"You have to cut off their heads!" shouted the officer.

That was alright. Ben tossed the gun into the car, reached in, popped the trunk, and walked over to it. Ten of them were making their way, slowly, up the hill toward him. He looked in the trunk. Goddamn, it was a shame that he couldn't use any of that good firepower. But, as with anything, it came down to the right tool for the job. He looked again at the approaching enemy. There were a lot of them, and they were moving slow. He picked up a machete, reground to a steeper angle, and honed razor sharp, that was encased in a holster. He undid his belt and slid the holster over it, then re-buckled. Then he picked up the other machete. He walked down to meet them.

The first one was, as he'd judged, no problem at all. A double-handed swing sent the head flying through the air. The head was still moving its eyes and snapping its teeth as it hit the pavement. The next one he tried one-handed. There was a bit more resistance, so that it was like cutting through cold butter still in the package, instead of room-temperature butter in a dish. But still easy enough. He drew the second machete and charged. He swung first with the right hand, and half a second later with the left. Then two more heads dropped to the ground. The fifth and sixth swings brought the two blades together on a single neck, and that was just for the hell of it.

Could he get two heads with one swing? He took a step sideways and lined them up. Then he swung. The blade cut cleanly through the first neck, but got stuck in the second one. Oh well, it was worth a shot. He let go of the machete and brought the other one through the other side. The severed head and the machete fell to the ground.

That left three. He could have disposed of them easily enough, but it would have been a waste of time. He picked up the blade which had fallen between two corpses and rushed down the hill. The man had found his axe again, but he looked ready to drop, in the face of some 35 foes. Ben watched as he screamed and took a desperate swing. It didn't connect with anything.

Ben stopped just before he reached the mob and took a deep breath. 35 was a lot of them. He could see into the bar, Finnegan's Pub. He and Linda went there sometimes. Sometimes they brought Jason, sometimes they didn't. He saw Mickey MacDaniels' corpse slumped over the bar, bloodied and torn apart. There were dozens of other corpses, too. Was it worth it? In a flash, he saw Linda and Jason, hugging each other, crying, crying over the death of daddy. They needed him, almost as much as he needed them.

"Run!" he heard the officer scream. "Save yourself! Find help, tell them what you saw!

Then he was back in Afghanistan. The mob was circling Stevens. Somebody threw a rock at his head. "Everybody GET BACK!" Stevens yelled. "Don't *make* me shoot you!" Then the knife was in Stevens' neck, and he fired a shot into the crowd. Ben was crouched in an alleyway, watching. He saw the knife go into Stevens' forehead. He knew the crowd was right to be angry, after the bomb, but Stevens had had nothing to do with that. Ben watched as the mob dragged him to the ground and thought of Stevens' family in Alabama. Gillian, her name was, and he forgot the name of the kids, but their faces floated in front of his eyes, faces he had seen a hundred times in photographs.

A soldier was best off not thinking. Once you started asking the questions, things got complicated. Then your ability to act became paralyzed. You had to go into it ahead of time with the faith that it would all contribute to the greater good. Once you were in it, you were in it.

An arm was reaching for him. He cut it off. He jumped into it all.

Chapter eighteen

It's hopeless, thought Nick, what have I done? At best, a few of the people had been able to escape because of them. But the rest were dead. There was only Nick, Hugh, Lucy, and Viki. And there was no way out. They were surrounded.

What the fuck had he been thinking? Why had it felt so important to him that he stay and fight them? Now he was going to die. That wasn't so bad, maybe, but he couldn't bear the thought of Lucy and Hugh, and Viki, dying too.

"Listen to me," he said. "I'm going to charge right there, toward the stairs. Maybe it will distract them, and make an opening for you guys to get the fuck out of here."

"No," said Lucy.

"Are you nuts Lucy?" said Viki. "It's our only chance."

"I'm not going to leave him," said Lucy. "Hugh, tell me you're with me. Tell me you can't leave Nick."

The circle surrounding them was getting tighter. "I... I'm scared, Lucy," said Hugh. "I don't want to die."

"It's alright, Hugh," he said. "Go. And drag Lucy if you have to."

Nick prepared himself. So he wasn't exempt after all, not from death. Had he lived a good life? He didn't think he had. But it hadn't been a bad life, either. It had just been a life, that's all. He'd done the best he could. Now the thing that made him saddest was thinking about the people he would leave behind, thinking about his mother. It would destroy her.

But there wasn't time to sort through his thoughts. The days of lying in bed and turning things over in his mind were gone. For good. "Lucy," he said. "I love you."

Then he grabbed her head and kissed her lips. It was good. It was better than he thought it would be. It was the best thing that had ever happened to him. He felt the bulge grow in his pants, then he pulled his head away and shoved her.

"Hugh!" he said. Hugh caught her as she tried to reach for Nick.

There was nothing else to do. He ran as fast as he could behind his shoulder into the circle of bodies. He wasn't able to pick up much momentum, but it was enough to knock one of them down. It worked. The zombie were confused. They broke their formation and started reaching for him.

He turned and saw Viki run through an opening. She made it out the door.

"Fuck this," said Hugh. He ran, but not toward the door. He ran through a different opening, and picked up the sword that was still gripped tight in Hal's dead hand on his severed arm.

"No!" screamed Nick. "GO!"

Then there was a zombie finger in his mouth, pulling at his cheek. He punched at it wildly until another hand come out and got his wrist. Then Lucy jumped on the one pulling at his cheek, stuck her finger in its mouth, and started pulling on *its* cheek.

"How do you like that, you fucker?" she said.

Nick stuck a knife in its throat with his free hand. He pulled with all of his strength, but he knew there was no way he could sever the head. Not one-handed. Then there was a hand on his thigh.

"Lucy," he said, "please go. Please try to get away."

Then she ripped away half of the zombie's face.

Hugh made it over to them and cut off two or three arms, enough to free Nick. Nick kept working on his zombie, and eventually he had everything cut but the spine. "Twist," he said to Lucy. Then she was holding the head. She threw it over her shoulder.

They were all together now, and the circle was forming around them again. Nick was tired. He had never been more tired in his life. There was nothing more he could do.

"I'm going to do it again," he said. "And this time, I want both of you to *go*."

Hugh took a swing with the sword and a zombie head went flying. "Please," said Nick. "Please."

Then he heard a scream coming from the front door. They all turned to look, including the zombies. But Nick couldn't see anything, beyond the wall of bodies in front of him. "Run!" said Hugh. They ran. Hugh made it first, past a zombie who was turned the other way.

Nick could see the door now. His mother was standing there, next to Hugh's mother, who was screaming. His mother was so *beautiful*. How could he never have seen that before? He ran toward her.

Lucy made it through, but just barely. One of them had grabbed her shirt, and it tore away, revealing her bra underneath. Nick felt himself stiffen again, and then he felt a hand grab his shoulder and yank him back. Then he was back in the center of the circle, alone. They descended upon him, arms reaching, grabbing whatever they could. One had him by the throat. One had him by the leg, and another by the other leg. They were pulling in different directions, tearing apart his clothes.

Then he watched in horror as one reached for his dick.

Chapter nineteen

Felicia cracked open Finnegan Pub's bathroom door and pointed her phone's camera lens through it. Through the phone's screen, she saw the results of the massacre, bodies strewn about, bloodied, missing parts, spilling out other parts that were supposed to be contained. It was the story of a lifetime, but what good was that if you didn't have a lifetime left?

She panned the room with the camera. There were no zombies on the screen. She opened the door a little more and stuck her head out. She saw the man, Pete somebody, lying on the ground with his head twisted around. Well, it hadn't been a bulldozer that had finally dragged him off his stool.

She crouched behind a booth and looked out the broken window, where two men were fighting valiantly – yes, that's the word, *valiantly* – against the mass of zombie invaders. She hid herself completely behind the booth except for the tip of the phone poking out, and watched the story unfold on the screen.

One of the men was swinging two machetes, with skill and purpose, hacking off heads left and right. Military, she guessed. The other man, she saw, was Duvlosky. He wasn't doing as well. He only got one head for every three swings, and each swing started a little lower, and came a little slower. Somewhere in her head, a voice screamed, *Do something*. But the other, sensible part, answered: I'm doing what I can; I'm reporting the story.

She watched. The military man was taking them out, methodically, one-by-one, dodging them, finding just the right ground, and striking. He took out one as she watched, two, three, four. On the would-be fifth one, he made a misstep. He brought up the machete in his right hand, but as he did so, his elbow came against one of the sex-zombie's (that's what she was going to call them, "sex-zombies") head. The obstacle hindered his motion and at once there were three hands grabbing his arm. He swung with his left, but it was a defensive swing, nothing to do with the hands on his arm. Then Felicia watched as his arm left his body, and she almost dropped her phone, but she didn't.

She heard him scream, and when she realized that the

audio had been muted, she said, "Shit." She covered her mouth with her hand. But it was too late. The sex-zombies had heard her. She watched through the screen as six of the thirty or so remaining turned their heads slowly, looked back into the bar, and started walking toward it. Four males, and two females, she noted, before she turned and ran back into the bathroom.

She locked the door and waited. "This is Felicia Jones," she said into the phone, "trapped in the bathroom at Finnegan's Pub in Clairmont, Maine, pursued by six of the sex-zombies. For the love of God, send help." She began uploading the video just as the door started to rattle.

She looked around, desperately searching for some kind of weapon. There was nothing there. The banging at the door was getting louder. Her phone made a noise. Somebody was commenting on the video she had uploaded. She looked at it. "Is this really happening?" it said.

Then another comment: "Good job, bitch, hiding away while that dude got his arm ripped off."

She sighed. There was always a critic. No matter what you did, there was always somebody there waiting to tell you that it was the wrong thing to do. They were like the sex-zombies, in a way, just intent on tearing you apart. She looked at one more comment: "Hang tight," it said, "help on the way."

She switched the phone back to video mode and pointed it at the door. They were slamming into it. The strike plate came flying off and struck her forehead. The door flung open. She backed into the stall and locked it. She climbed up onto the toilet. It was the only place she could go, the only place that was just a little further away from the door.

Another comment popped up on the top of the screen. "We're coming too," it said. Then another one: "Hold on, Felicia, just a few more minutes."

But there were no more minutes, Felicia knew. Thank

God she didn't have a family. It was fitting, in a way. She'd given her life to journalism, and now she'd be giving her death to it, too. The people deserved to know. There was nothing wrong with that, with letting the people know what was happening.

The door to the stall swung open. There they were. She lifted her phone and pointed it right at one of their faces. She had time to click "upload" just as the first hand started reaching inside of her.

Chapter twenty

Sarah Johnston awoke. It was dark, and cold. She was lying down on something hard and damp. Or she thought she was lying down. It was pressed up against her flesh. She felt naked. She couldn't see anything. Her head was swimming with pain. She pushed away from the hardness and dampness with her hands and then she thought she was standing.

"Hello?" she said, through a mouth dry with thirst. Her own voice sounded strange. It was like listening to it through a tape recorder. But where usually there were data and theories in her tape recordings to distract from the strangeness of her voice, here there was nothing. There was just the coldness, and the darkness, and the hardness and dampness under her feet. Her voice, speaking into the darkness.

"She's awake," said a voice. She recognized it. Then she recognized the *smell*. "We fixed you, didn't we?" the voice said. "You're not Cyclops anymore. I hope Mom and Dad let me keep you."

"Where am I?" asked Sarah.

"You're in your cage, silly," said the voice. "Mom and Dad'll be here real soon and maybe they'll let me take you for a walk."

THE ELECTRIC BONER

"Can I... have some clothes?" asked Sarah. "Can I have some water? I'm thirsty."

"Shut up," said the voice. "Pets aren't supposed to talk. Don't you know *any*thing?"

Sarah was shivering. "Please," she said. "Please."

"I *said* shut up!" said the voice. She heard the little boy bawl. "I'm trying to *help* you! Don't you want to be my pet, stupid?"

Sarah felt around. Everywhere she felt, there was more of the hard and damp material. Concrete? She tapped it with a finger. Yes, concrete. But was the little boy in the room with her? How was she hearing his voice through the concrete? With her hand, she followed one wall to the corner, and started to follow the next wall. Then she bumped into something. She felt it, and it was cold and hard, but not damp, and it was smooth. She tapped against it and it felt hollow and rang out. She followed its course with her hands, and then her hands were on something soft. She felt around, stretched out her arms and mentally measured it. It was a bed.

She didn't think she was still in the hospital. The hospital didn't have concrete walls, a concrete floor. She thought she was in a jail cell. She followed the wall to the next one, and sure enough, there were the metal bars. She felt her way back to the bed and sat down. It felt good. There was a sheet there and she wrapped it around herself.

What had her life been, up until this point? She had had a nice, thick bed, she had had nice warm clothes, both eyes, a big green water bottle always full of water. But it hadn't been enough for her, not nearly enough. Why not? she asked herself. What did you *want*? She couldn't answer the question, not really, not in the coldness and the darkness. She felt like a ghost. No, the *opposite* of a ghost - all body and no soul.

No, she told herself, it was not all in vain. She had been trying to solve problems, real problems, she had been seeking solutions that would make the world a better place.

But when she reviewed the data, that theory seemed false. It was more like she had been trying to solve some problem inside of herself, but instead of solving it, she had kept making it worse.

She felt alone. She had mostly always been alone, but it was just now that she felt it, blind, in her jail cell. Was there anybody in the world who would bring her a glass of water now? There was not. And why should there be? When had she ever brought anybody a glass of water? She felt now, in her cell, that she would walk across a lake glazed over with a thin layer of ice, she would walk across fire to bring somebody, anybody who was as thirsty as she was, a glass of water.

That was the only problem in the world. People weren't good enough to each other. When she realized this, she smiled, and would have cried if she had eyes. She *deserved* this, what was happening to her now.

She remembered that day, so many years ago, when her father had called to her from the doorway of the bar. She wished she could go back, and *run* up to him and hug him. She wished that Roland was there too, and her mother, to hear what she was about to say.

"It's okay," she'd say. "Sometimes things don't work out. I understand that now. You all deserve to move on, to try to find happiness wherever you can. To keep the good that's gone and cherish it, instead of spoiling it with burning hatred. Though I hope to never see you again, I love you all."

And she almost laughed. No. She would never be seeing them again, even if they were right in front of her face. But she missed them. Somehow, she even missed Jack Huskfield. It was all worthwhile, all of life was a worthwhile thing.

"You're boring me," said the voice. "You're not *doing* anything. Dance. Dance for me."

Sarah stood up and stretched one leg in front of the other. Had she ever danced before? She couldn't recall.

She leaned forward, further and further, until her forehead touched the cold concrete. Then she spread her arms out, as far as they would go. She slowly lifted her head and arched her back in, pushing out into the emptiness with her naked breasts. Thus she began a slow dance.

Chapter twenty one

When Mikhail saw his man go down, an impossible strength coursed through his body, beating back the impossible tiredness. He knew that it was the last of his strength, and after it was spent, there would be nothing. He charged with the butt of Marie stuck out in front of him, smashing into them. He bought Marie down on a neck that was bent over his man, and that cleared his view. The man was still alive, still moving, trying to lift his remaining arm against the four hands that were pulling it. Mikhail lopped two of them off with one swing, then lifted Marie. This was the final swing, he knew, his last chance. He brought her down and she got one more hand, and then he collapsed on the ground beside the man.

The man kicked his spiked boot at the elbow of the final arm holding him, and Mikhail watched as the arm tore apart at the joint there. Then, still on his back, the man began swinging his machete wildly to fend them off. It was an act of desperation, Mikhail knew. They were done. But they had brought half of them down with them, and that wasn't meaningless.

Then there were sirens in the distance. The noise confused them, the undead, and some of them turned to look. This gave direction to the man's swing, and he got another head that was bent over them with his machete. The head fell to the ground and came face-to-face with Mikhail. He pulled his knife from his belt and slid it through the dead eye, slowly. The teeth stopped snapping.

The sirens were getting louder. If he could only summon the strength to hold out a little longer, maybe he could make it. But all of his strength had been summoned and spent. He dropped his head back on the pavement and watched helplessly as a hand closed around his face.

It began squeezing, pressing just behind the eyes. It didn't matter. He had done his job, he had stalled the creatures long enough for help to arrive. The sirens were there. He felt fire in his head, thunder. But what about the others? he thought. The other fifty?

The hand relaxed its grip. Mikhail pulled it off his face and saw that his man had somehow made it back to his feet. His arm was gushing blood. He wasn't going to make it. He should be dead already, but he was still fighting, staggering around like he was drunk, swinging wildly. This was a hero, and Mikhail didn't even know his name. He wondered what his name was.

Then, suddenly, the creatures were leaving him, they were walking up the hill. Mikhail saw the fire truck pull up, saw the men with their axes jumping off it while it was still moving. Five men, six, seven, eight. Other cars followed, people from town, with whatever weapons they could find. One man whom Mikhail didn't recognize jumped out of his car wielding a two-handed sword, like they used in Medieval times. Everybody was swinging at once, heads were flying.

Then a hand was reaching for him, but it wasn't one of theirs. He recognized her. She'd been at his house once, when Marie had held a book club meeting. Kate, he thought her name was, or something like that. He took her hand and she helped him to his feet.

"You were brave," she said. Mikhail watched as the last head flew through the air. The men were going around, stabbing the severed heads to kill them finally. Mikhail saw that his man had collapsed on the ground.

"We need to get that man to the hospital, right away," he said.

"I'm afraid that's not going to help him," said the woman. Claire. Her name was Claire.

"There's still hope for him," said Mikhail. "He's still alive."

"No. I meant that something terrible has happened at the hospital. Everybody there is dead."

Whatever feeble feelings of victory Mikhail held left him at once. The hospital? But the other half of them had been going in a different direction. "That's where the rest of them went," he said. "Somehow. We have to stop them. We'll send this man to Jefferson. One of the firefighters will take him. Please help me over there, I need to tell them."

Claire smiled and slung Mikhail over her shoulder. "I'm afraid you have the wrong idea. It wasn't these... creatures that wrecked havoc on the hospital."

"What was it?" asked Mikhail. Johnston? But how?

"It was something much worse," said Claire. They had reached one of the firefighters, Kevin Woods.

"Take that man to Jefferson, to the hospital," said Mikhail.

"Jefferson? How come?" asked Kevin.

"I don't know. Something's happened at the Clairmont hospital. Just please, he doesn't have much time."

Kevin ran off to the man. Mikhail watched as he and Matthew Lahey lifted the man's body and carried it to a car. The car pulled off, the taillights disappearing into the night.

"What happened, Claire?" said Mikhail. "At the hospital?"

"This," said Claire. Mikhail watched as yellow claws grew from the end of her fingers. Before he could understand what was happening, her clawed hand was entering the back of Phil Kenzie. Mikhail spun away from her and watched at the hand came out of Phil's chest. "No!" he yelled, and fell to the ground from weakness.

He looked up and saw Joe Reed swing his axe and take Claire's head off. The head bounced on the pavement, and landed a yard away from Mikhail's head.

"That wasn't very nice," said Claire's head, "was it?"

Mikhail saw Claire's body walk over and pick up her head. She put it back on the severed neck, and Mikhail watched as the flesh rejoined. Then she picked up Joe and threw him up into the air. He went up high, higher than the top of the fire trucks, and then he started to come down, straight toward Mikhail. Mikhail tried feebly to lift himself, but it was no good. Joe landed on Mikhail's half-lifted back, and sent his head crashing hard into the pavement.

Chapter twenty two

Nick closed his eyes. He had been mistaken, hadn't he? Yes. That hand reaching for his dick, it didn't belong to some horrible sex zombie that would, very soon now, tear it from his body, just as the rest of his body was torn into an incomprehensible stew of bone and blood and organ... that's not what was happening at all. It was Lucy. They were going to consummate their love.

But he didn't think her hand would be so cold. She must have just come in from outside. And they were in his bedroom. And his Mom was on vacation in Italy for the month, finally enjoying herself, finally living life for herself, drinking a glass of wine, looking out on the sea, from the patio of some rich Italian man with a kind soul.

Then everything went cold. Ah, okay, so maybe they were outside for some reason. Maybe they had just come out of a movie theater and were so desperately in love that they couldn't wait until they made it somewhere inside, they just had to slip down that little alley and do it there and now.

THE ELECTRIC BONER

But why did he feel cold inside? Like his very blood was freezing? And why was she squeezing it so tight and pulling so hard? She must have never done it before, that's all. That's okay. Nick didn't know how any of it worked either.

Ah, that was better, some warmth. And the grip was loosening. They must have found someplace warm to go. Maybe a little too warm. Maybe a little hot. Like they were standing too close to a fire. Now it was like they were standing inside of a fire, and it was too hot and too bright, white, white. Then her hand was gone.

Nick opened his eyes and he was staring at a wide-eyed sex zombie. The zombie's eyes keep getting wider and wider, and then they burst in a splash of green slime. The whole head burst then, an explosion of green gore, and the body crumbled into gray ash.

Nick felt like all dick. Hard, throbbing dick. Powerful dick. Godly dick. He watched as another hand reached for it. The hand turned black, and the blackness flowed up the arm, and then its breasts swelled, grew and grew, and the zombie's white lab coat tore open at the chest from the strain, and Nick felt somehow even harder, like he was already well past the verge, and then the breasts popped like balloons full of green sludge and the rest of the body disintegrated into dust.

Like moths to a flame, more hands followed. Nick felt the pull. His boner was calling them, and they were answering the call. With each touch, he felt his power increasing, and soon there were zombie parts flying through the air; zombie feet, zombie arms, zombie dicks, zombie tits.

He stood up. "Come and get it you horrible fuckers. Come and get fucked by my electric boner!"

And they did. One by one, two by two, they grabbed for it. Noses sprayed forth green geysers. Mouths did too, and asses. They let out their death shrieks, their wails from Hell. For a moment, Nick felt sorry for them. Then he looked around, at his murdered classmates, at his friends by the door, still alive, staring at him now with open mouths, and he felt no more pity.

He eradicated them. 30 left, then 20, then 10. Then there was only one left. It reached, and Nick took a step back. Maybe he could capture it... him. Maybe there was a way to help him, to bring his humanity back. True, the scientists at the research lab hadn't been able to do it... obviously. But maybe somebody else could do it.

Nick looked at the zombie, then looked down by the zombie's feet. Emily Feldman's body was there. The valedictorian. She could have been anything, done anything. All kindness and earnestness. And that was all gone now, and her parents would find out what had happened, and things would never be the same for them. Things would never be the same for any of them, something huge had died here, something more than flesh.

Nick stepped forward. The zombie reached its hand, grasped his dick, and Nick felt the most powerful burst yet. The zombie swelled and stretched and all at once exploded in a splash of green guts and brains.

Nick turned and looked at Lucy, his mom, Hugh, and Hugh's mom. They were all just staring at him, mouths still open. "Are you guys okay?" he asked.

Hugh shook himself out of shock. "Jesus," he said. "Holy shit. The motherfucking electric boner."

"The what?" asked Lisa.

Nick's mom ran over to him and hugged him. The rush fading, Nick felt awkward standing there with his still erect penis sticking out like it was possessed (and it was), getting hugged by his mom. But she wouldn't let go.

"I'm fine, Mom, really."

"Does somebody want to tell me what this 'electric boner' is?" asked Lisa. Then she looked around the room. "You know what? Forget it. Let's just get the hell out of here."

Nick thought he saw the couch move. It seemed like

something was moving under there. It could be one of them, missing its legs or something, squirming around. He would have to finish the job. He broke free from his mother and walked over. He flipped over the couch and smiled. Mandy Perkins had crawled under there and curled into a ball.

"Mandy!" he said. "You made it! You're okay!"

"Depends on what you mean by 'okay,'" she said, unfurling herself and standing up uncertainly. "I'm alive. And I guess that's thanks to your... what did you call it? The electric boner."

Then everybody was laughing. It was a strange sort of laughter. Relief mixed with horror mixed with disbelief.

Nick looked at Lucy. She was staring at him. At his dick. All of his self-consciousness returned. He took off his torn sweatshirt and tied it around his waist to cover the hole in his pants where they had been ripped apart. He walked over to her.

"Lucy..."

She smiled her beautiful smile. "I told you it was okay," she said, "if you had a boner."

Chapter twenty three

There were two voices now. The boy's and a woman's. The boy was talking in a loud, whining voice, but Sarah couldn't make out what the woman was saying. She strained to hear.

"But *mom*, I've been so *good*! Can't I *please* keep her?"

"...this one here," Sarah heard. "How do you think that would work?... soon Papa..."

"I'll *die* if I can't have her, mom! I swear I'll take good care of her, I'll feed her and everything. Please!"

The voices were getting closer and Sarah could hear footsteps now. The sounds filled her world. The cold concrete was simply there, she felt it, it wasn't going to change. And the stench of herself, the stench of her cell was also fairly static, though she had become sensitive to the slightest changes in these, a draft coming from somewhere changing the hierarchy of scents in the subtlest way. The only news she could get was through her ears.

"We'll see," said the woman. "We'll see, okay baby? That's all I can promise. I'll take a looksee, okay?"

"You're gonna *love* her mom, I just know it! She was a Cyclops, but I fixed her, and she can dance and everything!"

As the footsteps drew nearer, the smell overpowered Sarah. Suddenly there was nothing else in the universe but that *smell*. It was even worse than it had been at the hospital.

"You!" said the woman.

Sarah stood up slowly from the bed she had been sitting on. "Yes ma'am?" she said.

"Oh that's good," said the woman. "Manners. I like that."

"I *told* you," said the boy.

"Hush now. Now, you. Tell me. Why shouldn't I come in there and tear apart your skull and feed you your own brain? Is there any compelling reason why I shouldn't do that? Tell me your worth."

"There's no reason," said Sarah. "I have no worth." She felt a flicker of her old self, her old impatient self: Let's get this *over* with! But the voice died quickly. She killed it. Whatever happened to her, she deserved it. She held that thought in the center of her brain, and it was enough to quiet her.

The woman laughed. "You've found yourself a good pet, boy. They'll all beg for death in the end, you'll see, but not this one. This one will kneel down and ask sweetly for more. You've done good, child, in seeing this. You may not understand it just yet, but you understand it well enough in your own fashion." The woman laughed. "Have at her," she said.

"Really, mom? *Really*? Thanks!"

Sarah stood still and heard a rattle and click of metal. She heard a squeak, and knew that they were opening her cell. Already cold, Sarah felt a rush of coldness beyond belief. Her skin tightened up and she felt her naked nipples harden. The stench grew larger, closer, and then it was on top of her, beside her, all around her. There was nothing else but the coldness and the stench.

She felt something colder than she had thought possible touch her wrist. It was a hand. It closed its small fingers and had her in its grasp. "Goodie!" said the boy. "Let's go play!"

She let herself be led. All she knew was the concrete under her feet and the stench. They walked and they walked. Their feet made almost no noise, and Sarah could hear herself breathing, and the slightest swish of her thighs, but nothing else. Her head was almost empty, there was only the thought: I deserve this. Finally, they stopped walking, and Sarah heard the same rattling as before. Keys, she thought. Then she heard another voice, a man's voice.

"Wha... what's going on here? What the *hell* is going on here?"

"We're gonna play soccer," said the boy.

"Soccer?" said the man. "What? Listen, boy, listen. You're Zack Ellis' boy, aren't you? You are! You know Stanley, my little Stan. He's in your class. Listen, he's got to be real scared right now. He's got to be worried about his dad. You can understand that, right? You can help me, right?"

Sarah heard the squeak of the door opening.

"That's a good boy!" said the man. "You must be scared too. Let's get out of here together, okay? And this woman... is she hurting you? Has she been...." His voice was replaced by a gurgling sound.

"Here," said the boy. Then something struck Sarah. It was warm. The warmth felt strange, in the midst of the total coldness. It felt like a miracle. The object bounced off Sarah and she heard it thump to the ground. In the same instant, she heard something else hit the ground.

"Pick it up," said the boy.

Sarah bent down and groped at the ground. Then she had it. At first she felt something warm and soft, but also somehow with a hardness to it, with a harness beneath the softness. She felt around and there were two depressions and also a protrusion. The depressions were very soft and the protrusion was too, but with a hardness at the base. It was a human head.

"Pick it up," said the boy, "and throw it up in the air and then we'll kick it. That's how you play soccer."

Chapter twenty four

Nick felt something coming. Something bad, worse than the sex zombies, worse than anything.

"Everybody needs to leave," he said.

"I tend to agree," said Lisa. "It's... I'm going to have nightmares for the rest of my life. Let's all go home. I'll call the police and tell them what happened here... or as much as I can explain anyway."

The thing was coming, fast. And at once, everybody else seemed to be moving in slow motion, like in a movie. Nick saw Hugh's mouth moving, but couldn't hear what he was saying. Then they were making their way toward the door one inch at a time, as Nick's terror mounted. It was like watching a movie where the killer creeps up behind the girl and no matter what you yell at the screen, the killer will kill.

Time resumed its normal pace just as the front door swung open. There was the evil thing, standing in the doorway, in the form of Officer Richaud, covered in blood. There was a bone, oddly clean and purely white, poking through his uniform at the shoulder. He stepped in.

"What seems to be the trouble here, folks?" he said.

"Hard to explain in a word," said Lisa. Nick realized that she didn't see what he saw, didn't see that Richaud wasn't Richaud, but a monster. "And you're hurt. The short story is that we're okay, the few of us who made it. So let's get you to a hospital."

The Richaud Monster grinned. "I'm afraid that's a lie. I'm afraid you're not okay. I'm afraid I'm gonna hafta put you all under arrest." The grin got wider, and his face seemed to stretch out to accommodate it. "Now, get those hands up in the air. Get 'em up real high like, I wanna see you touch the heavens above. Now put those hands up, or I'm afraid I'm gonna hafta eat 'em."

"What the fuck is this?" groaned Hugh.

"It's what you were born to do, little friend," said the Richaud Monster. His grin was now, impossibly, a foot wide.

"Leave," said Nick. "Leave now and maybe I won't kill you."

"Ooohh... we got ourselves a real wise guy, folks!" said the Richaud Monster. He reached out an arm. It kept reaching, further than an arm could reach, and kept reaching across the room until it rested its hand on top of Lisa's head. Then slowly he began twisting her neck, until there was a snap, and then kept twisting and twisting, until the head had made a full rotation, and then released her. Hugh's mom dropped to the ground, dead. Hugh dropped to the ground with her and put his arms around her.

Nick tore the sweatshirt from around his waist and charged, his dick still somehow erect, at the Richaud Monster, who gave him a look of curiosity and then amusement. Nick grabbed Richaud's hand and put it on his electric boner.

"Christ buddy," said Richaud, "that feels good! All tingly."

Nick's dick went soft in Richaud's cold hand. He suddenly felt weak and tired, the weight of everything that had happened sitting on him, like a collapsed building, a collapsed town, and he felt useless and doomed.

"The matter, kid? Get stage fright?" Richaud opened his mouth and laughed. Nick saw his fangs then, and caught a whiff of breath worth than any kind of imaginable death.

"Fuck you," said Nick.

"Maybe later," said Richaud, yawning now. "But if you don't put your goddamn hands up, all of you, I'm gonna rip this here pud off and chew it up and spit it out. You dig?"

Nick's mom's hands went up first, the Lucy's, then Mandy's, all in a state of shocked horror. "I'm going to fucking kill you," said Hugh in a choked voice, and then took his arms from around his mother and put his hands in the air. Nick looked into Richaud's eyes and saw endless darkness there. He raised his hands above his head.

"Now that wasn't so hard, was it?" said Richaud, letting go of his hold on Nick. "And I ain't talking about the kid's dick, either," he said, and erupted in laughter. Then claws grew bloodily from the tips of his fingers. He took one of them and drew it softly over Nick's armpit, where his shirt had torn and his flesh was exposed beneath his raised arms.

Nick had always been ticklish. His first instinct was to drop his arm and spin away. But something told him that if he did that, he would be dead. And he had to stay alive, to stop this thing, somehow. He clenched his teeth together and bore it out.

"Now," said Richaud. "Enough clowning around." He pulled his claw away from Nick's armpit and drew his hand into a fist. Then it was coming at Nick's face.

PART III

Chapter twenty five

What new Hell was this?

Mikhail opened his eyes and stared through the pain at the concrete ceiling. Why wasn't he dead? What cruel God was keeping him alive? A God with no concept of Justice, at least not a human concept of Justice. A God with no sense of mercy. That was obvious. That was third grade shit. Well, let God work away in His mysterious way. Fuck Him.

Mikhail lifted himself from the bed and looked at his cellmate. He was still clad in his firefighter getup, but he was missing a head. Mikhail felt the sadness wash over him, the sadness he felt whenever someone died, or whenever something awful happened to someone. It surprised him that he could still feel that. It occurred to him that the well of misery in the world was deep, and forever fresh, while the well of happiness was shallow and hard to come by.

He looked around the cell. He had been in there plenty, but mostly just to bring in some drunk who had done something idiotic. Looking around, he felt a sense of numbness wash over the sadness. It was just as well that he was here, locked away, unable to do anything. There was nothing he wanted to do. He supposed that if there had been some way to surely kill himself, he would take advantage of it. But he knew as well as anyone that the cell was clean of such suicidal instruments.

He sunk back on the bed and closed his eyes. He tortured himself with memories of Marie, of the first time he'd seen her. It had been at Bill's Beans just outside of Philly. She'd been sitting at a table, studying her books. He saw her right away and as he ordered his coffee in a polite and ordinary way, he was bursting with hot desire. He'd taken the coffee to a table and picked up a newspaper. There was his name, on the front page, surrounded by praise for solving the Jenson Murders. He studied her with his detective eye, over the edge of the paper.

Her body screamed out to him, but there was something else. It was the way in which she was completely absorbed in her study, biting her lip a bit, oblivious to anything else. He could have walked right over to her and stared blatantly and he didn't think she'd notice. She was writing furiously away in a notebook, as if her life depended on it. Mikhail saw the earnestness there, the earnestness that so rarely accompanied a beautiful body. Most of the women he had known, the beautiful ones, had always been playing some kind of a game. And Mikhail had always been playing some kind of a game too – a game, he had to admit, where he was most often the winner.

After all, it was kill or be killed, Mikhail knew that. He'd been earnest once too, with Beverly Masters. But that was way back in college, and he'd learned his lesson soon enough, when he found her sucking off his best friend, Evan Longley, whose family was rich. So Mikhail had made his notes, and changed his ways accordingly. The world was full of suckers. Beverly taught him that.

But this girl here, reading her book. There was something different about her. It was more of an instinct than anything. Mikhail had learned to trust his instincts. It was one of the things that set him apart from the suckers – that, and his shrewdness. And while usually it was his shrewdness that drove his evaluations of women, here now, in the coffee shop, it was his instincts. At once, he felt ashamed, unclean, impure, when he looked at her. At the same time, he supposed that she would be an easy one.

And, he reminded himself, it was probably all an illusion, a carefully studied trick. She was probably just like the rest, once it came to it.

Still, he didn't make his move that first time. Nor did his make his move the third time, or the fifth. The sixth time her saw her at Bill's Beans, he walked over to her and said, "Excuse me miss. I'm Mikhail Duvlosky, with Philadelphia Homicide, and I hate to bother you, but I think you can help me with a case." He showed her his badge.

She had been biting her lip, and it slid out away from her teeth. Her eyes grew very large and her face grew very serious. "Me? Help you? What… how?"

"May I sit down?"

"Please."

"Well," said Mikhail sitting down, "you see, I've been working very hard on this case, and I've just now gotten a very promising lead."

"What case?" she asked, her beautiful eyes growing larger and larger. Pure, shining eyes, deep and lovely.

"So far you're the main suspect."

Suddenly she closed her eyes in a squint. "Listen mister, I don't know what you're…"

"It's the case of my stolen heart," he said.

She laughed. It was a beautiful, honest laugh. It was a healthy laugh. "Does that line actually *work*?" she asked.

"You'd be surprised," he said smiling.

"I'm sure I would be… Mikhail. And I appreciate the effort, but I really have to get back to my studies. I like coming here because nobody bothers me, you see."

"Say no more," said Mikhail, smiling. "I'll let you go this time, but the evidence is starting to pile up." He stood. "Have a nice day, ma'am," he said and left.

That night, while he was fucking some broad he'd picked up at the Hot Spot, he couldn't get the coffee shop girl out of his head. He'd caught her name on the inside cover of one of her books. Marie. He was banging away and closed his eyes and Marie filled his head. He almost screamed her name, but he checked himself.

The next day, she wasn't there. He waited as long as he could, until the call came through about a new body. There was always a new body. It was relentless. The day after that, she wasn't there. Nor the day after that. He had scared her away. The girl who might have saved his soul.

On the fourth day, she was back, just the same as before. Mikhail walked into Bill's Bean, ordered his coffee, and pretended to read the paper. This time, *she* came over to *him*.

"Listen Officer Mikhail Duvlosky," she said. "I think you're probably an asshole, and the worst kind of asshole: one who can get away with it."

Mikhail laughed. "I'm caught," he said. "But don't you want to know what I think about *you*?"

"What do you think about me?"

"I think you bury your nose in a book because you're afraid of life."

"I bury my nose in a book because I want to *know* life," she said defiantly.

"Life is out *there*," said Mikhail. "On the streets. And it's behind closed doors, too, doors that eventually open up when I step though them, and get a firsthand look at what people are really like."

"I'll remember that," said Marie.

"Oh?"

"When they bring you in and put you on my operating table. I'll think, 'Silly girl, life doesn't depend on the internal bleeding brought on by a gunshot wound. The sun rises and sets in accordance to the eyes of an *asshole*.'"

Mikhail felt the laughter come, and it wouldn't stop. Then she was laughing too, they were both laughing up a storm and everybody in the coffee shop was looking at them.

"Listen," he said. "Let me take you out to dinner and try to plead my case. I almost went to law school, you know."

"I'm sure you can be very convincing," she said, smiling. "Alright. One dinner. If you still give me the screaming creeps after that, I'll call the police. Deal?"

"Deal," said Mikhail.

He opened his eyes and they were filled with tears. He heard footsteps drawing nearer. Then he saw the woman, Claire – or whatever kind of creature she had become – through the bars of the door. She was smiling.

"Officer Mikhail Duvlosky," she said. "Widower."

"You open that door," said Mikhail. "Open it. One of us is going to die."

"Is that what you want, you poor dear? To die?"

Mikhail didn't say anything. He stood up and walked over to the bars and spat in her face.

"That was... uncivilized," said Claire, wiping her face off.

"Open the door," said Mikhail. He was ready.

"I see sadly that you're eager to die, darling. I'm all too happy to grant your wish, after witnessing your bravery against those creatures. I would only ask: do you want your death to have meaning?"

"There's no meaning in death," said Mikhail.

"Come now, Mikhail, you know that's not true. There's a difference between the death of an ant and the death of a lion. That difference is the meaning."

"Maybe to the living, there's a difference," Mikhail said. "But the living die. And for the dead, there's no meaning. If you would grant me my wish, then grant me a swift death. I am sick of meaning."

Claire frowned. "What if I told you that you could trade your life for someone else's life? You die, and that other person, who otherwise would also die, gets to live. What would you say then?"

"I would like that," said Mikhail.

"So you see?" said Claire. "There's no need to go around spitting in everybody's face." She laughed. Then she withdrew a key from her pocket and unlocked the door. "Come now," she said. "Let's do this."

"Yes," said Mikhail. "Let's."

Chapter twenty six

Hugh was pacing his cell. He had already broken the bed and the toilet. There was nothing left to break. He had to keep stepping on the mattress, soggy with toilet water.

"FUCK YOU!" he screamed again. His voice was beginning to crack. He was thirsty and tired and weak, but he didn't give a shit. The fucker had killed his *mom*. Right before his eyes, while he was holding her in his arms. He had been fighting back the memories of her that came to him in jagged glimpses. He got a flash of being ten years old, it was Christmas, and he was unwrapping a present. It was the latest gaming system, now terribly outdated, but at the time it had been all that Hugh had ever wanted. He remembered his mother beaming with joy when she saw *his* joy, and his old man saying, "Well, I don't think the things are worth shit, so you got your mother to thank for this. God help us all." And he and his mother had laughed at that, in total delight.

"I'm going to fucking kill you," he promised the concrete wall for the twentieth time. In that wall, he seemed to see two yellow glowing orbs. "I'm going to rip out those fucking eyes," he said, "and make you *eat* them."

He slammed his fist against the wall. It hurt like all hell, but it made him feel a little better somehow. "Show your ugly fucking face," he said. "I'll rip it off and shove it in your asshole."

He didn't blame Nick. Nick had been on a roll with his electric boner. Hugh had thought that it would work, too, when he had seen that Richaud wasn't Richaud, but some kind of a monster. He would have done the same thing. Maybe if Nick hadn't shot off like that, his mother would still be alive. But it was no good blaming Nick, when it was the monster who had done it. Maybe he'd beat the shit out of Nick later, just as a release, but then he'd leave it at that. If Nick was still alive.

He paced the whole of his cell three more times and then he heard someone coming. About fucking time, he thought. He felt like he was ready to tear anything that was out there into a million pieces. The sound was getting closer, and his adrenaline was rising. It was unbearable. He felt ready to burst. Then a figure stepped out of the shadows.

"*You?!*" said Hugh. For a moment, he couldn't believe it. It was the scientist bitch. She was completely naked, with a heavy collar around her neck. He saw that the eye Marie had gotten was swollen shut, and where the other one was supposed to be… was only a black pit. "*You!*" he said. Now here was somebody who really did deserve some blame in the matter. He would be just as happy to tear her fucking face off.

"I know you," she said.

"I know you too, you dumb cunt."

"You're the boy who stopped me."

"Shut up!" said a kid, stepping into view. He was holding a chain that was attached to the scientist bitch's collar. "*Pets can't talk!*" he screamed.

"Who the fuck are *you*?" said Hugh.

"I'm your nightmare, potty-mouth," said the kid, grinning. He stuck a key in the locked door and swung it open.

"Good boy," said Hugh. "Now, the adults have something to talk about. Why don't you go play with some Legos or something?"

"Come on," said the kid. "Let's go."

"Fine with me," said Hugh. Then he was lunging through the air, with his hands outstretched. He got hold of the scientist bitch's neck just above the iron collar with both hands and started squeezing. It felt good. Her evil tongue stuck out of her head. Hugh tried not to look at her tits. He was afraid he would get a hard-on, and that would be fucked up.

Then a hand was around *his* neck. It yanked him away with amazing strength. He fell against the bars of the doors and saw the long yellow claws. It was the fucker himself! Good! Hugh spun around. He saw that the hand was attached to the boy, and not to Richaud, as he had been expecting and hoping.

So, there were two of them. But they were the same thing. Killing one would almost be as good as killing the other. Throw in the scientist bitch, and it would be enough to tide him over until he could find Richaud. Hugh jammed his finger into one of the kid's nostrils. It was a tight fit, but that's what he wanted. Then he pulled as hard as he could, and half of the kid's nose came off his face.

"Owie!" said the kid.

Then the claws were back around Hugh's throat. Then Hugh was up in the air. The little shit, about a foot and a half shorter than him, was lifting him up by the throat. Then he dropped. He heard the scientist bitch gasp.

"Mommy and daddy say I have to bring you alive," said the kid. "I don't want to, but I have to do what they say."

Hugh was on his ass. He swung out his leg, aiming for the kid's knees. He connected solidly with them, but it was no good. It felt like hitting the concrete wall.

"Stop," said the scientist bitch. "Please. He'll *kill* you!"

"*Pet's don't talk!*" screamed the kid. He yanked at the chain and the scientist bitch was on her knees. Hugh tried to get to his feet, but at once the boy-monster's hand was gripping his forehead. "Nobody listens to me cause I'm a kid," he said. "It's no fair." He squeezed Hugh's forehead, and it felt like he was going to crush the skull. Then he released it, and Hugh fell back on his ass.

"I'm gonna kill you," said Hugh. Then he was being dragged down the hall by his hair, slightly ahead of the scientist bitch, who was being dragged by the chain.

Chapter twenty seven

Mandy Perkins was huddled in the corner of her cell, crying. She wasn't drunk anymore. She had an incredible headache, and was scared just about to death. All she'd wanted was to go to the party and have some fun, maybe get a little tipsy, maybe find some boy who was also a little tipsy and make out with him. She didn't hold any illusions. She knew she was too fat for the popular boys. But the popular boys were dicks, and she didn't want them anyhow. James Rubin, on the other hand… he was smart, funny in his own way, and even kinda cute. And Mandy was just about to put the move on him, when suddenly one of those *things* jumped between them, and tore away his pants. At first, Mandy thought he was being raped by some insane scientist. And he had been raped, in a sense. His poor weiner was torn from his body as he watched through his oversized glasses.

Mandy had looked around her, had seen a mass of murderous bodies blocking her way out the door, and had wiggled under the couch. She watched for half a minute, and when a human organ plopped on the floor, maybe a liver, inches from her face, she had closed her eyes and covered her ears. A lifetime later, she had dared another peek, and had seen Nick Sherman taking them all out with his electric boner. Nick had seemed depressed to her when she had talked to him earlier, and all at once she understood why. It was because he was carrying around that crazy boner, and didn't know what to do with it. Mandy could sympathize. She knew what it was like to be different, to carry a burden around.

Still terrified and in sort of a state of shock, but seeing that the danger had apparently passed, she emerged from under the couch. That's when this new monster had made its appearance. So many monsters. And she had always thought that the kids who ragged on her for being fat were the monsters. She had watched countless horror movies, zombie movies where the message was that the true monsters were the human beings. And she'd always loved that. It made sense to her. But now, after tonight, she had suddenly changed her mind. *Fuck* all of that. *Monsters* were the real monsters.

There was no denying it: people could be pretty shitty. But at least they didn't go around ripping your genitalia off willy-nilly, or snapping your neck like a twig. Well, she supposed, some of them did. But that's not what all of those movies had been getting at. Those movies had been getting at the fact that people were mean and self-interested. And that was true enough. But there was something you could do about that. Yes, you lived in *their* world, you were born into it, but there were little sanctuaries, ways to live beyond it. You could still be happy in their world, you just had to stay away from the nastiest of the bunch. There were, after all, plenty of *good* people out there, too. You just had to find them, and stick with them, and if you came against those others... well, you could survive.

But the *real* monsters, the ones who tore you apart and had glowing yellow eyes... what could you do about them? She tried to huddle further into her corner, but she was far as she could go. She couldn't make herself any smaller. She was what she was.

Then he was there, at the door to the cell. The Richaud Monster. She remembered when he hadn't been the Richaud Monster. She remembered back to Junior High, when she had tried out for the basketball team. Of course, she hadn't made it. Richaud was the coach. He had come up to her after try-outs.

THE ELECTRIC BONER

"Mandy," he said, "you showed a lot of heart out there. Don't think I didn't see that. Heck, you showed more heart than the lot of 'em. Maybe another coach would put you on the team. And maybe I'd get fired for telling you what I'm gonna tell you, but I'm gonna tell it to you anyway. Heart is important, and it's the thing that sets the superstars apart from the rest of us. But it's not the *only* thing. Look, basketball is a *physical* game. You need a good body to play it, you need to be fast. Do you see what I'm getting at?"

"Yes," said Mandy. She did. And she always remembered that conversation. She supposed that she could be angry about it. She supposed that she could have had Richaud fired for it. But the fact was, she almost loved him for it. It seemed like all of her life, people had either been tiptoeing around the fact that she was fat, or else being cruel about it. This was the first time that she had ever heard somebody tell it the way that she had always felt it: that she was *good*, she just didn't have a particularly good *body*. It was the truth, and it was good to hear the truth. She didn't have a good body because she was good, and she wasn't bad because she didn't have a good body. That conversation helped her finally realize that. And in realizing that her entire existence didn't hinge on how people looked at her body, she felt a freedom. She hadn't wanted to play basketball, anyway. The "heart" that Richaud had seen had only been her trying to prove something to herself, or the world. She had been trying to prove the wrong thing, and she knew it now. More importantly, she knew that when she found the right thing to prove, she had the ability within her to do it.

"Don't be frightened, dear," said Richaud now, smiling. "You come with me now." He unlocked the door and swung it open.

"Where are we going?" asked Mandy.

"We're going to see the measure of your heart," he said.

Chapter twenty eight

Nick awoke and he thought through the fogginess that something was missing. He reached down reflexively and felt that his cock was soft. He *always* woke up with a boner. Something was wrong.

He opened his eyes and there was his mother's face. "You're awake," she said softly.

"He's awake?!" someone said. Was that...? Was it possible? Lucy? Here?

Then it came flooding back to him, the entire night – at first a glorious night, almost unbelievable. And then, the horror. Then, for a brief moment, a glory more glorious than anything he had ever known. And then, failure. He had gotten Hugh's mom killed. He leaned his head over the edge of the bed and vomited.

He sat up and looked around. "Where's Mandy?" he said. "Where... where's Hugh?" He felt weak. He laid his head back on the pillow, which was the shittiest pillow he'd ever felt, and closed his eyes again.

"I... don't know," said Fran. "We all came here together, and then they took us here and took them somewhere else."

"Are you okay Nick?" asked Lucy.

But Nick hardly heard her. Hugh. No. Please let Hugh be okay. He was starting to drift off again. It all came vividly to him, as if it were happening, the first time he met Hugh. He was at Janey's Dinner, he was in the fourth grade, sitting at the bar, waiting for his mother who was going to the bathroom. She had just told him the good news, that they were rich, over a Saturday brunch. He'd gotten a BLT. He didn't like breakfast, but he liked to eat a little later, once he'd woken up and gathered some energy finally and then had started to burn some of it off. Then

THE ELECTRIC BONER

food was good, and bacon best of all. And golden French fries, nice and crispy, with a nice smear of ketchup.

Going out to eat was such a rare treat for the two of them, ever since The Asshole had left. There was never enough money to go out. There was never enough money to do anything. Nick had learned the importance of money very early on. That's how you learn how important money is: by not having any. But this day, there had been enough money to go out, and once they were finished with their meal, Fran told him that they now had enough money to go out whenever they wanted, for the rest of their lives. Nick sat there, stuffed and happy. Fran was crying. Nick had seen her cry before, but never like that. Never when she was smiling like that.

Then she'd gone to the bathroom and all of a sudden he'd heard a voice next to him.

"You're Nick, right?"

He turned around and there was this kid. He'd never seen him before.

"You go to Dickens' School, right? I'm Hugh. I go to Gilly Pond."

"Hi," said Nick. He didn't know what else to say. He wasn't used to talking to other kids.

"Hi yourself. I think our parents know each other. I think everybody in this little rinky dink town knows each other."

"I don't," said Nick. "I don't know everybody."

"Don't worry about it. You're not missing much. Bunch of jerk-offs. You like comics?"

"Yeah."

"Good. Never trust a man who doesn't like comics. That's some free advice for you right there."

Nick smiled. "You check out that new series, Glasshook?"

"Are you nuts? That's the best one. Hey. What you doing right now?"

"I'm out with my mom. Aren't you?"

"Naw. They dropped me off in town. But everybody's being a wuss. Nobody wants to *do* anything."

"I… I can't. I've got to go home with my mom."

"C'mon man. Ditch her. What the hell are the two of you going to do all day anyway?"

Fran returned from the bathroom. "Oh," she said. "Hugh, isn't it?"

"The one and only, ma'am," said Hugh, smiling. "I was just talking to Nick here, and he was dying to go check out the comic book store, but I told him he should just probably just spend the day with his mom."

Fran smiled. "Oh? Well, I don't see any reason why he should do *that*. In fact, here's a twenty. Go buy some comics. Have fun."

Nick couldn't believe it. "Wow, Nick," said Hugh, grinning. "You got one cool mom."

"*Have*," said Fran.

"Huh?"

"'You *have* one cool mom." Fran laughed.

It was one of the best days Nick could remember. They had spent most of the twenty at the comic book store, and the rest at the candy store down the street. They had walked out of town then, along the railroad tracks, jacked-up on sugar and good stories and each other.

"Hugh," said Nick, stirring again. "Where's Hugh?"

"I don't know, honey," said Fran. "How are *you*?"

Nick sat up and looked around again. "Lucy," he said. "Mom. Where's Mandy? Where's Hugh? Are they okay?"

"I don't know," said Fran. "I don't know."

Chapter twenty nine

They turned the corner and Mikhail nearly ran into him. A sudden smile, a spot of light in the total darkness, spread across his face. "Richaud!" he cried. "Thank Christ.

THE ELECTRIC BONER

You're okay! Where have you…"

"Finding enlightenment, Lt," said Richaud. He closed one eye in a wink and when it opened again, it was glowing yellow.

"Shit," said Mikhail. "You too, huh? It figures."

"Don't be so glum, Lt," said Richaud, grinning. "We got something real *fun* planned for you."

Then they each had him by an arm, Claire and Richaud, and they led him down the hall. They were going to the reception area, he knew. He wondered what kind of reception was awaiting him. When they got there, he saw.

There were two kids tied to chairs with rope, and gagged. One of them he recognized as the MacMillan boy, the one who had been there when…. The other one was a girl, about MacMillian's age, and about twice his size. Both of their faces were red, soaked with tears. Then he saw another boy, about ten years old, step around the corner. He knew right away, his instincts told him, that it was one of *them*. The boy was holding a chain in his hand and gave it a tug and then he saw *her*. Sarah Johnston. She was naked, and somebody had taken her other eye.

Seeing Johnston and the MacMillan boy suddenly made him replay the whole scene in his head, in a flash. He saw himself sticking the knife in the back of his wife's neck. He saw himself tearing through her neck, her beautiful soft neck, and severing the head. He saw himself jamming the knife through the severed head.

"What is this?" he said. "I thought…"

"What did you think, darling?" asked Claire. "Did you think you deserved a gentle death? And why is that? Officer Richaud, do you think that your Lieutenant deserves a gentle death?"

"I got to say," said Richaud, "as a guy he wasn't that bad. I got to say that, for the record. Bit of an arrogant prick, you ask me, which you are, but in the end, not a bad guy at all."

"*Kill* him!" screamed the boy.

"Shush now, little one," said Claire. "Officer Richaud: are you saying that he deserves to be *spared?*"

"Well, I guess I am, Mama," said Richaud. "I guess that's just exactly what I'm saying. Only one thing though, Lt. What's my first name?"

Suddenly it occurred to Mikhail that he had *no idea* what Richaud's first name was. But that wasn't fair. He knew Richaud. He knew that he liked to go hunting, that he rooted for the Red Sox and the Patriots, that he had a brother somewhere in Alabama. It was no fair. He was simply *Richaud*. That's what everyone called him.

"If you're going to kill me," said Mikhail, "then kill me."

Richaud laughed. "Don't even know my goddamn name? It's Richard, by the way."

Mikhail couldn't help himself. "Richard Richaud?"

Suddenly Richaud's face grew dark. Literally. It became pure black, but for the two yellow eyes peering through it. "Is that funny?" he asked.

"A little," Mikhail admitted.

"Let's do this," said Richaud, and took a step back into a corner.

"Officer Duvlosky," said Claire. "You have before you two little teenage lives. It's your job to decide which one lives and which one dies."

"No," said Mikhail.

"Well then both of them die. Tommy? Kill them both."

The boy drew his claws and lifted his hand.

"*Wait*," said Mikhail.

"Heavens," said Claire. "Tommy, hold your horses. You've changed your mind, Mikhail? We knew you would. Of course, we wouldn't make you decide blind, pardon the expression Sarah dear. Tommy, be a dear and un-gag them."

The boy pulled the gag first from the boy, then the girl.

"Fuck you," spat out the MacMillan boy. "You fucking pussies. Give me Richaud. Untie me, and give me the fucker who killed my mom." Mikhail looked at him. It was like looking in a mirror. There was only one thing left in the boy, a burning, desperate hatred. Other than that, it was all empty. Soon, when the boy realized that there was no vengeance to be had, nothing that he could do to bring back his mother, there would be nothing. There would just be the emptiness, and then he would be just like Mikhail.

"You are monsters," said the girl, after gasping for air. "You are cancer. You want us to think that the entire world is cancer, but it's not. Do what you're going to do. It doesn't mean anything. We're the ones who get to make the meaning."

And suddenly, Mikhail could see Marie there, somehow, in the girl.

"If I do this, you'll kill me, too?" asked Mikhail

"That's what I said," said Claire.

"Hugh," said Mikhail, recalling the boy's name. "There's nothing I can say that will make this right, so I won't say anything at all. If there's an afterlife, we can talk it over there, and maybe we won't have to. Maybe you'll already understand."

"Can I *do* it already, Mama?" whined the boy.

"Fuck you," said Hugh. "Fuck all of you. You too, Duvlosky, you fucking pussy."

"Do it," said Claire.

The boy drew a single claw excruciatingly slowly across the girl's neck. She screamed at first, and then the screams turned to the wet gurgling sound of blood filling her throat.

"Was that fun for you, baby?" Claire asked the boy, once the girl was dead.

"*Yes,* Mama, *yes,*" said the boy.

"Now me," said Mikhail.

Claire laughed. "Oh no," she said.

"Yeah," said Richaud, stepping out of his corner.

"The fun's just getting started, Lt."

Chapter thirty

Daniel Ricksclyde was just beginning to become irritated by the urine soaking his trousers. He considered taking them off, but the thought of exposing himself called to mind at once the terror. He was wet. He was wet with tears, wet with sweat, and worst of all, wet with urine. It was so *undignified.* He fluctuated between feeling uncomfortable and feeling terrified. The one would replace the other, in a smooth cycle. It was as though he weren't in control of his mind. He, who had shaped the minds of so many youths.

He had come out of the Playhouse after a disappointing production of *Taming of the Shrew* and had borne witness to the slaughter up the hill a ways, in front of the bar there, where the degenerates liked to waste their time and destroy their minds. He didn't understand it. Then, before he could, the slaughter was upon him. It was one woman, Claire Peterson, doing the slaughtering. He knew her. He knew all of the parents in town, but he had never had her child in a class, on account of the fact that he taught *Advanced* Placement Literature, and the Peterson boy had been anything but advanced.

When Jane Flapperson's eyeball landed at his feet, that's when he soiled himself. "What is the meaning of this?!" he had shouted.

"You," Claire had said. "I know you. You're the one who teaches the books, the Great Books."

"That is correct, Mrs. Peterson," Daniel had said. "Now, if you will kindly…"

He hadn't finished his sentence. He hated incomplete sentences – unless, of course, they were done by a Master, with great effect. Now, sitting in the damp cell, he felt as though everything had become an incomplete sentence.

When he had first awoken, he had found himself in this insufferable jail cell, next to Maxwell Highfield. They were on the floor, and Maxwell was sitting up, rubbing his head. "Daniel," he'd said. "Do you have any notion as to *what* exactly is occurring?"

"Not the slightest," Daniel replied, noticing with dismay that his trousers were soaked.

Then there was a police officer at the cell door. "Thank goodness!" Daniel had said. "Law and order!" The officer opened the door, walked in, and took a bite out of Maxwell's face, with long, nasty yellow fangs. Maxwell screamed. The officer chewed, swallowed, and took another bite. He ate Maxwell. He ate Maxwell whole, all the while looking directly into Daniel's eyes with his own eyes, which flashed pure yellow.

When the officer was finished, he stood up, burped, and left the cell, closing the door behind him. Daniel was drenched in bodily fluids. "Wait..." he said meekly. "Please."

"Don't worry, bub," the officer said. "We'll be back for you."

Now, just as Daniel had made up his mind to remove his trousers and cover himself with the blanket from the bed – though on second thought, who knew what diseases were lying in wait in *that* thing – he looked up and saw that the officer had indeed come back for him.

"Up and at 'em, Professor," he said.

"Please," said Daniel, "I do not know who you think that I am, but I assure you that I am *not* a professor." He laughed nervously. "Perhaps, after all, this is only a misunderstanding, yes?"

"You're Ricksclyde, yeah?"

"Why, yes, I am. But..."

"Also known as Dick's Bride," said the officer, guffawing.

"Well I *never*..." began Daniel, but it ended up being

just another incomplete sentence.

"Up and at 'em. I just about digested your friend there, and I'm starting to get hungry again. You don't get that scrawny ass of yours *moving* right now, I might just fix it so it'll never move again."

"Please," whispered Daniel.

"Please what, Professor Dick's Bride? Please and thank you to not make me tell you again. *Move it.*"

Daniel felt a new rush of warmth run down his leg. It was actually comforting, at first, for the briefest of moments. He actually didn't want it to ever stop. But it stopped, and he felt it cool, and he smelt the stench rise up to his nostrils and mingle with the smell of dead meat and whatever foul odor was emanating from the officer. It smelled like a dead *soul*.

"May I ask where we are going?" asked Daniel, lurching unsteadily forward to the door.

"You may shut the fuck up is what you may do," said the officer. "There's gonna be plenty of time for chatting, don't worry about that. I mean, unless you don't just be a good old man and do what you're told. Don't do that, there won't be time for anything."

Daniel's mouth opened and closed. He followed the officer down the dark hallway. He wondered what time it was. He should be at home, with a good book and maybe a glass of wine. Suddenly, he realized with horror that he hadn't taken his heart medication for the night.

"Officer, sir," he said, "I hate to be a nuisance, but you have to understand. I need to take my medication. It is at my house." Daniel could feel his heart beating in his head. It was getting faster and pumping harder. It was going to explode. He was sure of it.

The officer turned and before Daniel could even see it, a hand was at his throat. "I *told* you to zip it." Daniel forgot about his heart troubles, forgot even about his pissy pants, and focused on his breathing troubles. Then the officer released his grip and as Daniel was gasping for air, he observed five long yellow grisly claws grow from the officer's hand. The claws reached for Daniel's face, right under his nose. He felt them go in, four through the upper lip and one through the lower lip. They each came out on the opposite side. Daniel tried to scream, but the scream was trapped in his mouth, which was held closed by the piercing claws.

Then the officer began dragging him along down the hall like that, with his claws embedded in Daniel's lips. Daniel pissed himself again.

Chapter thirty one

Lucy watched as Nick's mom wiped the sweat off his forehead. He was sick. It hadn't been a good night, no it hadn't been a good night at all. There were parts of it that were great, but on the whole, it was downright lousy. One part in particular stood out in her mind. Whenever she thought of it, she felt her face grow hot, and she felt a hotness somewhere else. It was Nick's part, and when she thought of it, she thought of doing something other than kissing him, something more than that, and she felt like she was going to explode.

"Is... is he going to be okay?" she asked Fran.

"He's going to be just fine," Fran said, but Lucy could tell that was holding back tears. "He's a strong boy." She wiped his forehead again with her sleeve. "Do you know what he said to me, when he was five years old? When I told him that his father was gone? He said, 'It's okay, mom. I'll take care of you.' Can you believe that? I couldn't." Then she *did* break into tears. "And he *has*," she said. "He *has*, without knowing it even. He's a *strong* boy, stronger than he thinks."

"I think you're right," said Lucy, remembering the way he had faced the things by himself, and destroyed them.

Fran wiped her face and turned to Lucy. "Do you think so, Lucy?"

Suddenly Lucy realized that Fran was the one who needed comforting the most, out of all of them. "You're damn right I do," she said. "I think he's so strong, that when he wakes up, he's going to go over there and bend those bar apart and then we can all go home."

Fran smiled. "I can see why he likes you," she said.

"He... said that?"

"He doesn't have to," said Fran. "I saw the way he looked at you earlier tonight."

Lucy knew it was true. She'd known it had been true all along. People were funny. They could hold a truth deep in their hearts, they could read the truth in the faces of other people, but hardly anybody ever *said* the truth, or *acted* like the truth was true. It was like walking around with a sock puppet on your hand, and you could only speak through that.

Nick bolted upright in the bed. "Lucy!" he screamed.

"I'm right here," she said.

He looked at her. "Lucy and mom," he said. "Where's Hugh?"

"I don't know, honey," said Fran.

"How about Mandy? Did she make it?"

Lucy thought he was acting more like himself now, like there was more of a sense of coherence about him, that his confusion was passing.

"I don't know, honey," said Fran.

"We're in jail," said Nick. "That fucker Richaud put us here."

"That's right," said Fran. "Are you feeling alright?"

"I *was*," said Nick. He looked at Lucy again. "Until you told her that I *liked* her. Thanks mom, you're the *best*."

Then Lucy felt like everything was somehow going to be okay. Fran started laughing. She laughed so hard that she started crying. Lucy couldn't help it, she started laughing too. Nick joined in.

"I guess you guys are wondering what the hell all of that was back there," said Nick.

"All of what?" said Lucy. "Do you mean the scientist things that were going around tearing everybody apart, or do you mean your electric boner?"

"Well," said Nick, "they're related, I think. See, me and Hugh…"

"Hugh and *I*," corrected Fran.

"Hugh and *I* came across this shed with some kind of green toxic… shit in it. We ran into that scientist, that Huskfield guy there. It was his experiment. That's what caused all of this. That Johnston lady… we led her right to it. That's what she used on Mrs. Duvlosky, that green toxic shit. It turns people into sex-zombies."

"Why didn't you tell me this before?" asked Fran.

"I…"

"Nevermind, honey," said Fran. "It's okay."

"And the electric boner?" asked Lucy. That's what she was most curious about, really.

"Well, um, see, I somehow got some of the green toxic shit, um, in my pants…"

"Somehow?" asked Fran. Nick just opened his mouth and no words came out. "It's okay, honey," she said.

"And then I just had it. This electric boner. But I guess it worked out. It saved us. It saved us… but it didn't save Hugh's mom. It didn't stop Richaud. I… did you see those *eyes*? And the way his arm just kept reaching and reaching?"

"So Richaud's not one of the sex zombies," said Lucy. "What is he?"

"I don't know," said Nick.

"And how do we stop him?"

"I don't know," said Nick.

"It's okay, Nick," said Lucy, smiling. "I like you too."

She watched Nick's face turn red. Then she heard a dragging sound come down the hall. Through the bars of the cell, Lucy could see a naked woman standing there, with an iron collar around her neck, one eye a black hollow nothingness, and the other one swollen shut.

"It's *her*," said Nick. "Johnston. Listen," he said to the woman, "you have to tell us what's going on here."

"XB15," said the woman.

"*What?*" said Nick.

"*Shut up!!*" screamed a new voice, and Lucy saw a boy appear by the woman's side. The boy punched her in the ribs. His eyes were just the same as Richaud's had been. Lucy shuddered. Two of them.

The boy unlocked the door, and swung it open. He threw something in.

"Here," said the boy. "Now you can play soccer with your friend." Then he walked away, and with a yank at the chain he was holding, the woman followed.

Lucy didn't even need to look at it to know what it was. She had seen several of them flying through the air that night. She didn't need to look, but she did anyway. It was Mandy's head.

Chapter thirty two

The yellow-eyed bitch shoved Hugh and Duvlosky into the cell, slammed the door, and locked it.

"I trust you'll be fast friends, the next time I see you," she said, smiling.

"Fuck you," said Hugh. "I'm gonna poke those goddamn yellow eyes out the next time I see *you*."

She walked away, laughing.

Hugh turned to Duvlosky. His face was pale, he looked sick. "Thanks a lot," said Hugh. "You were great back there. Laying on that shit about Heaven or whatever, getting ready to send me on my way."

Duvlosky dropped down into a corner, right into a

puddle of the toilet water that Hugh had unleashed some time before. He put his hands over his face. "I'm sorry," he said through the hands.

"Christ, Duvlosky, I guess I was wrong about you. I thought you were a *man*. Turns out you're just another goddamn pussy." Hugh briefly considered throttling him, beating the shit out of him to pay him back, and to have an outlet for his anger. But Duvlosky was too pathetic.

"She said she would kill me," Duvlosky said. "To put an end to it."

In a sense, Hugh could understand that. He didn't feel very enthusiastic about life just at the moment. But in another sense, a bigger one, *fuck that*. "Shit Duvlosky. Duvy. No hard feelings, okay? Just pull yourself together."

Not knowing what else to do, Hugh walked over and gave him a pat on the shoulder. He felt ridiculous.

Duvlosky took his hands away from his face and looked at Hugh. His eyes were red. For a painfully awkward moment, they just stared into each other's eyes. "Hugh, isn't it? Hugh MacMillan."

"That's right," said Hugh, "now you've got it."

They stared at each other some more. "Listen," said Hugh. "I'm sorry about Marie. I am. She was good. She was really good. She was the best."

"They got your mom," said Duvlosky.

Hugh felt the tears waiting behind his eyes. He held them back. "Yeah," he said at last.

"I'm going to get you out of here, Hugh," said Duvlosky. "I promise."

Hugh should have laughed. Any other time in his life, he would have laughed. Get out of there? How did the genius plan on doing *that*? But he felt something, some kind of vibe coming from Duvlosky, with his pale face and red eyes. Hugh knew he meant it. He even almost believed it. "Alright," he said.

"The next time they open that door," said Duvlosky, "and they will, I'm going to go right for them, whoever it is. You run."

"What about my friends? They're here too. Or I hope to Christ they are. I hope they're not…"

"You just run," said Duvlosky. "Get out of here and find some help. They'll believe you. They have to, after the massacre that happened downtown."

"And at Jake's house," said Hugh.

"Jake's house?"

"Jake Canter. His parents were out of town, he threw a party. *They* found it."

"Did… did many people die?"

"Everybody died, Duvlosky."

"How… how did you stop them?"

"The electric boner," said Hugh.

"Your friend… Nick. Is that what you mean?"

"That's what I mean."

"And these others… it was Richaud, wasn't it, that got you? The electric boner didn't work on him?"

The scene flashed again through Hugh's mind. Nick charging, him holding on to his mom, that arm reaching and reaching endlessly… "No," said Hugh, "it didn't work."

"And I watched her head get cut off… Claire Peterson… that didn't work either."

"What *are* these fucking things?"

"I don't know," said Duvlosky. "But I've got an idea it has something to do with that black liquid that Richaud found at Huskfield's house. At the time, it was only background noise, I didn't think anything of it."

They were silent for a moment, processing it all.

"When they come again," said Duvlosky, "I'm going to charge. You just run. Find help. Tell them what you know. *Then* you come back for your friends."

"What about you?" asked Hugh. He already knew the answer, but he had to ask. A part of him didn't want to go through with the plan. Even after Duvlosky had sold him out, he didn't want to see the guy die. Duvlosky had had it rough. And he was a good guy. He'd just been pushed past his limit.

"I'll be fine," said Duvlosky. "Maybe I'll get lucky and find their weakness."

"Yeah," said Hugh. "Maybe."

"I'm sorry about your mom. She raised a good kid. She must have been good."

"Marie was magic," said Hugh.

They looked at each other for another moment. "Shit," said Hugh, breaking the moment. "I wish I hadn't soaked the goddamn bed with that shitty water. I'm tired."

"Me too," said Duvlosky. "I've never been so tired in my life. But we have to stay awake, alert. It could happen at any time. We have to be ready."

Hugh nodded, but he felt his eyelids dropping down, heavy. He tried to snap them open, but they seemed to take forever in their opening. Then they slowly closed again and he sat down next to Duvlosky.

When he awoke, his head was on Duvlosky's shoulder. "Get ready," whispered Duvlosky. The adrenaline woke Hugh up in an instant.

"You sure about this?" said Hugh. Duvlosky nodded. "You're a good guy. I'm sorry I called you a pussy." He looked up and saw the boy standing there, with the scientist bitch at his side. Well, better the boy than one of the other ones, though Hugh knew it didn't make much of a difference.

"You," said the boy, pointing at Duvlosky. "Mommy wants *you*." He unlocked the door and swung it open.

Chapter thirty three

Daniel Ricksclyde must have passed out from the pain. When he came to himself, he was on the cold floor, on his back, looking up at four yellow orbs burning in the darkness.

"Papa," said a woman, "I told you not to hurt him."

"I'm sorry Mama," replied a man. Daniel recognized the voice. He recognized both of them. The woman was Claire Peterson and the man was the Neanderthal who had dragged him down the hall by his lips. "I kept telling him to keep his mouth shut, but he wouldn't listen." Daniel felt a hard shoe kick him in the ribs. "Hey, you, Dick's Bride. Can you talk?"

Daniel tried to talk, but he couldn't. His lips were on fire. When he opened his mouth, all that came out was a trickle of warmth down his chin followed by a hideous string of garbled sounds. More wetness, more failure to communicate.

"Come on now buddy," said the brute, "you're okay, ain't ya?" A cold hand gripped Daniel's shoulder and jerked him to his feet. He started to collapse again, but the hand held him up.

"Mr. Ricksclyde," said Claire. "I'm truly sorry about this. It was never my intention to harm you."

"She's right, Dick's Bride, that was my bad. Sorry about that."

"No more harm will come of you," said Claire, "I promise."

"That's right," said the brute. "No more harm, Mama. But what if he doesn't pass the test?"

"Oh, if he doesn't pass the test, then a lot of harm will come of him, Papa," said Claire.

"Lots and lots of harm then, Mama."

"But there's no reason on Earth why such a learned man wouldn't be able to pass such a simple test. Isn't that right, Papa?"

"That's just exactly right, Mama. Old Ricksclyde'll ace it for sure. He's one smart cookie."

"Why then let's proceed. Mr. Ricksclyde, if you would be so kind as to follow me?"

Daniel was only half-conscious, but he was able to

comprehend that he was about to undertake some sort of trial. He hadn't the faintest idea about what kind of a test it would be, or why he had to take it, but he understood now that there was nothing he could do about it. Dimly, from somewhere, he wondered: is this what some of the children in his classes felt like? As if they were being thrust unwittingly into some kind of a forced test that they didn't ask for, and that could have dire results? The thought surprised him. It seemed to come from nowhere, certainly not from the foundation upon which he had erected his life.

What if he had been wrong? What if he had been wrong from the start? What if everything about the educational system was wrong? What if everything about human society was wrong? What if the ideals he had constructed his life around had been false, illusionary? What if the whole thing was a matter of convenience for the few at the cost of ruined lives for the rest? Was that possible? It was. He didn't think it was true, but it was alarming enough to realize the possibility that it might be true.

After all, that was what some of the books said. That's what a lot of the books that he taught said. But it was one thing to have it typed out neatly in an outline in front of you, and quite a different thing to feel it in your gut.

Daniel vomited.

"See Mama? I told you he was difficult."

"Hush now, Papa. Mr. Ricksclyde, if you would kindly follow me."

Daniel weakly wiped the vomit from his mouth. Suddenly, all of his wetness and incomplete sentences didn't seem to matter. It was strange, he reflected, as he struggled to take a step into the darkness, with the brute's hand urging him on. Everything that you have spent your entire life thinking is important can, in an instant, seem to you the most trivial, petty thing. He wanted another chance. He wanted another chance at life.

He made his way down the dark hallway, dragging his shoulder against the wall for support. Occasionally, the hand would give him a shove, urging him on, and occasionally, he would see Claire's yellow eyes turn toward him to check his progress. At length, he could see a dim light ahead of him, and then he could make out the silhouette of Claire's body.

The hand shoved him into the light. He could see into a cell now. Three people were in there. Two of them were his students, Nick Sherman and Lucy Littleton. Nick's mother was also there.

"Ricksclyde!" shouted Nick.

"Mr. Ricksclyde!" screamed Lucy.

"Daniel," said Fran.

He looked at them. It touched his heart to realize that they were all somehow glad to see him, and at the same time, concerned for him. He had given a hard time to Nick, on many occasions. But it was only because Nick was such a smart boy, and could do so much if only he applied himself. Looking at them, Daniel's faith in his life was restored. He had done the right thing with his life. If he could change the structure of the world, and make life fair, then he would do it in an instant. But short of that, he could only play his small part. It was worthwhile to read the classics. It exposed the kids to the problems of the world, it helped them see things they might not otherwise see, helped them think in broader terms than they might otherwise think. Forcing them to write papers and holding them accountable for their work taught them to think in an organized way, and to learn responsibility. Daniel had done the best he could.

"Now, Daniel Ricksclyde," said Claire, "it is time for your test." Daniel looked at her. Her face was cruel. "Pass and you go free, and I set these three free. Fail, and you die."

Daniel calmed his heart. The truth is somewhere in

between, he thought. You did good, but maybe you could have done a little better. Maybe you made a little too much of things that weren't important, and didn't give enough attention to the things that were. But you had the basic idea. That will have to do.

"All that you have to do," said Claire, "is wrap your right arm behind your head and bring your index finger around over your face on the left side to touch your nose. That's all you have to do, but you have to do it while standing only on your left foot."

Daniel looked at Nick. "Mr. Ricksclyde," said Nick.

Daniel made a groaning sound. He couldn't get the words out. "Dan," he was trying to say. "Call me Dan."

"I'm sorry I was such a pain in the ass," said Nick. "And thanks. Thanks for trying."

Daniel nodded. Tears were welling up.

"Enough!" shouted the brute. "Do what the lady asked you to do!"

Daniel was able to reach his arm around the back of his neck. But as soon as he lifted his right foot, he collapsed on the ground. Claire bent over him. "Shame," she said. "I thought such a learned man would be able to pass such a simple test with flying colors." Then the long claw was out.

He didn't want to close his eyes. He heard the kids screaming, crying. He kept his eyes open. He watched as Claire made a cut down his torso. He watched her reach in and pull out his intestines. That was all.

Chapter thirty four

Mikhail rose slowly to his feet. It wasn't all an act. His strength had been drained and drained again, a thousand times that terrible day. But soon, at last, it would all be over. He turned his head and through half-closed eyes gave one last look at Hugh. He didn't want Hugh to die. That was all that he cared about. Mikhail knew that escape would be next to impossible, but it was better than letting Hugh sit around the cell, waiting in terror for what was coming.

"Come *on*," whined the boy-creature standing in the opened doorway. Sarah Johnston was standing behind him, naked and chained to a collar. Mikhail took a step toward them and then fell to his knees. That part *was* an act. The boy began to laugh, and then Mikhail was up and charging with his shoulder, just like he was back in high school, on the football team. The boy let out a shriek and fell down with Mikhail on top of him.

"GO!" screamed Mikhail.

"Shit," said Hugh, "shit." For a moment, it looked like he wasn't going to run. Then he ran. He made it out of the cell and Mikhail felt his heart lighten. There was hope. There was a chance. He felt the boy's hand close around his neck. Yes, he thought, yes.

The boy rose to his feet, lifting Mikhail by the throat. The world began to grow dimmer. He saw Hugh's silhouette, getting smaller and darker as he ran down the hallway. Then it suddenly dropped, and he saw that the boy had stretched out his free arm a distance of ten yards, and was dragging Hugh back by the ankle. No!

"I'm going to *eat* you!" screamed the boy. "I don't *care* what Mama says!"

Mikhail was struggling for air. It didn't seem to matter what the mind wanted, what the soul wanted – the body wanted to live. Then suddenly the boy released Mikhail and he dropped to the ground. He looked up and saw the boy grabbing with both hands at a thick chain that was pulled tight against his throat.

"Go," said a voice. It was Sarah Johnston's voice. "Both of you, go. I don't ask forgiveness, only that you go and try to live."

Mikhail ran. He made it to Hugh and lifted him to his

feet. They ran together down the dark hallway. "This way," gasped Mikhail as they came to an intersection. The back door was their best shot.

Just before they turned the corner, Mikhail looked behind him. He saw the boy standing in a faint light, holding Johnston's disembodied head by the hair, inches from his own face. Mikhail saw him lean in and bite off the nose. He turned away then, and kept running.

Mikhail knew the way, knew which hallways ended in locked doors, and which ones would bring them closer to the fresh air. He realized now that Hugh wouldn't have stood a chance alone, even if he had been able to make the initial escape. Finally, they made it to the rear entrance and Mikhail kicked open the door. The sun was just coming up. There was one squad car left in the parking lot, the one that Miller had always used. Mikhail ran over to it and found the hidden key near the muffler. He unlocked the doors and Hugh jumped in the back. Mikhail got in and tore out of the parking lot.

"Where are we going?" asked Hugh. "We have help my friends."

"We will," said Mikhail, though he wasn't sure where he was going. Jefferson maybe? And what could they do? What could anybody do against these invincible, monstrous creatures? Maybe it would have been kinder to let the boy die after all, instead of live with the grief that would haunt him for the rest of his life.

Then Hugh started laughing. Mikhail looked at him in the rear view mirror. "It's... Jesus Christ," said Hugh, unable to continue because he was laughing so hard.

"What, Hugh? What is it?"

"It's just, after all that, after everything that's happened... it was her."

"What? Who?"

"That scientist... lady. Sarah. She saved us."

Mikhail smiled sadly. "It's because of her that this whole horrible tragedy happened."

"Maybe," said Hugh. "But that's your problem, Duvy."

"My problem?" asked Mikhail. He was having trouble doing anything but focusing on the road. The important thing seemed to be to drive, to keep driving.

"At first I thought maybe you were a pussy. But you're not."

Mikhail smiled weakly. "So what's my *real* problem?" He drifted off onto the icy shoulder, but was able to correct the car just in time.

"Same as me, I guess. I mean, we're the guys who get shit done. We *know* how to get shit done, and we do it. And that's the problem. That we know." Hugh let out one more laugh, sharp and short. "We're too goddamn cynical, Duvy."

For the first time since Marie died, Mikhail Duvlosky laughed. It felt good.

Chapter thirty five

Nick hugged Lucy close as she buried her face in his chest. He watched as Richaud chewed on Mr. Ricksclyde's guts. He felt strong, as if he wouldn't let anything in the world hurt Lucy or his mother.

"How's that tingly little wiener of yours doing, kid?" asked Richaud before letting out a repulsive and wet-sounding belch. "Bet you got a stiffy, holding that sweet little hottie so close to you? Don't worry, old Richaud will take *good* care of her."

"You come near her," said Nick, "and I'll fucking kill you."

Richaud smiled and winked. "Now now," said the woman who had disemboweled Nick's English teacher. "Don't torture the boy. Can't you see that the three of them are a nice, happy family in there?"

"Just like us, Mama."

"Speaking of which," said the woman, "where's the boy? He should have been here with Lt. Duvlosky by now."

"What are you going to do with us?" asked Nick's mom.

"Be patient, dear," said the woman. "You'll have your chance soon enough, just like Mr. Ricksclyde had *his* chance."

Then the boy who had thrown Mandy's head in their cell appeared.

"Where's Duvlosky?" asked the woman. "Where's your pet?"

"I had to eat her, Mama, she helped them escape."

"They *escaped?*" hissed the woman. "You let them *escape?* The boy too?"

"Hugh?" said Nick. "It was Hugh, wasn't it? Hugh and Duvlosky. They're coming with help. They're going to kill you."

The woman laughed. "I doubt that very much, child," she said. She sighed. "It's no matter. It was Duvlosky's turn to be tested, but now that he's gone it will have to be one of you." The woman looked them over. "Hmmm.. you'll do. You. The mother."

"No," said Nick. "Leave her alone."

"You then, boy? Are you volunteering?"

"No!" screamed Fran. "Please. Take me."

"Ah, I'm never one to turn down a polite, civilized request," said the woman. "Papa, get her."

Richaud stood up and opened the door. Nick stirred. He was on the verge of jumping Richaud, though he knew it wouldn't do any good.

"Nick," said Fran, "don't do anything stupid."

"Listen to your mother, child," said the woman. "Mother knows best."

"Mom…"

"I love you, honey. I love you more than anything,

more than life itself. It doesn't matter if they take me. I'll be okay, because I'll always have you, and you'll always have me. You understand that, don't you Nick? Of course you do. You've always understood that."

Richaud put his bloody hand on Fran's arm. "Mom!"

"I'll be okay," said Fran. "Tell me that you love me."

"I love you mom. I love you, I love you, I love you."

"Then I'll be okay. Can I hug my son, ma'am? Can I touch my son one more time?"

"Go ahead," said the woman. Richaud released Fran and she walked over to the bed. Lucy let go of Nick, stood up, and gave them room.

"You take good care of him, Lucy," said Fran. "We both know how special he is."

"I will," said Lucy, sobbing.

Nick wasn't crying. Being brave meant being afraid but doing a thing anyhow. Fran leaned in and Nick hugged her. "I love you mom," he said. "I'm sorry if I was..."

"Shush," said Fran. "You were perfect. You're perfect."

"So are you mom."

"Aw shucks," said Richaud. "If I had a heart, I'm sure it'd be breaking right now." Then he put his hand on Fran again and yanked her away from her son. He shoved her into the hallway. Then they led her away, as she looked into Nick's eyes. Then she was gone.

"Nick," said Lucy, "I... I..."

"It's okay," said Nick. "I'm alright." He could still smell his mother, still almost feel her embrace.

"They're going to come for us next," said Lucy. "They're going to kill us."

"No," said Nick. "Hugh and Duvlosky are coming back for us."

"But what if they're too late? What if they can't stop them?"

"We're going to be okay, Lucy. I can feel it."

"Nick..."

"Yeah?"

"I know you're right. I can feel it too. But, just in case. Just in case something happens. I don't want to die like this."

"You're not going to die."

"But just in case, Nick. There's something I want to do first, before we die."

Nick almost asked her what, but then he looked into her eyes, and saw her smile shyly. He wasn't sure if this were a nightmare, or a fantasy, or what. Finally he figured out what it was. It was life.

Chapter thirty six

They passed a string of six or seven Jefferson police cars headed the opposite way, lit up in the early morning grayness. Duvlosky kept driving.

"Shit Duvy," said Hugh. "What are you doing? That was the cops."

"Fuck the cops," said Duvlosky. Hugh looked at him from the back seat. He looked better, somehow, more alive. Before, he'd looked like a corpse.

"Where the fuck we going, Duvy?"

"We're going to see the one-armed man."

"Right. The one-armed man." It was no crazier than any of the other shit that had happened. If there was an electric boner, then why couldn't there be a one-armed man? Still, Hugh didn't see how he could help, where the cops couldn't.

"I don't know his name, but I think he's at the Jefferson hospital. I hope to Christ he is."

"And what's this one-armed man going to do for us, exactly, Duvy – assuming we can find the guy?"

"I don't know," said Duvlosky.

Fuck it, thought Hugh, it's as good a chance as any.

Hugh watched silently as the trees passed by, covered in early morning ice. Everything looked so delicate. He thought back to when it all started, when he and Nick had been walking through the park, before they got to the shed with the green toxic shit. He remembered Nick saying something about how nice the still, cold bay was.

"Why can't we be content with that?" Nick had asked.

It was a good question. It was a good question, but in the end, it was a useless question. The green buds shot out of the sickly branches in May, and in October, the yellow and orange and red and green leaves fell to the ground. In January, the branches were bare again, and sometimes weighed down by ice, like they were now, sparkling like magic from the obscure light of the distant and early sun. That's just the way it was. That's just what happened. If you didn't like it, too bad.

Hugh smiled sadly. He couldn't quite articulate his thoughts to himself, but he knew that Duvlosky would understand. That's what it was. That he and Duvlosky could understand each other when neither one of them could make themselves understood through words. It was like how Marie, good sweet life-loving joyful Marie was the one who died, and grim-ass Duvlosky was the one who went on living. It was like everything was the *opposite* of what it was supposed to be.

Hugh shook his head. Goofy thoughts. The sort of shit that old Dick's Bride went on about, reading from old dusty books. But something wouldn't shake away. Somehow, he felt that he would even be glad to be sitting in Mr. Ricksclyde's class right now; he'd even be glad to see the old fart's wrinkled face. And his mom....

"You still with us, kid?" asked Duvlosky.

"Yeah," said Hugh.

"Good. Almost there now. Listen. We don't know what's going to be there. A lot of heavy shit has gone down, a lot of unbelievable shit. They wiped out the

Clairmont hospital, and we just don't know how far they got, or how many of them there are."

That was good. It brought Hugh back to the present. The present was shit, but it was all that counted.

"Don't worry about me, Duvy."

Duvlosky pulled into the parking lot of the Jefferson hospital. It was almost deserted. They parked and walked in. Duvlosky went up to the lady at the desk and said, "I'm Lt. Mikhail Duvlosky with the Clairmont police."

The lady rubbed the tiredness from her eyes and opened them wide. "Lt. Duvlosky?!" she said. "Everybody thought…"

"Just what have you heard?" asked Duvlosky.

"Well, there were some Clairmont firemen here, and they said… something horrible happened there. They said that you were there, fighting these… things. So we called the police, and they came, and tried to get in contact with you…"

"The firemen," said Duvlosky. "Did they bring someone? Someone with one arm?"

"Ben Clemmings," said the lady.

"Is he alive? Is he still here?"

"He's… here. His family is with him right now."

"I'd like to see him."

"I… I don't know, Officer Duvlosky. I don't think Linda would be pleased."

"Please. It's life or death."

The lady looked down at the desk and shuffled some papers. Finally, she cleared her throat and picked up the phone. "It's Janet," she said. "I have a visitor for Benjamin Clemmings. It's… a police officer." She listened, then hung up. "Okay," she said to Duvlosky. "He's in room 314. The elevator's down the hall to the right."

"Thank you, Janet," said Duvlosky.

Janet looked at Hugh, for the first time, with question marks in her eyes. Hugh nodded at her and then followed Duvlosky down the hall. They got in the elevator.

"Look," said Hugh. "Just what the hell are we going to do with this guy?"

"I don't know," said Duvlosky.

They rode up to the third floor. It was very quiet. They found room 314. The door was open, and Hugh could see a woman in there, and a little boy, and a pair of legs covered up by a hospital sheet. As they entered the room, he saw the rest of the body – what was left of it. Christ. The guy was in bad shape.

"Hello Mrs. Clemmings," said Duvlosky.

The woman turned her heard around sharply. "Who are you?"

"I was with your husband last night, when this happened."

"You," she said. "It's *your* fault! Go away! Get out of here, or so help me..."

"*Please,*" gasped the man from the bed. "Linda, please. Let him speak."

"You're a hero, Mr. Clemmings," said Duvlosky. "You saved my life. If you hadn't come, there's no telling how much of our town those things would have destroyed. You saved my life, and you saved our town, and yet I've never seen you before, I didn't even know your name until just now. I..."

"Look," said Hugh.

"Who are *you?*" said Linda.

"Hugh, please..." said Duvlosky.

"Fuck that," said Hugh. "We're wasting time. My best friend, his mom, and his... girl... are locked up in a jail cell in Clairmont. They're being held by three fucking monsters, different from the zombies. These ones, you cut off their heads, it doesn't kill them. We don't know how to kill them. We don't know how to stop them, or what the fuck they're going to do next. Can you help us, or not?"

"Get *out* of here!" shrieked Linda. The little boy started crying.

"Linda," said Ben, propping himself up on his one

elbow. "Please. My phone." Linda reached over to the table and handed Ben his phone. He dialed a number. "Clemmings," he said into the phone. "Shit's going down. Clairmont, Maine. Jail parking lot." He hung up and collapsed back on the bed. "Go back," he said to Duvlosky. "When you get there, there'll be help. Just say my name." He closed his eyes. "I only wish I'd made that call sooner, before I lost my fucking arm. Goddamn media. Never get it right." His voice was starting to trail off. "Goddamn fox," he said.

"Go," said Linda.

"Thank you," said Duvlosky.

"Yeah," said Hugh. "Thanks."

Chapter thirty seven

Lucy sat on the bed, leaned in, and kissed Nick. Their tongues swirled around in each other's mouths, soft and warm. Nick's cock was as hard as it ever had been. He closed his eyes and kissed Lucy some more. He never wanted it to stop. She ran her hands down his chest, his belly, getting closer. Nick pulled away.

"We can't," he said. He didn't want to say it, but he had to. It was number one currently on the list of things that he didn't want to do, saying that was.

"Yes," said Lucy, "we can."

"But my…"

"Electric boner? I don't care."

"It'll hurt you Lucy. It might even kill you, I don't know."

"I don't care," said Lucy. "Better the electric boner than that Richaud Monster."

"But Hugh and Duvlosky…"

"Won't be able to stop them. You know that Nick, don't you?"

"I... yes," said Nick. He had only been trying to give Lucy some hope, but he knew full well that they were going to die soon, in some gruesome way.

Lucy pulled her shirt over her head and undid her bra. It dropped to the floor, and there they were: two beautiful breasts, full and glorious, lovely, with the nipples drawn hard from the chill in the cell. Nick got even harder which he hadn't thought possible. It felt as though his cock wanted to pull away from his body entirely.

"Lucy," whispered Nick. Lucy took his wrists and placed his hands on her breasts. They were soft, and their touch sent a thrill through Nick's body. Suddenly, he wanted to devour them, and without much thought, he plunged at them and had a nipple in his mouth. Lucy moaned and ran her hands through Nick's hair.

Nick kissed his way up her chest, her neck, and found her lips again. She wrapped her arms around him and pulled him down, on top of her. "Take off my pants," she said. Nick fumbled with the buttons for a moment, his heart beating furiously, his dick throbbing with insane desire. Then he had them down and Lucy kicked them the rest of the way off. "Touch me," she said.

Nick ran his hands down her belly, down her hips, and grabbed her ass. Good god, it was lovely, everything felt so good to the touch, everything fueled his passion, made him want to tear into her, tear her apart, but at the same time protect her from everything, to treat her with the most delicate tenderness. He pulled down her panties and threw them over his shoulder.

He rubbed around the outside of it. It was wet and warm. He didn't know what he was doing, but he somehow knew what to do. He slid a finger slowly inside and moved it back and forth, exploring. It felt good. Such unbelievable wonders in there! Lucy moaned. "Now," she said, "I want you now."

Nick pulled out his finger and took a deep breath. He threw off his pants and underwear and there it was. He moved it toward Lucy's warmth. But when he tried to put it in, it just poked around the outside. The tip touched Lucy's inner thigh and he saw her head snap back. Her eyes closed tight and she let out a painful groan. Nick felt like dying. He had hurt Lucy. It wasn't going to work.

"I'm sorry," he said.

"Try again," said Lucy, opening her eyes. "I want you."

"I want you too, Lucy, more than anybody's ever wanted anything. But I don't want to hurt you. Maybe I can just use my fingers… maybe I can use my mouth. Maybe – "

Lucy grabbed his dick and slid it in. For a moment, he was senseless. Then he felt the warmth and the unbelievable comfort of Lucy. It was beautiful. She screamed and he started to pull out, but she grabbed him and held him in.

"Do it!" she screamed.

"Lucy, are you okay?"

"God yes, Nick, DO IT!"

Nick gave a shy thrust. The movement felt incredible, like he had entered a different world entirely, one apart from anything he had known. He was inside Lucy. He was making love to Lucy. He gave another thrust, this one a little more assertive. Something compelled him on, a momentum that he didn't seem to control. He thrust again and again, varying the speed and force, but building towards something.

"Yes!" screamed Lucy, "I love you!"

"I love you!" shouted Nick, "Oh God, Lucy, I fucking love you!"

"Fuck me!" said Lucy, "fuck me Nick, cum inside of me!"

Nick needed no further convincing. He looked down at her face. It was beauty itself, her head turned to one side, her eyes closed, her face flushed, as though she too were transported somewhere far away – but with *him*. It was only Nick and Lucy. There was nothing else. She opened her eyes and looked into his eyes and he felt something he'd never felt before. It wasn't the friction – you could get that from jerking it. It wasn't love, he didn't think, not exactly. It was something else. It was a deep connection, and the fact that it was happening with Lucy – who had always seemed unobtainable to him, whom he had wanted since he was able to want a girl – almost made his brains explode inside his head. Maybe they already had. Brains had little to do with this.

They kissed, and as they did so, Nick started to cum. She wrapped her legs around his back and he came, like an explosion of light, like the release of all tension everywhere, like the fucking angles lining up and strumming on harps. Lucy screamed and screamed and as Nick regained his senses, he suddenly remembered the pillow he had jerked off into, and the hole that he had burned into it. He pulled out right away.

Lucy's eyes were closed, but Nick could see that she was still breathing, heavily. "Are you okay, Lucy? Are you okay?"

She opened her eyes. They had a soft and vulnerable look to them, a look that Nick had never seen anywhere. "I love you," she said. Then she laughed.

"I love you, Lucy, but are you okay? Did I hurt you?"

"It hurt," said Lucy, "but I'm okay. Better than okay. It hurt, but it felt better than anything's ever felt." She smiled. "Come here and just lie with me for a bit." Nick lay down next to her. "I feel like there's something inside of me now," she said, "that wasn't there before."

"Maybe I got you pregnant?" said Nick. They both laughed.

"I'm glad we got to do that, Nick. I wish we could do it again. Again and again, always."

"Me too," said Nick. Then he felt something, a presence, ugly. He looked up and there was the monstrous boy, leering at them.

"You've been naughty," said the boy. He lifted a claw and pointed at Nick. "You. Mama wants you. We're gonna eat your mom, and you're gonna watch."

Chapter thirty eight

Richaud touched her cheek and it sent a warm thrill through his being. It wasn't a sexual feeling. Richaud was aware that such things existed and understood that they could be used effectively. He just couldn't feel them. What he did feel was the warmth of her fear, coursing through him, feeding him. That was his real sustenance - the Fear, the Pain. Eating the flesh was for show, to show them that he was something to be feared.

The woman was crying silently. Richaud smiled. "Don't worry dear," he said, "you'll get to see your son again. Maybe I'll pull out your eyeball and bring it over to him so you can get a real close look." The warmth increased. Richaud felt his claws grow a little longer, stimulated. He saw them scratch the woman's cheek, saw a trickle of red run down her face, mixing with the tears. It was all so delicious.

Suddenly, the touch grew cold. Richaud frowned and looked down at his victim, wrapped in a hundred feet of rope, like one of those things, he forgot what they were called. The things that turned into the other things and flew away. But *this* one wasn't going to be doing any flying. No sir.

She opened her mouth. "Officer Richaud," she said. "What *happened* to you? You used to be *good*."

Richaud laughed, but he felt very cold and uncomfortable. "Used to? Used to be good? There's no such thing, dear, neither as a 'used to' or a 'good.'" And that was the truth, or very near it. His memories of Before, of when he was weak, were all but gone. Now, when he tried to remember, there was only one thing.

He was standing in the darkness. Yes, that was right. And there was something there. It was The Fear, as strong as he had ever known it. Strong enough to reach from the past and come back to him, strong enough to cross over from the Before, when he was weak. Only it was strange. In the memory, The Fear gave him no warmth. It made him feel something strange, something alien. It confused him. How could that be? The Fear was a warm thing, a happy thing, the best thing there was. How could it make him feel bad?

He was standing in the darkness and there were things around him, the things with a lot of arms. That's right: trees. He was looking down at something, he was looking down at the Fear. It was a little boy, huddled up in the dirt, crying. He recognized the boy from Now, but then he was different. Richaud was different, too. The Fear was different. Everything was.

He bent down and picked up the boy, gently. "It's okay, Tommy," he said, "everything's okay now. I'm going to take you home. You're safe." The Fear grew a little weaker. It didn't make sense. Why was he trying to kill the Fear?

The memory disappeared into the darkness. It was gone. There was only Now, and suddenly, Richaud was very very hungry. He studied the woman's face. The Fear was gone, somehow. Well, he'd just have to call it back.

"But maybe we won't do that to you, dear. Maybe we won't pull out your eyeball and give it to your son. Maybe we'll pull out your *son's* eyeball, and give it to *you*. And then we'll pull off his little electric dick and make him eat it." That did the old trick. Richaud felt warm again.

Then Mama came back from the hunt. "They're gone, Papa," she said. "Our little special needs child let them go."

"That's okay, Mama, we've still got the three, and way I see it, we've still got the entire world."

"That's just right, Papa. The entire world. This is just a light snack before the feast."

"We just got to teach the boy not to play with his food, that's all."

"No dessert for the boy, Papa, until he learns his lesson."

"Speaking of the little shit, shouldn't he be here by now?"

"He'll be here, Papa. With the son."

Richaud felt another wave of the Fear coming from the woman. Oh. It was so very delicious.

Chapter thirty nine

Mikhail looked around the parking lot. It was just as they'd left it. There was nobody there.

"Well Duvy," said Hugh, "looks like your once-armed man was full of shit. Hey, you got a smoke?"

Mikhail found a pack of cigarettes in the car, handed one to Hugh, and lit one up for himself. "This is when somebody makes that joke, 'those things'll kill you,'" said Mikhail.

"Pretty funny, Duvy. Maybe we can kill the fuckers with your comedy."

"Take the car, Hugh. Take the car and try again. Try to find some help."

"And let you have all the fun? Fuck that. We're going in there together, and we're coming out with our friends."

"You'll die."

"Yeah, but we have to try, don't we? We've wasted enough time fucking around." Hugh took a deep drag and then snuffed the cigarette out in the ash tray. "Let's do it." He got out of the car and started walking to the entrance. Mikhail picked up the nightstick that he had found in the car, got out and walked behind Hugh.

One good blow ought to do the trick. Mikhail was weak, but so was Hugh. One good blow would knock the kid out. Then what? Drive him somewhere safe, and come back for his friends. They were probably dead already, and there was no sense in letting Hugh kill himself too. Hugh would never forgive him, but then how much forgiveness does a dead man need?

Mikhail lifted the nightstick, but when he tried to bring it down, it wouldn't go. Then something was moving it with an overpowering strength, and then it was out of Mikhail's hand and against his neck, choking him. Hugh kept walking and Mikhail felt a warmth in his ear and a voice whispered, "Who are you?"

The force on the nightstick eased up a little bit, so that Mikhail could gasp out a response. "A friend of Benjamin Clemmings," he said. The nightstick dropped to the ground and Mikhail turned around to see a man in army fatigues with all manner of weapons and ammunition hanging from his body.

Hugh finally turned around. "What the *fuck*?"

"He's with me," said Mikhail to the man.

The man looked at him, then looked at Hugh, then looked at the nightstick on the ground. "It's only that this is very dangerous, what we're about to do," Mikhail explained. "Is it just you?"

The man nodded. "Great," said Hugh. "One guy. That's all we get?"

"What's the situation?" asked the man in a husky voice.

"The situation," said Hugh, "is that there's three crazy fucking monsters in there that are impossible to kill, and they've got our friends."

"Impossible to kill?" said the man. "Did you try a grenade in the mouth? No? Then let's try a grenade in the mouth. Lead the way."

"I think they're using the reception room at the front entrance as their staging area," said Mikhail. "At any rate, there's a set of keys in the desk there. Third drawer down on the right, under a false bottom. Go for the keys, Hugh. If the monsters are there, we'll hold them off for you. Do you remember the back entrance? How to get there from the cells?"

"Yeah," said Hugh.

"If you find your friends, get them out that way. Our new friend and I will try the grenade trick. Sound good?"

"Yeah," said Hugh.

The man gave them each guns. "Locked and loaded," he said. "Just pull the trigger. Let's do it."

They strode in the sunlight to the door, with Mikhail in the lead and the military man bringing up the rear. Mikhail swung open the door and there they were, Claire Peterson and Richaud, standing over Nick Sherman's mother, who was wrapped like a cocoon in rope and lying helplessly on the floor.

Mikhail opened fire. It was an automatic. He landed a round of shots into Richaud's chest. With each hit, Richaud shook like a puppet on a string. Hugh added a volley of bullets to the foray, and then ran to the desk. Mikhail saw him find the drawer, find the keys, and run off down the hall. Where was the other one, he wondered? The little boy?

The military man was unloading into Claire, driving her back against the wall. Her body was opened up and oozing black blood. The man pursued her and, true to the plan, shoved a grenade in her mouth and then retreated. She blew into a million little pieces, splattering over the entire room with an incredible noise.

That left Richaud. Mikhail saw that he was smiling through the bullets and the blood. The military man joined his gun fire to Mikhail's, and they began disintegrating Richaud's body, one rapidly-fired bullet at a time. There was a hole one foot in diameter in the center of his chest. Still he smiled. The military man made his move. Mikhail stopped shooting so the man had room. He pulled a grenade off his vest and reached for Richaud's mouth. Richaud bit off the man's hand and shoved the hand and the grenade into the man's mouth. It went off.

For a moment, Mikhail could see nothing and hear nothing but ringing. He wiped the gore from his face and saw Richaud standing there, the hole in his chest closing itself back up. The ringing died down and he heard Richaud's laughter. Mikhail got off another round of shots, and then he was out of ammo.

"Nice try, Lt," said Richaud, flashing his hideous yellow fangs.

Chapter forty

Lucy watched as the boy swung open the door to their cell. She was dimly aware of being naked. But she didn't feel vulnerable. She had Nick there. They gave each other strength. Together, they were something else, something different than what they were apart. She held him tight. She could still sense him inside of her, a soft presence, without the intensity of when he had been physically inside of her, but none the less real and immediate.

She felt something else there, too, something not quite Nick, but something that hadn't been there before they had done the thing. It seemed to want to burst out of her, whatever it was.

"I won't let him take you," she whispered.

"It's okay, Lucy. Don't get hurt. Let him have me. What does it matter? I'm happy. If you get hurt, I won't be happy. Whatever else happens, I don't care."

"That's how I feel, too. I don't want you to get hurt. Why should you get the say in whose feelings matter more?"

Nick laughed. "Our first and only argument. Maybe

we would have ended in divorce. It doesn't matter. He came for me, so I'm the one who has to go."

"You would fight him, if he were coming for me."

"Yes," said Nick.

"Then let me fight. Let's fight him now, together. I only want to be together."

"Me too."

"So then it's decided."

"I guess so," said Nick.

"I'm gonna puke," said the boy-monster, approaching them.

"You're going to do worse than that, you little twerp," said Lucy.

"Mama said I couldn't hurt *him*, but she didn't say I couldn't eat *you*." The thing reached out a clawed hand toward Lucy's face. Nick jumped up and took hold of the wrist with both hands.

"That's it, you little shit," said Nick. He pulled the hand toward his penis, which Lucy saw was still erect.

"Ewww!" said the monster. "Gaybo!" The hand touched Nick's penis, but nothing happened. "Stop it! You're gonna make me eat you and get me in trouble again!" The thing put its other hand around Nick's throat. All thought flew out of Lucy's head, and there was only an incredible flash of a bright yellow light in there.

Without knowing what she was doing, she saw her own hand reaching toward the monster's face. Then it was on it, and she felt something inside of her surge, overwhelm her, and then the brightness wasn't only in her head, but in front of her eyes, coming out of her hand, seeping into the monster's face. She heard a sound like ten million crows cawing over ten million tires screeching and then the light was overtaking the monster's entire body and then, where a moment before there had been a terrible creature in the form of a little boy, there was now only a pile of black ashes.

Lucy collapsed on the bed and everything grew dark.

She felt empty, drained. She heard Nick repeating her name, over and over. Lucy Lucy Lucy. That was her. Little Lucy Lillian Littleton. She didn't feel little. She felt vast, as vast as the universe. And she felt like all of the vast empty spaces in the universe. She'd never felt like that before. She'd always felt the fullness of life, and she'd always been on the verge of bursting with that fullness. She'd finally burst. Now was only an empty endlessness. Was she dead? Lucy Lucy Lucy Lucy. No. She had only been emptied out.

Lucy, wake up.

She opened her eyes. Nick was there. She looked down at the pile of ashes.

"Are you okay?"

"Yes."

"What *was* that?"

"Nick..."

"Yes?"

"I think I can do it again. I think we can save your mom."

"Lucy... you... I thought you were dead."

"I just need..."

"We need to get out of here. The door's open."

"Your mom. We can save her. I just need... for you to fill me up again."

Nick gave her a questioning look. He always *was* a little slow, when it came to all that. Then he got it.

"Are you sure?"

"Fill me up. Quick."

"Well... I guess that would be alright."

Lucy laughed. "You guess so, huh?"

Nick smiled and leaned in to kiss her gently on the neck. They did it again.

Chapter forty one

THE ELECTRIC BONER

Hugh heard the explosion. Shit, maybe it worked. Maybe Duvy and that crazy dude would stop the fuckers after all. But… where was the other one, the little shit?

He ran down the hallway, not really knowing where he was going. He had his gun in one hand, and the keys in the other. He heard a second explosion, further away now. That was good. Maybe they were both dust.

Hugh found himself at an intersection, and went right. It was another hallway, this one full of cells. He walked slowly now, peering into each cell and trying to make something out, anything, in the darkness. The hallway dead-ended, so he made his way back to the intersection. Now he heard another round of gunfire. That wasn't good. If both of the monsters were dead, then why the shooting? Maybe the little shit had returned.

Now Hugh went left, and it was a row of offices that led to a locked door. He fumbled at the keys, trying them all, cursing each time one of them didn't work. Finally he got it and swung the heavy door open. There was another row of cells. He walked slowly down it, and then noticed that one of them was standing open in the distance. He gripped his gun a little tighter and made his way over.

There, in the open cell, he saw his good friend Nick Sherman getting it on with Lucy Littleton. He was really giving it to her. Hugh saw them both naked, fucking. He smiled and got a hard-on. He didn't know quite what to do. The door was open, they could leave any time they wanted to. Instead, they were boning. Nice, Nick. Nice.

Lucy screamed, Nick roared, and then it was over. Nick kissed her and rolled off. Hugh cleared his throat and they both looked up at him.

"Hugh!" said Nick. He jumped up, bare-ass naked, and gripped Hugh in a bear-hug.

"Shit buddy, is that an electric boner you got there, or you just happy to see your old pal Hugh?"

Lucy covered herself with the blanket and smiled. "Hugh," she said. "You're okay."

"That's up for debate," said Hugh. "But let's discuss it once we're the fuck out of here."

"Duvlosky?" asked Nick.

"Again. A great topic for another time. Let's go."

"No," said Lucy. "We have to help Nick's mom."

Hugh frowned. "She... if there's any help for her, Duvy's got it covered. Let's just save our own asses for a start."

"You don't understand," said Lucy. "I can stop them. I... have a power. Nick gave it to me."

"It's true," said Nick. "Look." He pointed at the floor and Hugh saw a pile of ashes. "That was one of them. The boy."

"You dusted him?" Hugh asked.

"Sure as shit," said Lucy, and she laughed.

Hugh looked again at the pile of ashes. "Shit. Alright. But for Christ's sake. Put on some clothes. I mean, at least Nick. You're okay, Lucy."

"Hey," said Nick. "Watch it. I'll kick your fucking ass from here to the moon to Sirius."

Hey. Not bad. The kid was learning. Hugh took one last look at Lucy's tits, then turned around while they got dressed. Then he led them back down the hallways. The gunfire had stopped. Everything was silent. Goddamn silence and darkness. Hugh was sick of it.

They reached the short hallway that led to the reception area. "Now get behind me," said Hugh, holding up his gun. "Who knows what's around the corner."

"Maybe you should get behind *me*," said Lucy.

"No thanks. I'll take a gun over magic any day." Hugh turned the corner. It was a bloody mess. He saw Fran, still on the floor, still tied up and squirming around like a fish in a sea of blood. He looked up and saw Duvlosky. Duvlosky was upside down in the air. Richaud, full of bullet holes which were closing themselves up, was holding him by the ankles.

"Put him down, asshole," said Hugh.

Richaud smiled. "Look at this. I didn't know they did delivery here. Lunch, with some left-overs for dinner."

Hugh was unsure. If he let loose with the gun, he might hit Duvlosky. And what good would shooting Richaud do anyway?

"Hugh," said Duvlosky. "Why are you still here? Go. Take your friends."

Nick ran to his mom and tried to untie her. It was no good. It was a fucking Gordian knot.

"Let him go," said Hugh, "and we might not kill you, Richard Richaud." Duvlosky liked that. Hugh saw him smile.

Then Lucy was walking toward Richaud. "Little girl," said Richaud. "Do you really want to be raped?" Then suddenly the smile left his face. "Wait. Where's the boy? Where's our little boy?" He dropped Duvlosky on the ground and turned to face Lucy.

"You've tortured us," said Lucy.

"You killed my mom," said Hugh.

"You scared us," said Nick.

"Why?" asked Lucy. "Why did you do all of this?"

Richaud shrugged. "It fills the darkness," he said.

"No," said Lucy. "*This* fills the darkness." She touched his forehead with her finger. The room filled with light. Richaud let out a terrible scream, worse than anything Hugh had ever heard. Then he crumbled into ashes.

Lucy collapsed on the ground beside his ashes. Nick ran over to her. "Hugh," he said, "my mom! Help her!"

Hugh bent down beside Fran and started to work away at the ropes. Then the black blood in the room began to swirl in the air. Hugh looked up. He had thought that he was beyond amazement, after all he had seen, but he watched nevertheless in amazement. The blood swirled in the air, and came together in the center of the room.

Then Claire Peterson was standing there.

Chapter forty two

Claire looked down at the girl. Whatever power the girl had used to destroy Richaud was now gone. She was drained. She was a husk. Claire smiled.

"What a brave little gang," she said. "And you deserve a better answer than the one that oaf gave. 'Why?' you asked. 'It fills the darkness,' he said. There is some truth in that. It wasn't wrong, only woefully incomplete. Since we're all neatly gathered here together, allow me to elaborate. As I say, you deserve that much. Before I obliterate you all."

Claire looked around the room. She sensed the hopelessness of them all. It filled her completely.

She began. "You can't squeeze blood from a stone, they say. How right they are, and how so very like them to state the obvious, and yet live their lives as if the truth weren't the truth. For what is human existence, I ask, but the act of trying to squeeze blood from a stone? That's your happiness, and when you look down finally at the end of your lives, you see that indeed you have a bloody stone in your hand. But the blood isn't from the stone. It's from your hands, from so desperately trying to squeeze out what isn't there.

"Take that as a prelude, if you will. You ask how we can be so cruel. I answer that you can't squeeze blood from a stone. Whatever we are, we've been sprung from you. If we're cruel, it's because you're cruel.

"You see me as Claire Peterson, and that's who I am. Oh, I confess, I remember little or nothing of my life before I became enlightened. I know that I made a mess of it. Do I need to tell you why? Haven't you guessed it? I won't repeat myself endlessly, like you do. If you're too thick to take my meaning by now, there's no help for you."

Claire looked around the room again. The girl had

regained consciousness, but she was still only a husk. There was a power in the boy, the smaller one, but Richaud had said that it was useless against them. All eyes were on her. For show, she grew her claws out until they touched the ceiling.

"It's almost a shame that I have to kill you all," she said at last. "You really are the best of the lot. By that I mean your sense of delusion is so finely honed that you think there's actually such a thing as love. There is no love. Or if there is, it's the passing of gas in the wind. It's there for a moment, loud and stinking, and then it's gone. But it's nothing real. It's nothing that lasts. The thing that lasts is pain. Love is a fart in the wind that you smell and think is real; pain is the reality of the stone in your hand.

"If it were love that were in your hearts, then you would see before you now a creature of love. I am your hearts. I am going to eat your hearts, too.

"Why is it that when a person appears rotten, you are so quick to make excuses for him? 'Oh,' you say, 'something terrible happened to him when he was a boy. It's understandable.' Or, 'Oh, he's an anomaly, a monster, not a fair representation of the rest of us.' I would only ask: did you squeeze blood from a stone with this one, or did you only squeeze blood from a sack of blood?

"But you try, you little dears. You try and you try. What are you trying to do? Be something that you're not. That's truly what it amounts to. If it weren't for the Law, you'd all be murdering and raping each other openly. And why does the Law exist? It's because you're all afraid of getting raped and murdered. You're clever in that sense, I'll give you that. You've found a nice little system that works for the most part. And when it doesn't work, you've got the system itself to blame for it. You've always got something or someone to blame, don't you?

"'Why?' you ask. I might as well ask the same question of you. Why do you pretend? If I had time, I could make you understand. As it is, you're still in denial that you're pretending. As I said, you're a brave little group. But you have your limits. And once past those limits, you'll turn rotten. If you hadn't proved so dangerous, I would take the time to educate you.

"As it is, I'm afraid that I'll have to dispose of you all quickly. The sad fact is that there is a whole world of people out there, and most of them are weaker than you, and easier prey. By 'weaker,' I mean simply 'less prone to delusion.'

"I hope that this brief lecture has allowed you at least a glimpse of understanding in your deaths. You've earned that much." Claire smiled and drew her claws back into her fingers.

"Hey," said Lt. Mikhail Duvlosky from the ground.

"Yes, Mr. Duvlosky? Do you have something very interesting to say to me?"

"Yeah. Fuck you."

Chapter forty three

"Fuck *me*?" said Claire. "That's just the problem. You're all such ingrates. I offer you enlightenment, and you spit in my face."

Duvlosky got to his feet. "You're right, Claire," he said. "People are shit. I learned that early and often. But I learned something else. Marie taught me. People can rise above the shit. People can be beautiful."

Duvlosky's voice brought Nick out of his trance. Claire's words had been like a spell on him, making him forget everything else. He looked down at Lucy. She was awake, but pale and weak-looking. "Lucy," he said.

"You have to stop her, Nick," said Lucy. "I... I can't do it again."

"I... can't do anything either, Lucy. I've tried."

"I can't," said Lucy again.

"Nick, listen," said Hugh in a whisper. "I've got to tell you something."

"What? What is it?"

"You were right."

"Right? About what?"

There was a terrible shriek. "What are you little shits up to over there?" asked Claire.

"Nevermind them," said Duvlosky, and he made his move. He dove at Claire and brought her to the ground.

Claire laughed. "Well," she said, "I tried. It's too bad, Mikhail, you would have made a fine pet."

"About that day," whispered Hugh. "When you asked me to touch your dick. I wanted to."

"Okay, Hugh. It's okay, I understand. But..."

"Look, I'm not gay. I mean, I don't think I am. I like girls. A lot. It's just..."

"It's alright, really, but Duvlosky needs our help. We're going to die, Hugh, all of us."

"You don't understand..."

Claire lifted Duvlosky to the ceiling with one hand. "Where's your love now?" she asked.

"...I'm saying that if I had to, I'd probably fuck another dude. I mean, if my life depended on it. Do you think you could do that, Nick? Do you? Sure you could. Lucy, get him hard."

Lucy understood. She rubbed Nick through his jeans. He was hard.

"I..."

"Marie..." gasped Duvlosky in a choked voice.

"Here's your love," said Claire. She plunged her claws into Duvlosky's throat.

Nick had trouble getting it in. It was too tight. "I can't do it," he said.

"Shut the fuck up," said Hugh, "and do it."

Nick did it. It was tight. "Ooohhh fuuucccckkk," moaned Hugh.

Claire dropped Duvlosky to the ground. "What is

this? What are you two doing?!" She reached across the room and took Nick's neck in one hand and Hugh's in the other.

It only took four thrusts. Nick looked into Claire's eyes as he came. They were opened wide in amazement. They turned pure black. Then they turned pure white. Then they were gone. Then everything was black.

Chapter forty four

Hugh fell to the ground as Claire disintegrated into ash. He looked around. They were all on the ground now. Fran was still tied up in the rope, still wiggling around. Lucy was still laying half-conscious after her bursts of light from before. Nick was collapsed unconscious but still breathing, next to the pile of ashes. Duvlosky was on the ground, staring up at the ceiling, blood gushing from his neck. Hugh yanked up his pants and crawled over to him.

"Duvy," he said, "we did it."

Duvlosky opened his mouth, but only blood came out. He was dying, fast.

"Mikhail," said Hugh. "Say hi to Marie for me, okay? Lucky I didn't get to her first, buddy."

Duvlosky smiled and reached over and grabbed Hugh's shoulder. Then the hand relaxed and Duvlosky was gone. Hugh felt the tears forming in his eyes. There was no use fighting them, not now. They poured down his face. Hugh kissed Mikhail Duvlosky on the forehead and then crawled over to Nick.

"Come on buddy," he said. "Wake up. I wasn't *that* bad was I?"

"Is he..."

"He's alive, Lucy. How are you? Fran? How are you?"

"Alive," said Lucy.

"Yes," said Fran. "How are you?"

"Just great." Hugh tried to get to his feet, but couldn't. "Don't suppose either of you gals have a joint on you?" he asked.

"Officer Duvlosky…" said Fran.

"Saved us all," said Hugh. "He was a good shit." He wiped his face dry and tried to stand up again. This time, he made it to his knees. "I don't know about you, but I'd be just as happy to get the fuck out of here."

He made one final monumental effort, and then he was up. He braced himself against the reception desk, and then remembered something he saw there, earlier, when he'd been looking for the keys. He walked around to the other side and there on the floor, where he'd thrown the contents of the drawer, was a pocket knife. He recalled it from somewhere. "SJ" was etched into its side. He grabbed it, walked over to Fran, and with a trembling hand flipped it open and started to cut her loose.

She emerged from the ropes, got to her feet, and ran over to her son. Hugh fell back to the ground. He looked at the knife again. Yes. It was the one that scientist lady attacked him with. It seemed liked six years ago that that had happened. Sarah Johnston, her name was. Hugh wondered if anybody would miss her. Hugh would miss her.

He lifted his head. Lucy had made it over to Nick now too. He'd be alright. Hugh dropped his head back on the floor and looked up at the ceiling. There were splatters of blood on it, some red, some black. His mother was dead. Everybody's mother had to die some day. Everybody had to die some day. It didn't matter if you were good or bad.

But then, maybe it did.

Yes, thought Hugh. That's *all* that matters.

NATHANIEL LEWIS

THE END

Printed in Great Britain
by Amazon